THE SHADOW OF THE MOTH

THE
SHADOW OF THE MOTH

A NOVEL OF ESPIONAGE WITH VIRGINIA WOOLF

ELLEN HAWKES & PETER MANSO

ST. MARTIN'S/MAREK   NEW YORK

Excerpts from *The Diary of Virginia Woolf, Volume One, 1915–1919,* edited by Anne Olivier Bell, © 1977 by Quentin Bell and Angelica Garnett, which appear on pages 192–193, 266–267, 278 and 279 in this book, are quoted with the kind permission of Harcourt Brace Jovanovich, Inc., and The Hogarth Press, Chatto and Windus. The quotations from Virginia Woolf's *A Room of One's Own,* © 1929 by Harcourt Brace Jovanovich, Inc.; renewed 1957 by Leonard Woolf, and *Night and Day,* © 1948 by Leonard Woolf, also appear with the permission of Harcourt Brace Jovanovich, Inc., and the author's literary estate, The Hogarth Press, Chatto and Windus. Grateful acknowledgment is also made to Holt, Rinehart, & Winston and Jonathan Cape, Ltd., for permission to quote from *Carrington: Letters and Extracts From Her Diaries,* edited by David Garnett, © 1970 (British)/1971 (American) by David Garnett and the Sophie Partridge Trust.

Design by Laura Hammond

Library of Congress Cataloging in Publication Data
Hawkes, Ellen.
    The shadow of the moth.

    "A St. Martin's/Marek book."
    1. Woolf, Virginia, 1882–1941, in fiction,
drama, poetry, etc. I. Manso, Peter. II. Title
PS3558.A817S5   1983   813'.54   82-17058
ISBN 0-312-71414-9

First Edition

10 9 8 7 6 5 4 3 2 1

For Anita and Frank

and

Blanche and Leo

THE
SHADOW OF
THE MOTH

[She] set to work to catch those unrecorded gestures, those unsaid or half-said words, which form themselves, no more palpably than the shadows of moths . . .

—*Virginia Woolf,* A Room of One's Own

1

Virginia Woolf took her favorite chair nearer to the fire. It was, alas, one of those dreary early November afternoons, the chill inside the sitting room as cold and damp as the gray heavy air shrouding London's streets. It was as if the world had come to a standstill, much like the horrible war itself. "The Great War," some called it, as stalled and mired, as dreadfully pointless a farce as her own life.

"Nineteen seventeen," said Virginia to herself, relishing the clarity of the numbers etched against the gravity of her mood. Still no change, no progress, could be measured, not here in Hogarth House nor across the Channel in the trenches. No, the enforced solitude of this Richmond suburb, the mindless task of setting type for the new printing press, none of it had had the prescribed effect. How could it, when she felt so ugly and frustrated?

Under the regimen of her special diet and extensive rest, she might be plumper, she might have fewer headaches and no longer hear voices. Leonard and her sister Vanessa might reassure her she was regaining her looks, yet they were lying. She was aware, painfully so, that the lines and shadows around her eyes weren't those of a thirty-five-year-old woman. Once her reflection had sometimes pleased her—the high arched forehead, deep blue eyes and full mouth—but now she knew that hers was the angular, haggard face of a woman besieged by a "mental affliction," every morning the bedroom mirror reminding her that a "nervous breakdown" had left its mark.

These, of course, were the doctors' labels. Virginia herself called it "a watery sleep," but never openly to Leonard. When they were first married, five years ago, she might have. Now he'd only think it was a symptom of her morbidity. Fanatical about the rules set forth by Dr. Maurice Wright, her Harley Street nerve specialist, he had become her keeper.

She was in the sitting room now, in fact, to take her nap before tea. She'd feigned sleep when Leonard checked on her, as usual hovering nearby to record her every move, and again she'd felt caged, especially as she'd discovered his code for noting her symptoms in his diary. With the aid of his Tamil and Sinhalese dictionaries, she'd deciphered the entries two weeks ago; in the midst of the expected references to a mild headache and her refusal to drink a second glass of milk, she'd been startled to find a chart of her monthlies. The doctor had diagnosed a connection between her irregular cycle and her illness, as if her body betrayed the instability of her mind. The notations enraged her. Was she never to have any privacy? Try suicide once, and you won't ever be trusted, she thought bitterly. Dr. Wright—the beast with the flaming snout, as she called him—yes, the good doctor with all his minions would come rooting into every private corner.

The room had grown darker. Virginia switched on the table lamp and sighed. Restless, bored, she was even losing interest in her new novel. The title she'd chosen—*Night and Day*—was fine, but if truth be told, she was tired of her heroine. The woman was too much like that side of herself she detested—cold, aloof, unsure of what she wanted, unwilling to take risks. Meeting this phantom every morning had only numbed her emotions and deepened her loneliness.

"That's enough," she told herself. "As Dr. Wright says,

'Think happy thoughts, practice proportion.' " She frowned. Irony wasn't the answer, and as a distraction she opened the afternoon's *Daily Mail.* "Ypres Under Siege," "Tommies Mired in Mud," "General Haig's Latest Plan," "Mata Hari's Last Words." Like gravemarkers in an old cemetery, the large black headlines put death at a distance, and she could feel nothing.

A moment later she came across a small, boxed story at the bottom of the third column, surrounded by commercial notices. She roused herself and reread it through several times before hurrying down the hall to her husband's study.

"Read this!" she commanded.

Leonard looked up from his desk. A small, wiry man, he had a congenital tremor of the hands for which he'd just received an exemption from the military. Now they shook more than usual as he spread out the paper, the column headline blaring, *"The Belgian's Suicide."*

He gave Virginia a sharp glance before reading:

London, Sunday, 4 November. Metropolitan Police removed the body of a woman from the Serpentine early this morning after Hyde Park pathkeepers reported it floating in the river. The woman has been identified as Anna Michaux, a Belgian refugee, age 46. Pinned to the woman's dress front was a note reading: "No mother, No father, No work." Scotland Yard reports no evidence of foul play and confirms death by suicide.

Leonard raised his head slowly, clearing his throat.

"Yes, a sad story," he said warily.

"That's what a woman feels when she's alone in the world. She mourned her father and mother and felt that without them, without work, life wasn't worth living, that there's no point in going on—"

He held up his hand for her to stop. "You're reading too much into this."

"It's all in her note."

"These tragedies are common now. She was a refugee, with nowhere to go.

"*That's* your response?"

"Didn't you see Lord Ladbrooke's letter to *The Times* last month—"

"What's that got to do with it?"

"He founded the Belgian Relief Committee, he knows their problems."

"So?"

"He was asking for help because the Belgians' plight has gone from bad to worse. Many of them have given up hope. Some blame the English for the war, some have turned to crime. Is it any wonder, then, that one of them—this poor woman—uh . . . well, couldn't carry on?"

"Which makes her *suicide* any less tragic?" Virginia emphasized the word he was afraid to say. "She knew exactly why she chose to drown herself."

"Please, Virginia, don't dwell on this. You'll bring on another headache." He reached out to take her hand but she pulled away.

"Look at her note. 'No mother, No father, No work.' Could any words be more poignant?"

"Exactly my point. You rush in here, your face flushed, talking about this woman as if you knew her. You're thinking about yourself, aren't you?"

She felt her anger rise. "Why is everything an inquisition?"

"I don't want to fight," he said with a pinched expression. "We'll discuss it after your nap."

She glared at him. There it was, the patronizing tone she'd grown to hate. His rules for reason and common sense were iron bars across her mind, taking away what she prized most—the freedom to look clearly at reality, unfettered and uncensored. Instead of illuminating the sky, he substituted

Wright's sense of proportion for her unquestioning obedience.

On the verge of tears, she grabbed up the newspaper and rushed back to the sitting room where she extracted her diary from a pile of books. In recent months she'd turned to it more and more.

Damn him, she thought, opening the marble-covered ledgerbook. Perhaps she *was* seeing herself in this unknown woman, but why not? She'd lost her mother when she was a young girl and still mourned her; her father, too, dead fourteen years now. Both of them had appeared like ghosts during her relapse last year. They were real and if another woman had grieved so, she wasn't as odd nor indeed nearly as obsessed as Leonard and the doctors might insist.

Taking up her pen she boldly printed, *"MONDAY, 5 NOV —THE BELGIAN'S SUICIDE"* at the top of the page. After a slight pause, she wrote in her galloping scrawl:

> *In the afternoon's* DAILY MAIL *a story that deepens my gloom. A woman drowned herself in the Serpentine, to her dress front she'd attached a note:* NO MOTHER, NO FATHER, NO WORK.
> *The words were addressed to no one in particular, yet she needed to tell the world how unhappy—*

Virginia raised her pen, thinking of the past two years, then added:

> *—how unspeakably lonely she felt. At 46 she still mourned her mother and father, just as I do. Not even marriage to Leonard has laid their phantoms to rest—*

She looked up and stared into the fire, her mother's face flickering before her. Then putting her index finger to her lips—the gesture was her mother's—she now wrote hastily:

My own mother's death when I was just 13 brought everything to an end. And when Father died, I felt muffled in gauze. This woman's note thus cries out to me, as if she knew that if her parents were alive she wouldn't have been lured by death.

She felt a slight chill, her pen leaving a blot on the page as she imagined the sensation of water closing over her head.

I once tossed a copper into the Serpentine, she continued, *but Anna Michaux threw it all away, in a final daring act.*

She cupped her chin, staring at the last phrase of the suicide note. " 'No work'," she repeated aloud as her pen scratched at the page:

If only Anna had had work she cared about. That's what Leonard fails to understand when he commands me not to write. Only my work banishes ghosts and keeps loneliness away. But it is difficult for women to find work of any kind, much less that which gives back a sense of one's self.

She paused to reread the black-bordered newspaper story before continuing:

The press exults in death now. First, the Belgian woman hacked to pieces in Bloomsbury and THE MAIL *raising the alarm about a 'Belgian Butcher.' Now they sensationalize this suicide, giving it a banner headline because they have nothing more bloodcurdling.*

She stopped, surprised by her choice of the word. "Bloodcurdling." She said it aloud. It was not part of her usual vocabulary. The tabloid was stirring her to melodrama too, it was that infectious. She dipped the pen in the inkwell and was about to write more when Nellie appeared at the door.

"Tea's up, mum," the servant announced. "Shall I call himself?"

Virginia nodded, adding three dots to the last sentence. Ever since keeping her first diary at 13, this was her reminder to continue later, even if she wouldn't always remember what more she wanted to say. But she knew this was different. She'd glimpsed a rare flash of her deepest feelings in this woman's final note.

When Leonard came in, she'd already put the diary away.

"It's all right," she said with a shrug when he asked how she was. "I shouldn't have bothered you." She ducked her head as if pouring out tea was occupying more than a small part of her mind.

❧ 2 ❧

Sam Josephs and Bobbie Waters were exchanging angry words in his glass-enclosed office at the rear of *The Daily Mail* City Room. Six feet one, he towered over the slim young woman. He was rangy and loose-limbed despite the weight he'd gained since being promoted from reporter to city editor two years ago. At 42 his red, curly hair was fading to a dullish brown but there was still a playful glint in his green eyes.

"The answer's still no. A hundred times," he said, staring down into her upturned face. "I'd be the laughing stock of the Yard, popping up with a pretty lass to view a butchered body. And a Yank, no less." He exaggerated his faint Irish brogue and then, to annoy her further, reached out to pinch her cheek.

"Be serious, dammit!" she said, pulling away.

Bobbie Waters was only 23 but considered herself an experienced reporter. With slanted blue eyes, rosy cheeks and blond hair cut into a silky bob, she was indeed pretty. But she disliked Sam's calling attention to her looks when she was trying to be professional. They had been lovers for four months but that was no reason for him to make fun of her ambitions. She had worked hard, first in New York, then in

London for *The Tribune* and his teasing this morning was infuriating. Still, she forced a flirtatious smile.

"Let's shock the Yard just this once?" Despite the abrupt, midwestern twang, her voice was attractive, with a slight agreeable huskiness.

"You'd faint dead away."

"No, I wouldn't. Besides, I have to see a few bodies if I'm ever going to the trenches." He was shaking his head again. "Come on, Sam! I don't ask many favors. Let me in on this, please?"

He sat down at his desk to sort through the stories already filed for the afternoon's edition. "I doubt *The Trib* needs something on the 'Belgian Butcher' anyway. American readers don't care about a refugee hacked to pieces in Bloomsbury. For that they have Chicago."

"I can sell it elsewhere. Don't you see? I'm sick and tired of the silly garden parties Draper always assigns. . . ."

She stopped. Sam was looking past her, and she turned. In the doorway stood a tall, thin woman in a long gray cape, her hair falling in wisps from her bun.

Bobbie was struck by the intensity of the woman's deep blue eyes and the self-conscious, ungainly walk as she strode into the room and announced herself: "I'd like to speak to you about a news story."

"You want society news. One flight down." Schooled in snap judgments, the editor turned away and pretended to be sorting his notes.

Bobbie saw the woman's eyes darken in anger. "You are Sam Josephs?" When he nodded, the woman thrust a clipping at him. "I'm Mrs. Woolf. I was told you wrote this."

Bobbie recognized the name immediately. She'd even read the woman's novel, *The Voyage Out,* the year before. But she'd imagined the author as middle-aged and rather prim and unattractive. She was surprised, therefore, to see instead a woman whose classic features seemed marred by the strange, sad look in her eyes.

She stepped forward and extended her hand. "Bobbie Waters, Mrs. Woolf. London Bureau, *New York Tribune*—"

"What about this?" Sam interrupted, pushing the clipping back across his desk.

"I hoped you could tell me about the woman."

"She turned up in the Serpentine late Saturday night or early Sunday morning."

"Is that all?"

He shrugged.

"Her note says she had no parents, no work. Where did the woman live? Didn't the police investigate?"

"The Yard's more concerned with the other Belgian, the one chopped up in Bloomsbury last week. That's what our readers like too—murder, not a suicide." He began to play with a horn-handled pocket knife, opening and closing it, punctuating his explanation with annoying clicks. "I don't usually cover this sort of thing, but I was walking in Hyde Park Sunday morning and noticed a crowd by the Serpentine. We needed a filler, see, so we slipped it in between the adverts. Ordinarily a refugee's suicide doesn't even run on the back pages."

He paused and began to pare his nails.

"What about Belgian refugees . . ." she said, then: "For heaven's sake, would you stop that?"

He closed the knife and set it aside. "Sorry. You were saying?"

"That the story deserves more attention. Don't the problems of refugees matter, especially now that Lord Ladbrooke is asking for contributions to his Committee?"

"Not with troop losses, the mud bath over there in Flanders."

"A soldier in the trenches is important, a refugee in London isn't?" Virginia leaned forward and tapped the clipping.

"This counts. The truth must be told. It doesn't matter whether it's a bombardment or a suicide."

A shadow crossed Bobbie's face. "Do you mean you've come here because this *was* a suicide?"

"Her note moved me very much."

"But suicide is an act of revenge," interrupted Bobbie. "A way of punishing the survivors." She continued to stare at Virginia with her wide blue eyes.

"I don't agree, Miss Waters, not at all." Virginia spoke sternly, but finding the young woman attractive and her vehemence refreshing, she gave her a slight smile.

"Let's not bother Mrs. Woolf with your personal theories, eh, Bobbie?" Sam's voice was gentle behind his impatience. He removed a typewritten page from a folder and passed it to Virginia. "That's the story before it was trimmed to one paragraph."

Virginia read the account. It wasn't much different from the published version, but it did note that Anna Michaux's immigration card listed her residence as "The Litchfield Arms Hotel, Dean Street." She copied the address into a small notebook, then asked Josephs if he knew anything more.

"I told you, I didn't pursue the story." He got to his feet. "And really, Mrs. Woolf, I'm sure there's nothing more to it."

"What will you do now?" asked Bobbie as Virginia hesitated, about to leave.

"I'm not sure. Go round to the hotel, perhaps." Virginia shot a puzzled glance at the young woman. "Why?"

Bobbie shrugged, unwilling to say more.

Josephs watched Virginia depart, a scowl on his face. The desk telephone rang and he grabbed the receiver. While he talked, Bobbie leafed through the Michaux file. Suddenly she read with concentration.

"What the hell do you think you're doing?" demanded Josephs, hanging up.

"I *thought* you were in a hurry to get her out of here. And I know you play with your knife when you're edgy. Or lying."

"Mind your own business." He pitched the file into a drawer.

"All she wanted was information. Why give her a run-around?"

"Don't you realize who she is?"

"Of course I do. I've even read her novel."

"Then use your head. Who knows what a woman like that would do with the story. Perhaps she'll use it—"

"What difference would that make?"

"A bloody lot. The Yard wants the lid kept on."

3

"Don't know'er," the hotel clerk muttered without looking up from his game of solitaire.

"I beg your pardon?" said Virginia, inwardly flinching at the sordid, sour-smelling lobby of The Litchfield Arms. One of several dilapidated hotels along Dean Street in Soho, it had once catered to prostitutes and transients, but now housed refugees waiting out the war with little money and less hope. Three of them were sitting on the lobby's torn, stained sofa, watching Virginia.

"Never 'earda 'er," the clerk repeated, slapping another card on the counter. His face was sallow and pockmarked, as unhealthy and defeated as the hotel. Virginia put her hand across the card.

"If I might have your attention," she said in a haughty voice. "I know Anna Michaux lived here."

The man raised his head. "I don't bother with names. I take two bob, put 'em in a room. They don't pay up I run 'em out."

"Perhaps I could see your register?"

The clerk laughed. "She thinks it's the ruddy Savoy, she does. I don't keep no book, lady, I don't ask no names, I don't see nothing."

Virginia turned and started across the lobby. Someone touched her arm as she reached the doorway. She turned to find a gray-haired man looking into her eyes.

"Excuse me, Madame, I may be of help to you?"

It was one of the refugees. His clothes were threadbare but neat, and his tall, thin figure was further distinguished by a dapper white mustache.

"You are looking for Mademoiselle Michaux?" He spoke with an accent, keeping his voice low. "She moved away last spring, I think."

"Do you know where?"

He shook his head. "She found work somewhere. The Belgian Relief Committee near Victoria Station, they gave her a job I think." He paused, then his face brightened. "You could ask Mademoiselle Ickx, Marie Ickx. She lives here; they were friends. Perhaps she will know.

"Oh? Which floor?" asked Virginia, turning back toward the stairs.

"She may be away. I have not seen her for several days."

Virginia wrote out her name, address and telephone number on a page from her notebook and handed it to him. "Will you ask Miss Ickx to ring me?"

"*Bien sûr,* Madame Woolf," he said, glancing at it. "As soon as she returns. But you try the Relief Committee, too. They should know Mademoiselle Michaux's new address."

"I will," she said, choosing not to contradict him. She glanced back at the clerk, certain he'd been listening. But now he looked down and played another card.

Virginia found the offices of the Belgian Relief Committee on the first floor of a sooty red brick building but a block from Victoria Station. Refugees were seated on long wooden benches stretching the length of the dingy yellow room. Many had satchels and boxes at their feet as if they'd been stranded at some outlying railway depot. Few spoke, waiting miserably for their names to be called.

Virginia went to the rear of the office where she introduced herself to a round-faced, older woman behind a desk.

"Ah, yes, Mrs. Woolf," said the woman. "You were Virginia Stephen, weren't you?"

Virginia arched her eyebrows in surprise.

"I'm Katharine Ladbrooke," the smiling woman explained. "I knew your father and your Aunt Fisher, too. I expect you read my husband's plea in *The Times.*"

Virginia nodded, thinking to herself that for all his altruistic sentiments, Lord Ladbrooke himself was much too busy to attend to the actual problems of refugees. Instead, Lady Ladbrooke would be expected to see to the day-to-day details of running the relief committee.

"I hope you have a place for one of these unfortunates," the woman was saying. "Perhaps an upstairs servant?"

Virginia winced. Like so many well-born women doing "charity work," Lady Ladbrooke carried her class assumptions with her, and naturally she expected Sir Leslie Stephen's daughters to keep a full staff of servants.

"There should be no problem in finding you someone suitable—"

"I think it's marvelous what you're trying to do here," Virginia interrupted. "I'm sure you meet a number of Belgian women. . . ."

"It's really more my husband's doing," Lady Ladbrooke said. "Alex established this office soon after the German invasion in '14. He realized that these poor people would be coming over here in droves needing our help. Of course, he's so taken up with banking matters, the Prime Minister's War Budget, you know, that I'm forced to run our office here. Why, Lloyd George treats him like a member of the Cabinet, always ringing him for advice." She flushed proudly, then remembered herself. "Now, Mrs. Woolf, what position did you say you have?"

"Actually, I'm inquiring about a woman named Anna Michaux."

Lady Ladbrooke sorted through her box of index cards. "The name's familiar," she murmured, "but I don't find her. Are you sure she registered with us?"

"Perhaps I'm wrong. But there's someone else. A Marie Ickx. Is she listed?"

"Ah, yes," she said, pulling a card. "Though she already seems to have a position."

"Oh? With whom?"

"As a waitress. Unfortunately it doesn't say where." She stopped and looked up. The front door had banged open and a voice called out, "Mrs. Woolf?"

Virginia turned. It was the young American from *The Mail,* Bobbie Waters, who rushed past the seated refugees.

"A man at the hotel told me you'd be here," she panted. "I've got to talk to you about Anna Michaux."

The woman's face was flushed and her shining eyes aroused Virginia's interest. With her heart beating more rapidly than the intrusion might have warranted, she bid Lady Ladbrooke goodbye and allowed Bobbie to lead the way outside to a nearby tea shop.

"But why would he lie to me?" asked Virginia after the American had denounced Sam Josephs for withholding information.

"He said the Yard told him to keep the case quiet."

"The Yard? But I thought the case was 'insignificant'."

"It may have to do with her employer."

"But her note said, 'No work.' Why would she say that if it weren't true?" The back of Virginia's neck began to tingle.

"I thought it was strange, too. Unless, of course, she was let go. She was Sir Henry Cranford's governess, you see."

"I don't understand."

"Cranford—he's a leading arms manufacturer. Adviser to Lloyd George. Definitely a big wig." She took a sharp little breath. "Look, Josephs will be furious if he knows I've told you. He promised the Yard to keep Cranford's name out of it. But it was Sir Henry who reported her missing and who identified the body!"

Virginia held her gaze, aware that the young woman was waiting for a response. She'd let her mind wander. It had happened in the past often enough, succumbing to the charm of a spirited woman. It was the magnetism of her first love, Madge Vaughan, and then of Violet Dickinson, the tall, eccentric Quaker who'd been a second mother to her. Her sister Vanessa could tease her about Sapphism, but she knew she often felt what men feel about women and now it had come without warning, a tremor of passion, a stirring of erotic attraction.

"I'm sorry, Miss Waters," she said. "I'm afraid I wasn't following."

"It's simple!" Bobbie said impatiently. "Cranford's such a mugwump, he's the reason the Yard's hushed it up."

"Mugwump?" Virginia couldn't help smiling. "Oh, I see. He has influence."

"Right. But just because he *wants* it kept quiet doesn't mean you can't ask him about his governess. Especially if he fired her. If that's why she drowned herself, he might even feel a touch guilty."

"I doubt he'll answer my questions. Why should he after the Yard kept his name out of the newspapers? Besides, the old gentleman at the hotel said she had a friend there, Marie Ickx. Another Belgian. She ought to be able to tell me something."

"But it can't hurt to ask Sir Henry himself. The worst he can do is say no." She pushed back her chair. "Look, I've got to cover a soldiers' tea in Mayfair. Ring me at *The Tribune* tomorrow if you do decide to see Sir Henry. Believe me, the note *is* puzzling and I'm curious to hear how he explains it." Her eyes darkened as she gave Virginia a parting look. "Really, you may actually have stumbled onto something important."

Virginia nodded, saying nothing. A quiver of excitement went through her. Fear, too. And desire. She sighed and followed the American out the door.

Back at the offices of the Relief Committee Lady Ladbrooke still sat at her desk. As soon as Virginia and Bobbie had left a man put down the newspaper he'd been reading and crossed the room to the rear. He was tall and broad-shouldered. His close-cropped hair accentuated large, flared ears and the square, block-like shape of his head, despite his overall size, seemed far too heavy for his body.

"That woman you was talking to?" he said in a rough voice to Lady Ladbrooke.

"Mrs. Woolf you mean?" She was sorting registration cards and did not bother to raise her head.

"Was she asking about Anna Michaux?"

Lady Ladbrooke nodded. "To hire her, yes, but I can't find her listed. Someone named Marie Ickx, too. Why? Do you know Miss Michaux?" She looked up with a helpful smile. But the man was already closing the office's front door.

4

"Sir Henry never sees anyone without an appointment."

The elderly, pinch-faced secretary was seated at a large desk in the reception room of Cranford's Chester Square townhouse. He had already looked Virginia up and down, and as though taking cues from some imagined Dickensian forebear, now allowed as how he might be able to schedule an appointment within a fortnight. He opened a large date book. "What's the nature of your business?"

Virginia stared back at him. The man made her feel ragtag and out of place. Belgravia often had this effect on her, even as she valued the charm and self-confidence of the upper class. But this morning the pilastered townhouses surrounding the square had annoyed her. It was as if the residents had chosen to ignore the realities of the war, or anything more serious, more consequential than the promptness of their morning tea.

"I must speak to Sir Henry today," she repeated, summoning her most peremptory tone. "It's about his governess."

The secretary's eyebrows arched above his spectacles. "Perhaps you'd better take a seat." He gestured to a salon chair against the wall and disappeared through the nearby door.

Virginia was surprised by the alarm she'd seen in his face, but even more intriguing, now, was his sudden reappearance.

"You may go in, Mrs. Woolf."

Sir Henry rose from his desk and crossed the thick blue Kurdistan to take her hand. For a heavy man he had a lively step. His high domed forehead and smooth cheeks had the sure, polished look of success, and a crisp white handkerchief was perfectly folded into the breast pocket of a well-cut pin-striped suit.

"I'll be slightly delayed," he said to his secretary. "Tell Mrs. Murphy I'd like luncheon at noon."

"You're forgetting Wade's demonstration of their new device," the secretary said, hovering at the door.

"Put it off until tomorrow," he said, closing the door and returning to his desk. Its surface gleamed in the sunlight spilling through the French doors behind him. He clasped his hands and leaned forward with a smile.

"I wasn't sure you'd agree to see me," said Virginia.

"It's a pleasure. Your friend Mr. Keynes speaks so fondly of you."

That her precocious friend, John Maynard Keynes—already the economic darling of the Treasury Office—would know Cranford came as no surprise. But Virginia sensed that their mutual acquaintance was not why she'd been ushered in so quickly. The friendly note struck her as false. "Didn't your secretary tell you why I'm here?"

His smile faded. "I gather you knew her?"

Virginia shook her head. "I read about her in the newspaper."

"Ah, and I was hoping you could help us."

Virginia gave him a puzzled look.

"If she'd been a friend, well, there was the thought you might have an explanation. It's upset us all, especially my two daughters. My wife's taken them to our house in the north to help them forget. . . ." His voice trailed away as he withdrew to the privacy of his grief.

"She was still working for you, then?"

"Of course. Did you think otherwise?"

Virginia felt her stomach knot. The man seemed unaware that this assertion called the phrase "No work" of the suicide note into question. Did he really not know? Or was he lying? she wondered as she kept her voice calm and continued:

"Did she seem that unhappy?"

"Not really, though my wife did notice she was listless, not her usual self since last August. I'd just hired a chauffeur for my new motor car. . . ." he paused; a note of pride had crept into his voice. "Anyway, we considered suggesting that she see our physician."

"But you didn't?"

"We didn't want to intrude." He went to the table on the far side of the room where he picked up a small, gilt-framed photograph. "Anna fled Brussels after the German invasion, leaving her homeland behind. I suppose that explains her depression."

His remark struck her as glib but she let it slip by. The photograph would be her first chance to see the woman, as if a glimpse of the face might reveal the story behind the suicide. Virginia half-rose from the chair. "May I see that?" she asked eagerly.

He turned and stood behind her, holding the picture as she studied it. "That's Anna with our two girls," he said, looking over her shoulder.

Virginia was struck by her frailness. The woman's dark hair was braided on top of her head and her face was turned slightly away from the camera. There was a shy, vulnerable look—much like her own expression when anyone pointed a camera. There were traces of shadows, lines under the governess' eyes as well.

"That was taken last August at our country house," Cranford said, returning to his desk. "If only we'd taken her mood more seriously. . . ."

"I suppose we all feel that when someone dies . . . all the things we might have said or done." Her voice faded as she peered more closely at the photograph. Across the right corner there was a handwritten inscription: *"Pour mes jeunes filles."* The script was fine and angular, almost spidery.

"Anna wrote this?" she asked.

He nodded. "She gave the photograph to my daughters as a present."

Virginia studied the slant and style of the handwriting: it came to her in a flash; she saw tension and reticence in the pale script, just as she'd noticed in Anna's eyes. Was it fear? she wondered, imagining the governess hesitating as she touched the pen to the photograph. Why? But she could hardly discuss psychology with the woman's employer. The man unquestionably took an uncomplicated view of emotions.

"There was nothing to indicate suicide beforehand," he went on. "But when we packed up her things—only a few books and clothes—we realized how meager her life was. I suppose many Belgians feel that way. Our Relief Committee can give them food and shelter but how do we cheer them up? Offer inspiration?"

"Relief Committee?" Her head came up in surprise. "The one near Victoria Station, Lord Ladbrooke's group?" When he nodded, she narrowed her eyes. Why hadn't Lady Ladbrooke recognized Anna's name then? Even if she couldn't find a registration card, hadn't she heard about the governess? She was even more startled as Cranford continued:

"Alex has done a marvelous job. I'm not much for charity, but he runs it like an employment agency, and I agreed to serve on the board. My wife sometimes helps Lady Ladbrooke in the afternoons. In fact, that's how we came to hire Anna. Alex met her at the Committee and suggested her."

"But what about her note? Why did she say she had no work?"

The smile faded; still, he didn't seem especially startled. "I wondered about that, myself. But as I told the Yard, perhaps she meant no translating work—what she did before the war. Perhaps being a governess seemed beneath her."

"Perhaps," she murmured. "Her friends would know, though."

He shook his head. "She had no friends."

"What about someone named . . . Marie Ickx?"

"I don't recognize the name. No, she seemed a recluse."

"But she did go out Saturday night?"

"I was at a meeting, didn't realize she was gone. My daughters found her bed empty Sunday morning, and I called the police."

"That's how you learned about her death?"

"They'd already found her, yes. I had to identify the body." There was a slight quaver in his voice. "Ghastly sight. Just awful."

Virginia looked up. She had begun to write in her notebook and now she caught the pained expression on his face. "But do you know what actually happened? I mean, when she did it? And how?" It was something she needed to ask, as if through the answer she might experience walking into the Serpentine, one foot before the other until the water closed over her head.

Sir Henry flushed slightly. "I was rather a coward, I'm afraid. The police made a full report but I didn't wish to see it. Have you?"

She shook her head.

"Then I don't understand." He gave her a narrow look. "Did the police suggest you come to me?"

Virginia hesitated. "No. I spoke to the reporter who was there when the body was found. He wrote the story."

"Mr. Josephs, wasn't it? I was glad to see he omitted my

name. A man in my position . . . ." He left the sentence unfinished. "Mr. Josephs isn't pursuing the matter now, is he?"

"Not at all. He called it a 'filler'."

"How sad," said Cranford with evident relief. "Anna's life reduced to one paragraph." He shook his head. "I can't pretend I like reporters."

"That's why the story upset me. It seemed so stark and unsympathetic."

"Mrs. Woolf, I must ask—are you planning to write about Anna?"

"Because of this, you mean?" she asked, catching his glance at the notebook.

"Keynes told me you're an author. I haven't read your novel, but now I shall." He walked back to the French windows, staring out at the terrace and rocking on the balls of his feet. "I do try to keep up with cultural things," he said, turning back. "Life can't be all business even in a national emergency. That's why I've joined the committee for the National Preservation of the Arts. Alex suggested it. Your friend Keynes is on the board as well."

"Yes. Maynard's in Paris now, buying for the government from the Degas collection."

Cranford smiled. "And doing a splendid job. I admire that young man. Interesting friends, too. He's told me about his Bloomsbury parties. Not wild about the politics, mind you, but they seem good fun, all you writers and artists."

Before she could say anything, there was a knock at the door, and a short, plump woman stepped into the room, wearing a starched white apron over a black dress.

"Yes, Mrs. Murphy?" asked Sir Henry.

"Luncheon is at noon," she clucked. "Now it's getting cold. And never mind that his Lordship is waiting outside."

"Ladbrooke?" said Sir Henry in surprise.

"Yes, Henry, I hope you don't mind," said a gentleman

from behind Mrs. Murphy. Ladbrooke was tall and almost reed-like, and silver-gray hair accentuated his pale, narrow face. "I've something urgent to tell you," he said, strolling across the room. "Your secretary thought you might have a moment."

He paused in front of Virginia and looked down at her with cool, gray-blue eyes. "I'm sorry to interrupt."

Sir Henry quickly introduced them and Virginia shook Ladbrooke's hand. "I met your wife just yesterday at your Relief Center. She knew my father."

"Of course. I should have remembered. My wife told me how pleased she was to see one of the Stephen girls after all these years. She hopes you'll call on us soon."

"That would be lovely," Virginia replied with a smile. "But I shan't keep you any longer, Sir Henry." She put away her notebook. Sir Henry was quick to help her on with her cape and escort her to the door.

"And what about your luncheon, sir?" the housekeeper asked.

"Hold back, Mrs. Murphy, please." He laughed, adding to Virginia, "With my family away my housekeeper likes to play mother."

"No, no. It's my fault for taking so much of your time," said Virginia, "but I do appreciate your seeing me about Anna."

"You knew Anna?" the housekeeper asked. "Maybe you can explain it then. There she was, dressed up in her best hat and gloves, matching shoes and handbag too, all smiles about seeing a friend. Next thing I know she's dunked herself in the river. It don't make sense. And her a proper Catholic too!"

"Mrs. Murphy, please!" said Sir Henry.

She gave him an injured sniff and strode away.

"Servants don't know their place anymore," grumbled Sir Henry. "I'm afraid she takes her food as well as her religion a little too personally."

5

"The housekeeper's right," said Virginia. "It doesn't make sense. Why would Anna dress to meet someone if she were planning to drown herself?"

Bobbie Waters puffed on a cigarette. They were at a rear table in Lincoln's Inn Buffet. Bobbie had suggested the place, and not only did Virginia want to share what she'd learned, she was eager to find out more about the young woman, even to listen to her American twang.

"So, whom was she seeing?" asked Bobbie. "A lover? Was there a quarrel?"

"I doubt it. The housekeeper said 'a friend,' but Sir Henry said Anna had no visitors and rarely went out. He'd never heard of Marie Ickx, either." She paused to let the waiter serve their sherries. The restaurant was the favorite of professional men from the City and the two of them were the only women in the crowded room. Aware of the curious glances at them, Virginia lowered her voice.

"As for Sir Henry himself, he's the sort of man I dislike on instinct. He reminds me of my half-brother George, the kind of chap who's very conscious of the impression he's making. He was very careful to show how sensitive he is, how much he cared about Anna. I wasn't convinced. I don't think 'No work' referred to her job as a translator, and he snapped at his housekeeper when she mentioned Anna's meeting."

Bobbie had been listening eagerly. "You think that's why he wanted to hush her up?"

"That's my guess. Also because she said Anna was a good Catholic."

"Well, Catholics do commit suicide. It could mean very little." She stubbed out her cigarette. "Any idea why Lord Ladbrooke was there?"

Virginia shrugged. "Business, I suppose. Sir Henry practically jumped to attention. The *nouveau riche* in awe of the aristocrat." Her voice trailed off as Bobbie placed a large envelope in front of her. "What's that?"

"My surprise. Open it."

The envelope was filled with papers.

"Look at the top one first," commanded Bobbie. "That's the coroner's report."

"Where did you get it?"

"From Sam's desk. This morning he wasn't around and—" she grinned "—let's say I 'borrowed' it."

Virginia looked back at the report, reading it quickly.

CORONER AND WARRANTS OFFICE REPORT
METROPOLITAN POLICE, CITY OF LONDON

Name of deceased: Anna Michaux
Address: 5 Chester Square
Employment: Governess (Sir Henry Cranford, same address)
Circumstances: Body found 10:23 A.M., Sunday, 4 November, 1917, Serpentine near arched bridge. Fully dressed (shoes and handbag missing, not recovered). Note pinned to dress: "No mother, No father, No work."
Identification: Caucasian female, 46 years old. Dark brown hair. No distinguishing scars. Special visa card in coat pocket: No. 1183-602*E-BEL,* issued 29/8/1914 to Anna Michaux, Bel-

gian refugee, Litchfield Arms Hotel (temp.). Identity confirmed by Sir Henry Cranford, employer.

Autopsy: Bronchial Pulmonary: 1.8 litres clear water; lobar congestion; water saturation peritoneal cavity: .12 litres clear water.

Oesophagus: clear
Duodenum: clear
Haemoglobin: Type A
Epidermis: No bruises. Slight discolouration at neck
Approximate time in water: 6–8 hours
Approximate time of death: Midnight–4 A.M.
Verdict: Death by drowning, suicide

"I suppose it confirms suicide by drowning," said Virginia when she'd read it a second time. She gave an involuntary shudder. Never had her fantasy of "an easeful death" been so dramatically, so coldly contradicted.

"No, it only proves she was in the water, not whether she died there. I did some reading. The examination wasn't thorough. They should have measured water in the blood." Bobbie waved her hand impatiently. "Even more important is that 'slight discolouration at the neck'."

"What does it mean?"

Bobbie leaned back in her chair and lit another cigarette, watching Virginia as if to gauge the effect of what she was going to say: "I think the woman was strangled—strangled first, *then* thrown into the water."

Bobbie's words came at her like a runaway horse. Suicide she could understand. She even sympathized. But murder? It opened the door to her terrifying fear that humans were basically violent, ready to swing an ax, plunge a knife, fire a gun. How many times on the underground had she seen a homicidal glint in a stranger's eyes? How often had she imagined an ugly, pockmarked man following her, ready to tear at her flesh? It was part of the nightmare that had plagued her since childhood—the leering man, the screeching harpies lurking in the shadows. No! She shook her head, trying to rid herself of the images. "No, no. I can't—I won't—believe it!"

"It's not that crazy," Bobbie insisted. "Remember Cranford's evasiveness, plus what the housekeeper said. There's the coroner's report, and now, look at the pages from Sam's notebook. Obviously he thinks there's something wrong too."

Virginia shuffled the pages with a trembling hand. Josephs' penciled script ranged haphazardly across the page as if he'd been writing standing up. There were designations of time in military form, descriptions of the body and several references to "BB."

"What's this 'BB'?" asked Virginia.

"The Belgian Butcher," Bobbie explained. "You know, the Belgian woman who was cut up in Bloomsbury last week. He thinks the two deaths are related."

On the next page, Josephs had written, "Marie Ickx, Litchfield Arms?"

Startled, Virginia looked up.

"You see," Bobbie said. "Sam knows about her too. We'll have to find her first."

Virginia shook her head. "She's still away. When I rang the hotel this morning that disgusting clerk was ranting about her owing for her room. . . ."

Bobbie slapped the palm of her hand on the table. "So! We have two Belgian women dead and coincidentally, a third, the only friend of one of them, is missing."

The waiter brought their plates of sole and Virginia cleared the papers. She took a few bites, still without looking up. She felt pushed into a corner, uneasy and agitated. However attractive, however intelligent this Bobbie Waters was, she was also too insistent. She wanted instant agreement and Virginia couldn't give it. Not when the thought of murder was sending waves of panic through her.

Bobbie waited, not touching her food. "Sam thinks it's

more than a suicide," she repeated. "Which is why he lied. He wants it as his exclusive story. He'll pretend he's protecting us, you know, mouthing nonsense about women reporters not writing about crime. But when someone tells me what I can or can't do, I fight back."

She picked up her fork and waved it defiantly. "I learned that the hard way. When you want something, you have to go after it. My father was a reporter but he didn't want me to be one. 'Just get married,' he said, but as you can see, that didn't stop me. I left Iowa and wangled a job at *The New York Tribune.* On the society page, granted, but when the war broke out, I announced I wanted to go to the Front. My editor said, 'No, no, not for ladies.' He let me come to London only because Ed Draper, the head of our bureau here, needed someone to cover stupid garden parties and charity balls. Still, I intend to show him—and Sam—and my father too that I can cover any story I want. You can't be a real reporter if there are things you aren't allowed to see. I mean, think of the women who couldn't be doctors because the body was taboo. Or women painters who have had to paint cows instead of nudes."

She took a deep breath. Virginia couldn't help smiling. Calculated or not, the outburst had stirred her. How often she'd talked in a similar vein. The American's declaration of her ambitions, her fervor were beyond reproach. She'd spun out an emotional tie, and Virginia felt unable to brush it away.

"I agree with you," she said, "of course. Still—"

"Good. I'm glad to hear it."

"It's fine to want to prove yourself. But is this the right occasion?"

"Why not?"

"Because first of all you don't know that it wasn't suicide," Virginia began lamely.

Bobbie stared at her. "Are you only interested in Anna if it was?"

Virginia heard the question as an accusation, and she didn't know what to say. How could she admit that the suicide note had drawn her because it had made her feel less alone, less strange? That bizarre or not it was almost comforting? It was an emotion she could hardly interpret for someone so young, so ambitious and full of plans. Abruptly, she pushed her half-eaten meal to one side.

Bobbie waited, sensing the tension in Virginia's face.

Virginia sighed. "I can't really explain it. I have my reasons for being interested in the woman's suicide. You seem to hate the very idea, though. Of a suicide, I mean. And not just because it doesn't make a compelling news story either. There's something else."

"What else?" Bobbie's voice rose. "It's an important story if some maniac is killing Belgian women. . . ."

"Was it your mother?" Virginia cut in, watching Bobbie flinch. "My own mother died when I was young, too. I know how difficult that can be." She paused, softening her tone.

"You mentioned only your father before. Is that why you're so angry? All memories of her locked away?"

Bobbie looked down at her plate to hide her welling tears. "My father told me she died of pneumonia when I was three," she said in a shaky voice. "It wasn't until last year I found out the truth. An old friend of my father at *The Tribune* mentioned my mother's suicide. Father was furious when I told him what I'd heard, but he still refused to talk about it."

"That's why you called suicide an act of revenge?"

"My father seemed so sad and bitter. He'd blamed himself all those years. No matter why she killed herself, he was the one who had to live with it."

Tears spilled down her cheeks. Virginia reached into her bag and handed her a handkerchief. "Maybe suicide was a real choice for your mother." Virginia paused, aware that she found Bobbie's vulnerability appealing. The mask of the hard-bitten reporter had slipped. She was a woman who grieved for her mother, who'd discovered that the meaning of life was indeed ambiguous.

"You mustn't blame the victim," she went on. "When I read Anna's note, I didn't think she was a coward. I could imagine why she felt her life was over."

"But you came to Sam to find out more."

Virginia shrugged. "Perhaps because I wanted to prove I wasn't reading too much into the suicide note. My husband said I was. I suppose I needed to reassure myself I wasn't."

"And now you're satisfied? Despite all the things that make no sense?" Bobbie wadded Virginia's handkerchief into a ball and threw it down on the table.

The gesture of frustration touched something in Virginia. Not that she'd ever believed in the maternal instinct, but she found herself wanting to protect Bobbie, to encourage her in her desire to shape her own life, just as she herself had been sustained by other women, just as she'd committed herself to her writing. Spreading out her handkerchief, she refolded it into a neat square and looked up with glittering eyes, as if she had just awakened from a light sleep.

"No," she said. "I'm not at all satisfied. But we're both making a mistake. We can't force this or twist it into our own version of reality. The idea of murder frightens me. But I know I mustn't hide from that. Nor can you hide from the possibility of suicide. We can't change the facts to suit our needs. It wouldn't be fair to Anna Michaux, it wouldn't be fair to ourselves," she paused and added for emphasis "—to ourselves as writers."

At first Bobbie looked surprised. Then she blushed with pleasure. "You mean you do want to go on with this?"

Virginia nodded. "Agreed?" She offered her hand.

"You bet. And I know just what I want you to do next."

Virginia laughed. "Oh, Bobbie, if necessary, you could probably make an armored tank polka."

6

Deputy Commissioner Nigel Allington of Scotland Yard's Special Branch reread the report. His brow was creased, his face rigid with anger. There had been another bombing, this one adjacent to Piccadilly Circus. Like the one last week at Harrod's, it bore the unmistakable stamp of the Irish. But whether it was German saboteurs or Sinn Fein home-rulers, he knew that the average Londoner wouldn't care. The death toll stood at seventeen and primed by the press, the public would simply blame his Special Branch for not preventing it.

Allington had returned to his office after a severe dressing down from his superior, Sir Basil Thomson, Head of the Yard. Thomson had listed Allington's failures over the past year. Poor methods of surveillance, ineffective infiltration of political groups, lack of informants. And Allington knew that though he was still head of Special Branch, his authority was diminished, just as he knew that Sir Vernon Kell, Head of MI_5, was the one responsible for his losses.

Kell had in fact been present in Thomson's office to witness Allington's humiliation. An anonymous dandy, he was unknown to the public by name or looks. He had stood smiling triumphantly, straightening his cuffs, as Thomson announced the assignment of an MI$_5$ officer, one Angus Clarke, to light a fire under Branch.

The rivalry between Allington's Special Branch and Kell's military intelligence group had grown ever worse over the past year. Kell had been permitted direct access to the Prime Minister, and now, with this morning's assignment it was clear that Sir Basil Thomson had capitulated to pressure from above. Despite Allington's laurels at Eton and Oxford, the successful years in Tonga and New Guinea, his promotions for quelling the riots at Dartmoor as Head of the National Prison System, his power was now severely undermined, his effectiveness openly called into question.

Allington slammed down the morning's bomb report. "That's what we need from Munitions," he barked at his assistant, tearing a page from a notebook. "And tell Bomb Division I want those tests in an hour. Match the wrappings with the last Sinn Fein bombing and we'll know it's the bloody Irish. And if that bastard Kell comes on the line, don't tell him a thing. Meanwhile you'll have to clear out that office." He gestured to a small adjoining room. "We're going to have a visitor from MI$_5$. Don't stand there. Get going."

"Yes, sir. But there's Mrs. Woolf, you said you'd see her nearly an hour ago."

"Mrs. Woolf. . . . nearly an hour ago," he repeated the words, seemingly unaware of what had become a persistent verbal tic. "I don't have the time. Still, I'd better not ignore the wife of an old acquaintance. Give me ten minutes. I'll ring for her when I'm ready."

Virginia was sitting downstairs on a wooden bench in the dingy gray hallway, still fidgeting. Bobbie had made the idea sound so logical. "Just pop round to the Yard and ask to see the case report," she'd instructed. "You can lie and tell them you knew Anna Michaux. And besides, you'd better report Marie Ickx as a missing person." She herself couldn't do it, she explained, since several Yard men knew her and her visit would be reported to Sam.

It was Virginia's first visit to Scotland Yard. The slate-gray building loomed as a sinister presence over the Strand, its tall iron gates a forceful reminder of dark crimes and merciless violence. She'd felt afraid, climbing the steps, as if she were entering a secret, threatening domain. Yet, inside, she found it boringly ordinary, with no hint of the evil she felt must penetrate the walls. Instead, people scurried in and out of offices, just as they would in any private firm. A sergeant at the duty desk had asked her business, then informed her that Deputy Commissioner Allington, an old friend of her husband, would see her himself as soon as possible. She'd had to wait close to an hour now before being escorted upstairs to the Deputy Commissioner's office.

It was a long, high-ceilinged room, and furnished like a gentleman's study, it made a point of the occupant's rank. The tall leaded windows cast patterns across an Oriental rug and on the rear wall behind the desk hung crossed spears and several Sepik River masks beneath a mounted elephant tusk. Photographs filled the remaining space, several of them showing Allington in the midst of shorter aborigines.

In the flesh the man had obviously thickened with the years, and at the corners of his round blue eyes were lines of age and fatigue. His gray-streaked brown hair was cut short in military style and he sported an exaggerated waxed mustache beneath a bulbous nose.

The mementos on the wall matched Allington's pukka sahib manner. As he stood to greet her, Virginia guessed that Leonard had known him in the Colonial Service. Allington soon confirmed this.

"Ah, yes, Leonard Woolf, one of our best men in the East," he said after asking her to be seated. He gave her an appraising look and stroked his mustache. "So you're the woman he threw it all over for? Such a romantic story."

Virginia flushed. She knew Leonard's resignation from the service in Ceylon had provoked nasty remarks at the Colonial Club about "the penniless Jew" marrying into one of London's more distinguished literary families. The gossip had reached her own ears, thanks to her half-brother George Duckworth, himself displeased with her marriage. Now she nodded pleasantly, however, and agreed to give Leonard the Commissioner's regards.

"I gather you've come about a Yard investigation," said Allington.

"I'm not sure Special Branch can help."

"I'll do whatever I can," he assured her. "My primary responsibility is internal security. But when I heard you were here, I thought to see you myself. If I can't answer your questions, then I'll direct you to the appropriate officer. My assistant mentioned a woman's suicide. Someone you knew?"

She wasn't sure, but his eyes seemed kind. She decided she didn't have to lie. "No," she said, placing the autopsy report in front of him. "I wondered if the Yard could add anything to this. I mean, can you tell me if it truly confirms suicide by drowning?"

"Suicide by drowning," he repeated her words as a murmur, scrutinizing the report. "Yes, I'd say so." Then he looked over the rim of his glasses, a scowl pulling at his mouth. "Strange you should have this. Where did you get it?"

Virginia shifted uneasily in her chair. "Someone from the press had it, I believe, from the investigating officer." She fell silent. Through the room's cathedral windows came the sounds of the afternoon traffic on the embankment below.

"Someone from the press," he repeated. His verbal tic was beginning to annoy her. She supposed it was an affectation that gave him time to think.

He gave her a piercing look. "Our boys can be free and easy with reporters. Still, I notice the woman worked for Sir

Henry Cranford, and I'm sure he'd want to avoid publicity. This Fleet Street chap, he's not going after this as a story, is he?"

"I wouldn't know," she said, alerted by his wary tone to keep both Josephs and Bobbie out of the conversation. He seemed to know Cranford and she wondered if, in fact, he'd already heard about the case. "I came to the Yard because there seem to be some unanswered questions."

"Oh? For example?"

"First of all, she went out the night of her death dressed in her best clothes, apparently excited about meeting someone. Second, she was Catholic. And also, even though she was employed by Sir Henry her note said she had no work."

He stared at her over the rim of his glasses. "Where'd you get this information?"

"From Sir Henry."

He nodded and reached for the house phone to issue an order to his assistant. "We do want this handled properly," he said when he'd hung up. "If you'll just wait until I can adequately brief myself?" She nodded, saying nothing.

Within a few minutes a clerk arrived with a file. The Commissioner read aloud from the typewritten report: " 'Anna Michaux, age 46, found in the Serpentine, 4 November. Identification: immigration card with address, the Litchfield Arms'—one of those dreary refugee hotels in Soho," he added without looking up. "According to Sergeant Second-class V. S. Stewart of Hyde Park Barracks, 'time of death estimated between midnight and four A.M..' "

"There's nothing about her background?"

He turned to the second page. "Only this: according to Immigration records she fled Brussels in '14. There's a sister—one Elise Robert, a Mrs. Jacques Robert, now living in Paris."

"How did the police find that out?"

"From Sir Henry. I gather when he identified the body."

"Sir Henry!" She sat straighter in her chair, unaware that

she was raking the fingers of one hand across the palm of her other. "But that can't be. He told me she had no family." This morning she'd had the impression Cranford was lying. Here was proof. The nape of her neck tingled as she stared at Allington.

"Perhaps Sir Henry simply meant she had no family here in England. That's probably why he arranged for the funeral himself. Quite decent of him, really."

Virginia hesitated a moment. "Is it true the Yard ordered his name kept out of the news story?"

Allington seemed irritated that she was questioning Yard procedure. "It's not that unusual with public figures. Sir Henry is an advisor to the Prime Minister. He may have requested it or the Yard may have extended the courtesy. In any case, it's why I stressed the need for discretion once I saw he was involved." He glanced down at the file. "Oh, it's Sam Josephs at *The Mail,* is it? He was in the park. God knows, he should know enough to respect our wishes. I'm sure he was given the coroner's report confidentially."

"But you do feel it proves suicide?" asked Virginia, choosing to let him assume what he liked about Sam Josephs.

Allington removed his spectacles and pinched the bridge of his nose with his thumb and forefinger. "It seems quite in order, yes. The tests indicate she'd been in the water for several hours." He replaced his glasses. "You're not suggesting anything else, are you?"

"Aren't there other tests? How do you know whether she jumped from the bridge or walked into the water and held herself down?"

"You've been reading too many mystery stories," he said with a barely disguised chuckle. "No medical examiner can determine exactly what happened. Even Dr. Spilsbury could only guess, and he's the best pathologist we have. Evidently there were other clues." He paused to check back in the file.

"Here it is, fingerprints on the railing. Certainly that's enough to show she'd jumped into the Serpentine. Besides, Sir Henry himself has apparently expressed no reservations—" He was interrupted by the ring of his desk telephone.

"I told you, Moffit, MI$_5$'s to be kept out of it," he shouted. "It'll take them twelve hours to come up with anything and by then I'll have Bomb Division's report."

He paused, then burst out: "I don't care what Clarke is demanding. Bring him right here when he arrives."

He hung up. "Now what was I saying?" he asked, trying to hide his shaking hands by clasping them on the desk. "Oh, yes, just this. I hope Sir Henry doesn't think we sent you round."

"Not at all. He seemed quite willing to talk about Anna. His housekeeper, too—" she stopped, remembering a detail. "The coroner's report said her shoes were missing? Why? And what about her handbag? Did the police find it? Her gloves, too? If she left fingerprints, she must have taken them off. What about the slight bruise on her neck?"

Allington took his time reading through the file. "There's nothing here. But I'll check with the investigating officer. I daresay the missing clothes floated down river. As for the bruise, she may have hit herself on a rock, some object in the water." He paused. "On the face of it, Mrs. Woolf, this wouldn't be an important case but for Sir Henry. He's an old friend and, as I say, I'll speak to him directly. I don't want him unnecessarily alarmed." He gave her a reassuring smile. "At any rate, I doubt any of it warrants reopening the case."

"But there's one thing more. She had a friend at the Litchfield Arms, Marie Ickx, a Belgian. She's been missing for several days. Put that together with the Belgian refugee murdered in Bloombsury last week and I'd say there's very good reason to go on."

"Not really. Call it a coincidence. Chalk it up to the number of Belgians now living in the city. About the missing woman, I'll have the Soho precinct look into it. Her name again?"

She spelled out Marie Ickx for him.

"Now, Mrs. Woolf, as for your suspicions," he removed a small piece of paper from the file and held it up, "we do have conclusive evidence: the woman's suicide note."

"That's strange, too. Why did she say, 'no work' when—" She stopped, peering at the note. "Let me see that." She took it out of his hand before he could refuse.

The once blue paper was mottled with water stains. Still visible were large, round letters formed by a thick pen. "No mother, No father, No work." The words jumped out at her; flamboyant spirals trailed from the "w" and "k" in "work."

"No!" The suicide note trembled in her hands. Her face felt tight, her voice a throaty whisper as she repeated, "No, no. Impossible!"

"What do you mean?"

She riveted Allington with her eyes. Her voice rose; she seemed to be speaking in short bursts as her doubts of the morning took shape: suddenly she felt afraid again.

"This isn't her handwriting. I've seen Anna's handwriting . . . on a photograph, and she didn't write this! Someone else did. Someone who wanted it to look like suicide."

7

Virginia was hardly in the mood for her sister's party that night even though she'd spent the week before convincing Leonard she was well enough to attend. As much as she had resisted, she now agreed with Bobbie's suspicions. If Anna hadn't written the note, then who had? And why? Commissioner Allington's promise to give the case his personal attention seemed half-hearted. He had been kind enough, but even her announcement had hardly alarmed him. His final, "We'll get to the bottom of this," was just too predictable and had prompted her to stop by Dr. Wright's office in Harley Street, a visit that had set her head pounding.

"Nothing wrong, I hope?" the doctor had greeted her. "Leonard's medical exemption was passed, wasn't it?" He gestured her to the armchair which she'd called "the dock" ever since first coming to him.

"Your letter got him permanently exempted," she replied, "two days ago." Forcing a smile, she had then taken the autopsy report from her handbag, aware that he was staring at her.

"You seem thinner, my dear. Have you been losing weight?"

"I don't think so. I've—"

"I don't want you below nine stone. I was happier when you weighed twelve."

"I was disgustingly fat. But that's not why—"

"And remember, only three hours of work a day. We don't want a relapse."

"I know what I'm supposed to do," she said impatiently. "Though I'll never finish my novel at that rate."

"That's not my concern. Put yourself on an even keel, then we'll discuss your writing schedule. Leonard suspects that writing your first novel caused your breakdown. All that dwelling on your parents, imagining your character's death. That's not happening again, is it?"

She gave him a wary look but shook her head.

"Well, it isn't like you to drop in without an appointment. Your monthlies? Are they regular? No headaches? No melancholy thoughts?"

Despite the quick shake of her head to each question, he continued. "There's no reason you can't keep up a happy frame of mind. Leonard and I hoped that your leasing Hogarth House and starting the press together would keep you away from too many friends and parties. As I've said, the people we're most fond of often aren't good for us. So if Hogarth House and Richmond aren't isolated enough, if setting type doesn't keep your mind off yourself, then another visit to Miss Thomas's nursing home will be in order."

She eyed him narrowly, wondering if this was a threat. Had Leonard read her diary and told him of her interest in Anna? She took a deep breath. "I'm here to ask you about this," she said quickly, sliding the autopsy report across his desk. "In your professional opinion, does this confirm suicide?"

The doctor's face became rigid as he read the report. "How in God's name did you get hold of this?"

She waved her hand. "That's not important. Would you

just explain those terms? The woman may not have drowned herself and—"

"Hold on there." He stood up and paced back and forth behind his desk. "I won't allow this. You're disobeying, aren't you?"

It was the word "suicide," and, no, he wouldn't allow it, couldn't, since her interest in the woman's death was so obviously symptomatic of her own morbid obsessions. The customary speech about food, sleep and "keeping things in proportion" soon followed, interminably like some stentorian roll-call. She listened, trying to control herself. Finally she could bear it no longer and snatched up the autopsy report. "You and your bloody sense of proportion can go to blazes," she shouted and rushed from the office. Outside on the stoop, she turned back. She could see him through the office window, already talking on the telephone, undoubtedly to Leonard.

"You should have rested for the party tonight," scolded Leonard when she returned to Hogarth House.

She had gone to the library, then to buy stockings, she explained. She wasn't about to tell him about her interviews or her throbbing head, though she suspected he was testing her. But Leonard said nothing about a call from Wright, and in her bath she wondered if she was mistaken. He had been hovering for so many months, watching for any sign of depression, that she was bound to mistrust the most innocent remark.

She looked down at her long thin body as she sponged her shoulders. It was true, she had lost weight, but she was glad. Her body felt like her own again, not that of the heavy matron Leonard and Wright wanted to make of her, so much so that last summer she'd felt like a white, unpalatable block of lard. And still, they were always ready with yet another glass of milk or a plate of porridge, not to mention the smelling salts and Veronal.

Calmer, the headache gone, she took her time dressing, all the while thinking of Anna Michaux. If the Yard refused to investigate, what could she and Bobbie do? She felt frustrated, and even her new apricot brocade dress couldn't lift her spirits. On the train into town Leonard again remarked that she seemed tired and oddly quiet. A few gossipy remarks about her sister seemed to convince him that she'd put on a festive mood, but she was conscious of her own forced laughter.

The party was well underway in Maynard Keynes's flat at 46 Gordon Square, launched with several bottles of the economist's champagne. Not that Keynes had relinquished his parsimonious ways. He'd lent his rooms to Virginia's sister, Vanessa Bell, and her lover Duncan Grant, who were in town for an exhibition of their paintings at the Omega Workshops, a gallery for both paintings and crafts. They'd pillaged Keynes's wine cabinet, though, intending to celebrate Duncan's vacation from farm work, the national service assigned to most conscientious objectors.

Vanessa rushed out to greet them on the landing. Like Virginia, she was tall and wore her hair in a bun. But her face and figure were fuller and softer, and with her large blue eyes and gentle mouth, she was considered the greater beauty. Now she took Virginia's hands and whirled her around as she'd done often as a child.

"Oh, Billy Goat, it's grand to have you back at our parties!" She gave Leonard a perfunctory kiss and pushed them into the crowded sitting room.

Virginia saw some of her oldest friends scattered among the guests. Duncan waved from one corner; Lytton Strachey was in the center of a group of young men, rising above them in both height and voice. In another corner stood the painters, among whom she saw Mark Gertler shaking a fist at Roger Fry, the art critic and founder of the Omega. On the sofa sat Virginia and Vanessa's younger brother Adrian, trying to look at ease with his wife Karen but still stiff and self-conscious as always. The other guests were strangers. Undoubtedly, they'd heard that Vanessa was reviving the old Bloomsbury evenings, the war and the blackout curtains be damned.

Virginia moved aimlessly among them, stopping to smile distractedly at the friendly jibes of several younger women who often made appearances at Bloomsbury evenings—"the cropheads" as she'd named them for their stylishly bobbed hair. Ordinarily she would have found them attractive in their emerald and amber dresses. Now, she retreated through the wide archway to the less crowded inner room where she took a seat alone on the sofa.

"Hello, 'Ginia. Looks as if you need a drink."

She looked up and smiled, relieved to see Roger Fry leaning over to hand her a glass of champagne. Once Vanessa's lover, Fry was the man Virginia most trusted. She knew she could confide in him without his repeating things to Leonard. There was a fundamental integrity to him, a sense of self-possession, which the others lacked.

He sat beside her. "Your novel worrying you? Nessa tells me you're writing again."

"I've only just started. But that's not it." She glanced warily toward the front room. "I've been trying to find out about a woman, a Belgian refugee who—"

She stopped. Vanessa was guiding Leonard through the crowd. Her blue-green diaphanous dress shimmered in the dim light. She more than lived up to her nickname "Dolphin" as she leapt from one group to another with grace and playfulness.

"Duncan's the lucky man now," Roger muttered as he continued to stare after Vanessa. Then he gave Virginia a conspiratorial smile. "What were you saying? I don't think Leonard will interrupt."

"Catch on rather quickly, don't you?" She swirled the champagne in her glass and studied the bubbles as they broke the surface.

"Doesn't it ever bother you that we're all so isolated?" she asked. "We go through days on end, working, eating, sleeping, finding the same little pleasures in life. But we never consider how fragile it all is. Then something happens to break through our screens. . . ."

"What's this to do with a Belgian woman?"

She took a sip of champagne, telling him about the news story and suicide note.

"So that's why you don't want Leonard to know about it?"

"Quite. He was terribly upset when I first showed him the story. Said I mustn't dwell on suicide, that it would make me sick again." She rolled her eyes in exasperation. "But I've discovered some things that just don't make sense. Now I can't believe it was a suicide. In fact, there may be a connection to that other Belgian woman who was killed here in Bloomsbury."

"Oh, no, Virginia, not you too!" Standing over them was her old friend Lytton Strachey; she knew he was in especially high spirits, having finished a large portion of his new book which he was calling "Eminent Victorians." Still, she found herself annoyed by his affected speech and foppish gestures as he hooted across the room to Dora Carrington. A sturdy young painter with a shiny red-gold bob, Carrington, as she was called, was devoted to him and quickly came to his side.

"Now, Mopsa," said Lytton, "I want you to tell Virginia how you solved the Bloomsbury Butcher Case."

Carrington blushed and shook her head, aware of Virginia's pained expression.

"Then I'll read your letter myself." Lytton's voice rose to his famous nasal whine. "Or at least those parts fit for public consumption."

Virginia knew the flamboyant writer well enough not to try to stop him. One of her first male confidants, he'd once even proposed marriage but the next morning they'd both realized how unsuitable the match was. Despite his widely proclaimed homosexuality, Carrington loved him and he basked in her daily adoring letters. Retrieving a piece of paper from his tweed jacket, he pushed his glasses up his nose, cleared his throat, and began to read.

" 'After you left, the conversation became lurid with abortions and limbless bodies. The ten-month versus the nine-month birth case and menstruation were discussed. Then the horrid murder of the Bloomsbury Belgian, and how one would dispose of a body if one committed a murder. In the end' "—he tugged at Roger's arm—" 'it was decided that Roger would embalm it, fake a mummy case and sell it as an antique at the Omega!' "

"But how did you know?" hooted Roger. "I've learned that trick from Dr. Spilsbury!"

The name brought Virginia up sharp. Spilsbury! Allington had mentioned him that very afternoon.

"What's this about Dr. Spilsbury?" she whispered in Roger's ear.

From the front room there came a swell of laughter.

"You'll never believe what Clive's doing now!" cried Lytton over the noise as he glanced toward the front door.

Virginia and Roger craned their necks to see. Clive Bell was Vanessa's husband—though now in name only—and he'd arrived at the party with a woman draped in bright yellow silk and looking, Virginia thought, like a canary.

"My God, he's really brought Mary," she said aloud, recognizing Mrs. St John Hutchinson, a cousin of Lytton's rumored to be Clive's new mistress.

But Virginia was even more startled when she saw Lord Ladbrooke move to Clive's side.

"Oh, no," she muttered.

"What?" asked Roger.

"You know how Clive loves to name-drop. Only this

time he's dropped the name in our laps. That's Lord Ladbrooke. I met him this morning. Don't say anything."

Clive and Mary sauntered over. "We ran into Alex at the Savoy Grill," Clive said without a pause, "and I thought we'd all pop round. . . ."

"Who?" asked Virginia, nudging Roger.

Clive glanced over his shoulder.

"*Lord* Alex Ladbrooke. The man talking to Leonard."

"A Lord, did you say?" It was an old game, boasting of titled friends. Clive, she felt, used it to put distance between himself and his Midlands commercial family.

"He's an old friend of Mary's," Clive continued. "A distinguished family, I must say. Alex sits on every City committee you can think of, and Lloyd George wouldn't spend a guinea without consulting him. By the way, Roger, he has a perfectly wonderful art collection."

"What in blazes do you think you're doing?" Vanessa interrupted, swooping down on them.

"Well, really, Nessa, we're all adults. . . ."

"I don't mean Mary. This party's for our friends. Not for strangers who provoke political arguments."

Clive glared at her. "Even if I have to be out at Garsington, I share these digs. I still have some rights here. Besides, Lord Ladbrooke is a friend."

"You'd better look after him then. Leonard and he are already arguing about a negotiated peace."

"If Woolf's spouting off again, it's not my fault." As he hurried away to the front room, Virginia whispered to Roger, "I want to talk to you about this Dr. Spilsbury."

Before he could reply Lord Ladbrooke appeared at her elbow. Clive quickly came up behind them and a look of surprise crossed his face as he heard Ladbrooke say, "Mrs. Woolf, what a pleasure."

Frustrated, Virginia introduced Roger.

Ladbrooke beamed. "Roger Fry! Can't tell you how

much I've enjoyed your essays. Ever since your Post-Impressionist exhibitions at the Grafton I've been collecting Cézanne's." He guided Roger a few feet away. Clive glared after them. "How do you know Ladbrooke?" he demanded.

"I met his wife yesterday. Then this morning I ran into him at Sir Henry Cranford's."

"Don't tell me you know him too?"

"Not really. Do you?"

"No, but rumor has it that Maynard's making a few private purchases from the Degas collection for one and the same. For himself, too. I call that rather dodgy."

"Sounds more like sour grapes."

Clive raised his voice to make sure Ladbrooke could hear. "My point is that people sent to Paris should know more about art than Maynard to advise either the government or Sir Henry."

"Oh? On what basis is someone qualified?" asked Ladbrooke, turning back to Clive.

"For example, there are certain principles of aesthetics which I discuss in my book. . . ."

As Clive began to lecture, Virginia took Roger aside. "I'm not in the mood for Clive's version of your ideas," she said as she drew him out on the landing.

"Clive getting your goat again?" he teased.

"I'm just tired of his silly intrigues."

"I wouldn't be too hard on him. Besides, I think you're more concerned about your Belgian woman than Clive's worn-out poses."

Once again he'd read her accurately, just as he always had, ever since she'd traveled with him and Vanessa in Italy and Greece. Part of it was his unbounded receptivity; like a bright purple sea urchin, she thought, pulling into itself any bit of life that passes its way. But he also genuinely liked women, making him more responsive, certainly, than Lytton or any of the others she'd maliciously dubbed the "Bloomsbury buggers" for their hostility toward women. With Roger she could be honest; he seemed to draw from her emotions that she had sometimes not yet admitted to herself.

"When I first read the news story, I kept thinking how she had thrown it all away," she began at Roger's urging. "Like a coin you toss into a river, perhaps. Then I decided to find out more, I felt I had to."

"Why?"

"To understand what brought this woman to realize she still mourned her parents, even in middle age. I'd been trying to explain that feeling to Leonard. So I thought if I could discover the details of her suicide, I might be able to prove I wasn't so odd; that it isn't so strange to yearn for death at some time in your life. . . ." Her voice trailed off. Then she spoke with force: "That's why I first went round to *The Mail.* But my questions have only made it more complicated. And I think . . . yes, I'm frightened. I'm sure the woman didn't write the suicide note. I saw the note itself this afternoon, and it was definitely not her handwriting. It could mean she didn't kill herself and—"

"Wait. Don't get excited, start from the beginning."

Virginia listed the discrepancies discovered during her interviews with Cranford and Allington and Bobbie's doubts about the autopsy report. "That's why I want to know about Dr. Spilsbury."

"I'm not surprised. He's famous for his new diagnostic methods."

"Look here," she said with excitement as she took the autopsy report from her bag and unfolded it. "Could Spilsbury tell if the coroner's tests in this case actually prove anything?"

"You're asking quite a lot from a written report. Still, drownings are Spilsbury's specialty. His most famous case was the man who drowned a number of wives but the Yard couldn't prove it. Spilsbury devised new tests to demonstrate that someone can be forcibly submerged in water with no signs of struggle. I could show him this report. But it has to be tomorrow. I'm going to Paris on Friday."

"Take it with you tonight then. Ring me in the morning." She paused, thinking. "I'm convinced Cranford was hiding something. Perhaps Spilsbury will find the reason here, in the report."

"Perhaps; at least he'd know what's missing. If he himself had performed the autopsy he'd have been able to determine whether the governess held herself under water or whether she—" he gave Virginia a sharp look—"was forced under or knocked unconscious. . . ."

"And that's called murder!" It was Clive, lounging in the doorway, his arms folded across his chest. "I thought the two of you were up to something. So this is why you called on Sir Henry today, Virginia? His governess drowns herself and you suspect foul play."

"Dammit, Clive. If you so much as mention this!"

"I'm sure Leonard would love to have an earful. But no, I won't say a word, I promise. As long as you tell me why you think Sir Henry's lying."

"Go to blazes, you bloody extortionist!"

"That was probably a mistake," said Roger after Clive chuckled and sauntered back into the main room.

"I know," muttered Virginia. "But why is he always interfering and stirring up trouble?"

"Virginia!" Predictably, it was Leonard, now at the door, holding Virginia's cape in his trembling hands. "We're going home. Now!" he announced.

"What's this? My punishment?" she asked dryly, giving Roger a sidelong glance. Clive was a few feet behind Leonard and with a smile whispered to Lord Ladbrooke who stood beside him. "Thanks *so* much, Clive," she shouted.

"Don't make a scene," said Leonard. "All I want to know is why you lied to me. You said you didn't care about that woman's death."

She stared at him for a moment, tears of frustration welling up in her eyes. "If you'd try to understand, I wouldn't have to lie." She grabbed her cape from him and ran downstairs. At the front door she turned and called back to Roger, "And do what you promised. Tomorrow!"

In the morning Leonard retreated from her icy silence to the printing press in the basement. She waited by the telephone in the front hall and answered Roger's call on the first ring. Hearing the rhythmic clank of the press from downstairs, she told him she could speak freely.

He sounded excited as he rattled off the reasons why Spilsbury thought the autopsy was inadequate: There was no measurement of the blood's dilution by water, nor was there any indication of diatomes and algae penetrating the body. The heart's left ventricle hadn't been examined, a test that showed whether the deceased had died in or out of water. And finally, the coroner had failed to investigate the discoloration on the neck.

The details sent a shiver down Virginia's spine. "So the report doesn't prove suicide?" she said.

"Not at all," said Roger. "That's why Spilsbury wanted another autopsy."

"You mean he'll exhume the body?"

"That's the problem. There is no body! Anna Michaux was cremated."

"What!" Her knees were weak. The earpiece felt like lead in her hand. "Impossible!" she cried. "Anna was Catholic." She forced herself to think. "Did Sir Henry agree to it?"

"That's even stranger. There's no record of any order."

"Oh Christ!" she muttered. There was only one reason: no body, no evidence. No evidence to prove—"Roger, do you know what this means?"

"Yes. . . ." He hesitated as if his silence would compel her to say it.

"It wasn't a suicide. It was just made to look like one. It

was. . . ." The word caught in her throat. "She was killed!"

She fell silent, her breathing shallow as she pictured Anna's face.

"Virginia, are you there?" asked Roger in alarm.

"Yes," she whispered. Then her voice turned vehement: "Why would anyone kill her?"

8

A motor car moved through the deserted streets of Le Havre in the early hours of Sunday morning. Inside Henri Giraud shuffled the papers his driver had handed him, then snapped his attaché case shut and leaned forward to peer into the rear-view mirror. It wasn't necessary, the driver had proven his skill often enough in the past. But tonight Giraud felt the need to reassure himself. Sleepless for the last two nights, he had shadows under his brown eyes and lines around his full, soft mouth. His jaw was set as he closed his eyes and rubbed the scar on his left cheek.

His body felt the car slow. He jerked himself upright.

"Any problem?" he asked in French.

"A dog in the road," the driver replied. A stubble of beard covered the lower half of his face, but Giraud knew that like the rest of his men the driver dressed like a French workman in order to move easily about Le Havre. It was a disguise to which he too sometimes resorted.

The car twisted through the last of the labyrinthine streets leading to the Place Frederic Sauvage and drew up in front of a Norman manor house. Instructing the driver to return in an hour, Giraud mounted the broad steps to the entrance where a guard saluted and stepped back to let him pass.

Once a private residence, the house had been converted into offices for the Belgian government-in-exile. Sandbags were stacked waist-high along the corridors, the windows were shuttered with iron plate, and on each landing stood an armed guard. Echoing down the stairwell from the top floor came the clatter of telegraphy machines, all in use despite the hour.

Giraud hurried to his third floor office. His name was stenciled in large letters on the glass door and, in smaller print, *"Bureau des Renseignements."*

Inside, the walls were covered with maps and several pieces of dusty furniture had been pushed to one side to make room for two desks and their chairs. Behind the larger desk was a small oil painting by Corot, a landscape, at which Giraud hardly glanced as he sat down to read the messages left for his review.

Ten minutes later, the decoding of a wire from Paris brought a worried look to his face. Where had he heard the name before? And why had this person come? Whatever the reason, the information changed things. His trip would be delayed at least 24 hours. He had to be patient, both patient and careful, he reminded himself for the third time that day.

Identical row houses fronted the neat, tree-lined streets of the Paris suburb of Issy. Virginia found Number 20, rue de Lafayette, quite easily. Her decision to accompany Roger to Paris had been impetuous, the result, she knew, of Spilsbury's all too damning view of the autopsy procedure, as well too her need to expunge any lingering doubts. Ignoring Leonard's objections, she'd suffered the stormy Channel crossing and spent Saturday morning locating Anna's sister, Mme. Jacques Robert.

No one answered the door at Number 20. But convinced she must see Mme. Robert, she sat down on the top front step and, oblivious to the stares of passersby, smoked a cigarette.

"What are you doing there?" a woman called to her from the bottom of the steps. Despite her fleshy face, Virginia recognized the deep-set, somber eyes she'd seen in Anna Michaux's photograph.

Virginia explained in French why she'd come.

"But I told the police all I know," the woman sighed. She came up the steps and fiddled with a key in the lock.

"I think you'll want to hear what I have to say," Virginia insisted. "Your sister may not have killed herself after all."

Startled, Elise Robert hesitated, then invited Virginia in and gestured her to an overstuffed armchair. She took her time unpinning her hat, as if trying to compose herself. "Now, what do you mean? The police told me it was suicide, pure and simple."

"Scotland Yard closed the case, true. But there are some questions. . . ."

"I'm not interested," she said. "If you're a friend of Anna's, take it up with the police."

"You might be able to help. If you could tell me about Anna, her friends in London?"

"I didn't even know she was in London. I hadn't heard from her since the beginning of the war. Frankly, I was just as glad. I hold her responsible for our parents." The woman paused, her anger now mixed with sorrow.

"Please tell me, what happened?" asked Virginia.

Elise Robert shrugged. "What is there to say? Anna was too busy to help them. When the Germans invaded, my sister should have taken them out of the country. I begged her to."

"You couldn't do anything?"

"I was already living in Paris with my husband. He's in the army, an engineer." She glanced at his photograph on the chimney piece. "Anna never approved of Jacques. She said we were bourgeois. She was the free-thinker, with her job in the publishing firm and her political friends from university. Yet when it was necessary she failed my mother and father." The bitterness returned to her voice. "Perhaps she finally realized what she'd done."

"You're a Catholic, aren't you?" The woman nodded. "Then how can you think suicide is God's will, or a form of retribution?"

"I don't want to talk about it." She stood up and walked to the front window. Her back was to Virginia but she was trembling.

"Did you tell Sir Henry Cranford to have her cremated? Were you that angry?"

Elise Robert whirled around to face her. "Of course not. I wouldn't betray my faith that way. Her employer must have known that she no longer believed."

Virginia shook her head, but Elise Robert ignored her and picked up a worn, leather-bound book from the side table. "Here. This arrived yesterday. No letter, nothing. Perhaps it was her parting gesture." She handed it to Virginia and returned to the sofa.

The book was an edition of Michelet's *Louis XV et Louis XVI*.

Virginia thumbed the pages. Then she went more slowly. On most of the pages there were words underlined. "Did she think you'd be interested in French history?"

"Of course not. She must have known the book would upset me. You see the publisher?"

Virginia turned back to the frontispiece. *"Editions du Nord,"* she read aloud.

"That's where Anna worked in Brussels. She helped start the firm with her lover; she was his editor and translator. I never met him. But that's why she couldn't be bothered with my parents. She and Giraud—Henri Giraud was his name—they went to Le Havre together, to work for the government-in-exile. That's where he is now. The Minister of Information. A Belgian patriot. Ha! What did he care about my parents!" Tears glittered in the woman's eyes.

"I'm sorry. It must be painful." Virginia stood, her mind already made up. She had another plan.

"Will you be going back to London?" the woman asked.

"Eventually. Why?"

"A detective from Scotland Yard, an Inspector Brown, came last Tuesday. He wanted to know if Anna had sent anything. Particularly books, he said. This hadn't come yet, so perhaps you should take it to him. If it matters so much."

Once more it made no sense. If the Yard was treating it as an insignificant case, why send a man to France? Perhaps it was important enough to involve Special Branch. But if so, why hadn't the Yard asked the French police to see Elise Robert? Another thought occurred to her, and she shuddered. Perhaps Brown wasn't a Yard detective at all, but only pretending to be in order to claim the book.

Virginia put the book in her handbag. "I'll show this to Scotland Yard. It may indeed be important." Mme. Robert made no response. "I don't know if this is any comfort," Virginia went on. "But it's possible that Anna felt guilty about your parents. At least, if she wrote the suicide note, she was still mourning their deaths."

Elise Robert glared at Virginia through her tears. "My parents aren't dead. They're in prison somewhere in Germany!"

The train trip to Le Havre was absolutely necessary. If Anna's parents were alive, the suicide note was an outright lie. Now, sitting in the train, Virginia felt her throat constrict as murder became an inescapable conclusion, and she tried to concentrate on the other travelers in the compartment. All four were soldiers, one wearing a bandage around his head, another with his arm in a sling. None was over 20, she guessed, all of them with the glazed look of trench fatigue. They spoke among themselves but in French too colloquial for her to follow.

This was the double tragedy of war, she thought, as she watched them pass a bottle of wine. If not death, then their memories of battles; always to think of war as heroic, a ritual of manhood, just like the men sitting in London offices who romanticized the Hindenburg Line as an extension of Eton. Either way it was an evasion, a hopeless, perverse repetition of history.

The soldiers disembarked at one of the countless checkpoints along the route, clambering from the compartment, pulling their equipment behind them. Virginia turned back to study Anna's book but could make no sense of the underlinings. The marked words were neither difficult nor ambiguous.

Soon the motion of the train lulled her to sleep. As she dozed, French phrases flickered through her mind. She heard Anna's name; she was walking in a forest. In a clearing she saw a large abandoned house, and drawn to it, she ran through the woods and up the front stairs. From the attic she heard a woman weeping. She called out Anna's name, then heard a voice from outside: "Stop her. She's going to jump." She ran up the stairs. The attic was filled with old furniture and trunks. A woman was looking out an open window. "Anna!" Virginia heard herself shout. "Don't! Your parents aren't dead." The woman turned. It was her own face smiling back at her, she was the woman at the window. She felt exhilarated as she stepped over the ledge, leaping into the open air. She was floating downward, spinning through wisps of clouds, the wind billowing her hair behind her. There was nothing to stop her—no weight, no time, no space. No division between herself and the sky, immense and gentle and infinite.

Suddenly she was jolted awake. They were in Le Havre, the train hissing and motionless at the station platform. Dazed and disoriented, she asked a taxi driver to take her to the nearest good hotel.

Her head still hurting, she went to bed as soon as she was given a room. The dream haunted her. Was it a warning? Had

Leonard been right to suspect she was reliving her own suicide attempts through Anna Michaux's death? When she'd jumped from a window in Violet Dickinson's country house she'd had the same floating sensation, the sudden release from anger and guilt at her father's death. Hours later she'd awakened with no awareness of hitting the ground. But the memory of floating stayed with her. She'd always thought that drowning would feel the same—the purest experience of freedom—and she supposed that's why she'd been so taken by Anna's suicide.

But it was no longer a question of imagining Anna's drowning in the Serpentine. There was the certainty of murder, something cold and public.

She slept fitfully that night and awakened early, realizing again what it was that had prompted her to leave a note for Roger and rush off to Le Havre. Although it was Sunday morning, the offices of the Belgian government were open. She asked for Henri Giraud at the reception desk. The soldier on duty directed her to the third floor.

Mounting the stairs, she saw a man watching her from the third floor landing. He was extraordinarily handsome, dressed in a dark tweed jacket, a blue jersey and gray flannel slacks. To her astonishment, he came forward and greeted her. "Mrs. Woolf? I'm Henri Giraud." He escorted her into his office.

She could well imagine Anna Michaux falling in love with him. No government official she'd ever met had so attractive a sweep of dark brown hair across his forehead or such large, almost black-brown eyes. She guessed he was about 50, judging by the gray at his temples and the lines around his mouth. A thin scar on his left cheek lent an even more exaggerated cast to his Byronic looks.

"I want to ask you about your friend Anna Michaux," she said, taking the chair in front of his desk.

"Oh, I see. A reference, I suppose." He'd been lounging in his desk chair and now leaned forward and picked up a pencil. "I'll be glad to—" He stopped, noticing Virginia's pale face. "What's the matter?"

Virginia took in a deep breath. "I'm sorry, I supposed you'd heard. Anna Michaux is dead."

"Dead? My God!" His face went rigid. He shook his head, trying to absorb it. Virginia thought she saw tears in his eyes.

"What happened?" he asked after a moment.

"The police say she drowned herself. Her body was found in the Serpentine, the river running through Hyde Park."

"She must have been very depressed. The war. . . . She'd been unable to return home, unable to find work. Oh, damn." He looked at her steadily. "She was a dear friend."

"So her sister said."

"You've seen Elise?" When she nodded, he smiled ruefully. "I suppose she told you Anna and I were lovers. We were, a long time ago. But we remained friends. She helped me start *Editions du Nord.* Then she went to London and I didn't hear from her very often. A few letters in the beginning, but recently nothing. Damn! I should have suspected something."

"It wasn't suicide!" said Virginia evenly.

"What?" She saw his hands tremble. "But you said the police—"

He listened intently as Virginia recited what she had discovered, ending with the false suicide note. "You see she did have work. And her parents are alive too."

Giraud swept his hand through his hair. "But Anna thought they were dead. She told me. Perhaps Elise hasn't been told."

"Possibly," she said. "Anna hadn't been in touch with her sister until she sent the book, just before her death."

"Book?"

She explained. "Your edition, in fact."

"Anna always liked Michelet. Perhaps she was translating it for a British firm."

"It has some strange underlinings in it, and someone claiming to be from the police inquired about it, the London police. I'm taking it back to the Yard."

"Do you have it with you? Perhaps I could make sense of the underlinings."

"No, I left it in my hotel room."

He paused, then sighed again and looked at his watch. "I'm due at a meeting, but I'd like to go on with this. You must have other reasons to suspect Anna's suicide. . . ."

"There's the autopsy report."

"Then can you meet me tonight, say here about nine-thirty? We can have a late dinner, I'll have food brought in."

"May I bring a friend? Roger Fry."

"The art critic?"

"Yes. He's been helping me. In fact, he knows more about the autopsy report than I do. He's arriving from Paris on the evening train. He rang me this morning, worried that I'd come here alone."

"By all means, bring him." He rose to escort her out. "And please be careful," he said at the top of the stairs. "Mr. Fry is right. These days Le Havre isn't the safest of cities."

Giraud's warning seemed sensible. In the café where she went for lunch a man with a beard and a fisherman's cap seemed to be watching her. Also, signs of the war were all around. Military machinery atop lorries, petrol drums ready for export, refugees and troops alike seemed to fill the streets. She was probably only imagining it, she told herself, but there still seemed reason for uneasiness and she chose to spend the afternoon in the hotel room where she compiled a list of the underlined words in Anna's book.

She could translate the French easily since she was quite familiar with Michelet's work. Once, in fact, when Lytton had denounced it as a vile book, she'd insisted that Michelet's style was thoroughly masculine and one which she'd emulate if she wrote histories. Still, she took little pleasure in the writing now since the list of underlined words revealed nothing: neither why Anna had sent the book to her sister, nor why she'd liked this volume, nor even why she'd marked these pages so randomly.

Perhaps the words had private resonances, thought Virginia, like the sympathetic chimes of a bell. She tried to imagine Anna's own reactions, plunging beneath the surface of the words to the unconscious, to what she called the hidden caverns of the mind. But staring at the words seemed only to pin them to the page; like moths their wings shriveled and turned to dust.

Frustrated with her lack of progress and eager to get back to Giraud, she was dressed to go out when, as arranged, Roger appeared at the door direct from the station. She'd already made a reservation for him for the room next to her own and followed him inside.

"Don't unpack. We have an appointment with Giraud at nine-thirty."

"Good God, Virginia, I'm exhausted. Besides, weren't you seeing him this morning?"

"There wasn't enough time to discuss everything so he suggested dinner tonight. Please, you must come. He wants to hear about the autopsy report."

He agreed with a sigh.

Because the nighttime restriction on taxis was already in effect, they set out on foot, Virginia leading the way to the street that fronted the harbor. To their left, the bay was slick and still with tendrils of fog curling around the fishing smacks and shrouding the upper decks of the Southampton ferry moored at the end of the quay. Near the sea wall a mangy dog nosed at fish crates, while in the dark shadows of the pier dock workers were stacking a shipment of ammunition.

"What's that?" asked Roger, suddenly stopping.

"I don't hear anything."

"Listen. Those thuds from across the water. It must be shelling in the trenches. We're that close to the Front!"

"Sounds more like charwomen thumping heavy tapestries. . . ." She pulled Roger onward, telling him about her visit with Giraud that morning. "He's intelligent and attractive. I'm sure you'll like him," she said.

"You're that taken with him? After what, ten minutes? Is that why you're looking so elegant?"

"Don't be silly," she snapped. "I know you'll agree once you meet him. He even has what I think is a Corot in his office."

As they turned away from the harbor and crossed the Place Gambetta, Roger pressed her for more details about the painting.

"I wonder how he came by that particular one," he said when she'd described the landscape. "Schwartzheimer in Antwerp took six Corots off an Alsatian through some shady dealings with the Schaeffer Gallery in Paris. Some people suspect it has some ties to the Germans." He paused, noticing that Virginia had begun to shiver.

"Want my overcoat?"

"No, thanks. I'm not cold. Just frightened. I suppose it's the blackout."

Roger glanced up at the darkened windows above the heavily gated shop fronts. "That's why I wasn't happy to find your note yesterday. This is hardly the place for a woman."

"You're beginning to sound like Leonard. Stop it."

"And he, indeed, sent a wire today. He accused us of lying and ordered you home."

"How did he find out the real reason for my trip?"

"My fault, I'm afraid. I mentioned it to Vanessa. She probably let it slip to Clive, who'd be sure to tell Leonard."

"You should know you can't tell Nessa anything. What did Leonard say?"

"You'd think it was a military order: 'Return home at once. Will not tolerate—' Wait, I'll show you."

"Here," he said, retrieving a cable from his coat pocket. He struck a match and held it up so that she could see. "Only a few years ago he was a man of the world in Ceylon with his hunting and his sweepstakes winnings. Now he's a maiden aunt. Here."

" 'Your lies, your subterfuge,' " Virginia read aloud.

"How long are you going to put up with it?" He dropped the match, then lit another. "You're not a child, and his tone with me is—"

Suddenly he blew out the match and peered into the darkness behind them.

"What's the matter?" she asked.

"I thought I heard footsteps." They both listened. There was only silence.

Then from beyond the last turn came a series of small explosions. They recognized the sound of an engine starting up.

"That's funny. We didn't pass a motor car," Roger whispered. "But I heard one as we crossed the square."

Virginia's eyes were wide. "Do you think we were followed?"

"Look!" he said.

An open car was just rounding the corner. As it moved toward them they could see that next to the driver another man was standing, a gun balanced on the rim of the high windscreen.

"Oh, my God," cried Virginia. She jumped back, pulling Roger into a doorway.

The headlights of the car came on, blinding them. Frozen in its beams, they flattened themselves against the side of the building.

Suddenly a third man leapt from a entryway halfway between them and the car. He was running toward them, silhouetted in the beams of the headlights, his macintosh flapping at his sides. In his right hand they saw the glint of metal. Another gun, pointing at them as he ran.

"Get down," cried Roger, throwing Virginia to the ground and covering her with his body.

Shots rang out over their heads. The running man stopped in midair. He let out a shriek and spun in his tracks. He weaved drunkenly, trying to aim his pistol at the figure in the car. Flashes of light burst from the muzzle of the automatic gun held by the man standing in the auto. A staccato of shots echoed down the narrow street.

The man in the macintosh screamed again. Bent double, he stumbled backward until he collapsed.

Virginia was pinned by Roger. At first she thought he'd been shot. She shifted under him, and he moved aside into a crouch. She sat up and leaned against the wall, her throat constricted by fear.

The man lay on his back not three or four yards away, dark stains spreading across his shirtfront. She could see that he wore a fisherman's cap and had a growth of beard. He was the same man she'd seen in the café. She gulped for air, trying to speak, but her mouth felt like cotton batting. A wave of nausea washed over her.

The man moved, trying to struggle to his hands and knees. His breath came in rattling gurgles. He groped toward her, his fingers clawing at the pavement to pull himself forward.

"Get up," said Roger, "we've got to move." He pulled her to her feet, then braced her against his side. The car lurched toward them. Over the sound of the engine, the man standing beside the driver shouted at them in French: "Stay where you are."

The car stopped in front of them, only inches away from

the body. The driver leapt out and glanced up and down the street as the gunman rushed to the wounded man and bent over him.

"Est-il mort?" asked the driver in a sharp voice.

The gunman did not reply. He picked up the man's hand-gun from the pavement and shoved the figure over onto its back. Then he aimed the revolver at the man's head. There was an explosion. A small black hole appeared in his temple.

"He is now," said the gunman. He rose and gestured toward the motorcar. "Hurry up!"

Virginia's hands went up to her face. She let out a high, piercing scream. The driver stepped forward now and grabbed her wrists in one large hand. *"Taissez-vous,* Madame Woolf! *Vite!"*

Her name cracked in the air and stopped her as sharply as a slap in the face.

"How do you know—" Her question ended with a moan as her knees gave way and she slipped to the ground.

9

Bobbie lay in the curve of Sam's arm watching him draw
feathery circles around her right breast, but when she groaned
in pleasure his hand stopped, falling leadenly to his side.

She propped herself up on one elbow and looked into his
face. His eyes refused to meet hers. She reached under the
comforter and stroked him. He grunted slightly.

"Am I boring you?" she whispered.

"Sorry, love, I'm not in the mood."

"Do tell? You've hardly said a word all evening. And
now this. It isn't like you."

He got up and walked to the armoire in the dimly lit
bedsitter. She watched him, admiring his tall, wide frame and
his smooth white buttocks. Their affair had begun four months
before, taking more and more time each weekend to indulge
their pleasure and forget the dreariness of war. Sam had never
hidden his experience with other women and pleased by Bobbie's growing abandonment, he usually took the time and care
to satisfy her. But tonight was different. Was this her punishment? she wondered as she watched him hunt for two clean
glasses among the clutter of dishes in the kitchen alcove.

"Doesn't your daily wash up for you?" she called, sitting
up and pulling the quilt around her shoulders.

"She's visiting a wounded cousin. I'm saving up for her return." He swore as he stumbled against a table. The table lamp came on.

"Christ!" She shielded her eyes against the sudden glare.

"I can't find glasses in the dark."

"I'll rinse some out. Hand me your robe, it's cold in here."

She sat on the edge of the bed, her arms folded across her bare breasts. He went to the window and peered out around the edge of the heavy blackout curtain.

"Sam?"

He did not reply.

A voice shouted up from the street below: "Light showing up there."

He dropped the curtain back in place.

"Sam, talk to me. What the hell's the matter?"

"I'm tired, that's all. Chasing down stories, listening to everybody's idiocies. . . ."

"There's more to it than that."

"I've a lot on my mind," he muttered, grabbing his clothes from the sofa.

"You've been in a rotten mood ever since I mentioned Mrs. Woolf's trip to Paris."

"I told you to stay out of it. You've done precisely the opposite." He rolled his eyes in exasperation. "Why you want to get mixed up in this is beyond me. Unless you like being wooed by that Bloomsbury crowd. Rumor has it your precious Mrs. Woolf is a Sapphist."

"So what? You think it matters if she's a lesbian?"

Bobbie hadn't told him about the missing cremation order or about Virginia's certainty that Anna Michaux hadn't written the suicide note. Now she was sure he was hiding something too; his remark about Virginia was a stupid ploy. It wasn't going to work.

"Am I dismissed, m' lord?" she asked as he pulled on his jacket.

"I want a drink at the tavern."

"I thought you were tired of Fleet Street."

"Stay here if you want. I'm going."

"All right, all right," she said, "just let me get my clothes on."

They took the short walk through Crane Court to the old Cock Tavern in silence. The pub's back room was filled with reporters and as they elbowed their way to an empty table there were greetings from every side.

Without a word, Sam turned his chair to speak to a man called Arch, a writer for *The Black and White*. Harry the barman brought them their pints along with his familiar complaints about Lloyd George's watered beer.

Bobbie sipped at her bitter and waved to a short, dark man two tables away. The Parliamentary correspondent for *The Daily Mail*, Frank Delnot made a point of teasing her about women's suffrage. He got up and took a seat beside her and began his customary banter.

Ernest Purser soon joined them. The crime reporter, also from *The Mail*, was renowned for his aristocratic airs and black silk top hat. The latter he'd just removed, the former he never shed.

"If it isn't the Duke of Dartmoor," said Delnot.

"At your service. Hello, Miss Waters." He gave her a bow. "Mind if I sit down?"

"Only if you take my side on the women's question."

All the while Bobbie had watched Sam out of the corner of her eye. He was still in conversation with Arch who was known for his left-wing sympathies. She'd already overheard snippets about the situation in Russia. Now Delnot and Purser were arguing about Lenin and the Bolshevik revolution as well. The latest bulletins had stressed the possibility of a separate peace. Kerensky had fled Russia, and Delnot had heard that he was already in London.

Bobbie only half listened, still incensed that Sam was

treating her as if she had no right to pursue the story. She'd show him, she told herself.

"There's something I want to ask you," she whispered to Delnot.

"Sounds intriguing." He grinned. "Problems with our friend over there?"

"No, this is business. What do you know about Sir Henry Cranford? Ever run across him through your friends in Parliament?"

"Your bureau chief want a story about him?"

"Maybe. I'd like to find out more about him first."

"I can't tell you about Cranford's personal life. I know his father made farm machinery, but Sir Henry converted the company to a munitions plant almost as if he'd predicted Sarajevo. God knows where he got the financing, but he set up a second works and made alliances with Maxim's and Armstrong-Whitworth on the Continent."

"Is that why he's so influential in the government?"

"That was Ladbrooke's doing."

"*Lord* Ladbrooke?"

He nodded. "Anyway, I gather he took Cranford under his wing. Introduced him to the right people, including Lloyd George."

Bobbie leaned forward. Here was a track to follow, the ties between Ladbrooke and Cranford, Ladbrooke's obvious power and influence. Was there a connection to the cover-up of Anna's death? Her mind was leaping ahead, her face flushed with excitement as she pursued her hunch.

"I know Ladbrooke's a Conservative. What about Cranford's politics?"

"Who can say? Look at the Coalition Cabinet. You know the joke, 'Lloyd George used to be a Radical, he'll someday be a Conservative, now he's the leader of the Improvisatories.'"

Bobbie forced a laugh. Then: "But isn't it odd that so many contracts go to Cranford's firm?"

Delnot looked annoyed. "You Yanks would think of bribery. But there's no scandal here. Cranford's always the lowest bidder." He shrugged. "Of course, he's smart enough to see what's in it for him after the war. But there's been no profiteering, and if that's what your chief's after he'd better look elsewhere."

He was more irritated than Bobbie had expected. Yet it was predictable, too. How many times in the last few months had she trod on sensitive British toes? She should have known. Now Delnot ignored her and turned back to Purser.

"Pulled all the visas for the Socialist Conference in Stockholm," Purser was saying. "Leonard Woolf has an angry letter in *The Times* today, denouncing Lloyd George for harassment."

Delnot shook his head. "The government has a point. Swedish neutrality's a joke. They're providing the Kaiser with lading lists of armament shipments. Not that our boys found them out. MI5 and Special Branch are far too busy chasing knockwurst in the Midlands. It took the Belgians to discover the espionage."

"The Belgians?" asked Bobbie.

"Ah, ever the reporter," said Delnot, winking at Purser. "The Belgian government has its own MI5. A ragtag group, but efficient. Everybody's in the spy business these days."

"That's the truth," said Purser. "Last week Special Branch picked up a poor bloke because of his Austrian accent. Turned out to be a Scotsman with a speech impediment."

Bobbie laughed, then looked over at Sam. He and Arch had been joined by a short, stocky man with thinning ginger-colored hair.

"Who's that?" she asked Delnot.

He glanced over his shoulder. "Clive Bell. He's one of that little group over in Bloomsbury. Fancies himself an art critic, but likes the press, as you can see."

"Oh, Christ," muttered Bobbie. She knew the name:

Virginia had recited the story of her brother-in-law's interference at a party last week. And now Sam was bringing Clive Bell over to her.

"I asked Sam to introduce us," he said as he shook her hand. "I hear you're Virginia's new conquest. Didn't know you were a reporter." He smiled, then chattered on: "How nice you're helping Virginia with her investigation. I hear she called on Sir Henry, even went to the Yard. Now she's off to Paris to see the governess' sister."

"Goddammit," interrupted Sam. "You didn't tell me she'd gone to Sir Henry."

Clive grinned. "So you're involved in this suicide story, too? Well, I don't mind telling you, Leonard Woolf's furious. He didn't know the real reason for his wife's trip to Paris, not till I told him. Now he's had strange telephone calls from another Belgian woman, someone named Marie Ickx, frantic to talk to Virginia."

"Marie Ickx!" exclaimed Sam. "Now you've really gone and done it, Bobbie."

"I can explain—"

"Damn you!" he shouted. He turned to Delnot. "Do me a favor, Frank? Take the lady home." He spun away and pushed through the crowded tavern.

"Sam, wait." She tried to follow, but Bell grasped her elbow. "I'd be honored to escort you."

"Do you mind!" She thrust Bell's hand aside and rushed to the front door. Sam was already gone. None of the men at the entrance had seen which way he'd turned.

10

Virginia's throat ached. The smell of ammonia stung her nose and as her eyes fluttered open she saw Henri Giraud leaning over her, holding a bottle of smelling salts. She struggled up from the sofa.

"Roger?" she asked hoarsely. He took her hand. She looked across the room. There on the wall was the Corot, the landscape. "What happened? How did I—"

"You fainted. My men brought you here," said Giraud.

"Your men!" She looked up at Roger in dismay. "You mean—"

"Yes. His men shot that bloke in the street." He turned to Giraud, his face ashen. "And I think you'd better explain. We were nearly killed. . . ."

"Please." Giraud's voice was hard, his mouth set in a thin line. He rubbed the scar on the side of his face. "The keys to your hotel rooms, we need them." He held out Virginia's handbag.

She dug out her key and handed it to him.

"What the hell is going on here?" insisted Roger.

"The Southampton ferry leaves in forty minutes," said Giraud. "I want you on it. My men will pack your things and meet you at the pier." He held out his hand. With a petulant look Roger gave up his key as well.

"That should prevent any immediate problems," said Giraud after escorting the driver to the hallway.

"This is outrageous," Roger exploded. "Your men killed that chap."

"Before he shot the two of you, yes."

Virginia was too stunned to speak. The words pounded in her head like the staccato burst of gunfire in the street.

"He followed you," Giraud went on. "When you left my office this morning."

"You had her followed too?" said Roger.

"A precaution, M'sieur Fry. Aren't you glad we did?" He turned his attention back to Virginia. "One of my men spotted him when you left here."

She nodded weakly. "He was in the café where I had lunch."

"Right. Then he stayed in the lobby of your hotel all afternoon and trailed you both on your way here. Apparently you did something to make him act."

"I don't know what," she said with a slight shudder, still shrinking from the image of the dead man's face.

"Didn't M'sieur Fry hand you a note?"

"It was only a cable from my husband."

"Doesn't matter. With the trenches only 150 kilometers away, any piece of paper passed on the street may be valuable information to a German agent."

"A German agent!" exclaimed Roger. "But then why haven't you called the police?"

Giraud heard the doubt in his voice. "We know he worked for the Germans. The police will simply dismiss it as a common street shooting—Le Havre's specialty."

Virginia had been watching him closely. Now she burst out, "Perhaps he was trying to stop me from asking questions about Anna's death. . . ."

"No," he said with an impatient shake of his head. "They took you for British couriers." He paused a moment, his voice softening. "While we wait, M'sieur Fry, tell me about the autopsy report."

Roger hestitated, but then relented, describing Spilbury's objections. When he had finished, Giraud said: "So, Mme. Woolf, your doubts are confirmed by the medical examiner?"

"Definitely. I don't believe it was suicide, even if you do."

"She was always hard on herself. When we worked together, I'd often have to tease her out of her moods."

"But the person who saw her that night said she seemed happy," insisted Virginia in frustration. Like everyone else, Giraud was much too ready to dismiss her doubts.

Giraud shrugged. "Perhaps she was only pretending. Besides, a woman she apparently knew, a Marie Ickx, mentioned she was upset in a letter to a man here in our office."

Marie Ickx's name struck a match in the shadows of Virginia's fears. She stood up. "Then I've got to see him. Marie Ickx has been missing from her hotel for over a week."

She saw Giraud stiffen. "He no longer works for us. I've no idea where he is now." He stared into her eyes. "As for this Marie Ickx, I don't know her. Anna herself never mentioned her to me. So just let the police sort that out."

His irritation took her by surprise. She glanced at Roger.

"Just what I've been thinking, Virginia. Leave it to the Yard." As if to absent himself further, Roger walked behind Giraud's desk to study the Corot.

"Do you like it?" asked Giraud before she could say anything.

"Did you get it in Amsterdam? Or was it through Schaeffer in Paris?"

"Schaeffer?" snapped Giraud.

"The Schaeffer Gallery, it's—"

"I know, the one on rue Brea." Giraud eyed him a moment. From the street below there came two toots from the motor and Giraud reverted to his clipped manner:

"I'm afraid we don't have time to discuss acquisitions," he said sharply. "The car's waiting."

On the ferry Virginia returned to the subject. "Did you notice Giraud wince when I said Marie Ickx was missing? And he was definitely upset when you asked about Schaeffer."

Roger sighed. "Please. I've had enough. Your imagination's gotten the better of you." He looked away and closed his eyes.

Feeling deserted, she said nothing. She pulled her suitcase from under her seat. Her clothes had been hastily packed by Giraud's driver, and she rummaged through them, first casually, then frantically.

Finally she shook Roger awake.

"Dammit, it's *not* my imagination," she said. "Someone's stolen Anna's book!"

❧ 11 ❧

"But you could have been killed!" exclaimed Bobbie.

"Giraud tried to convince us it was a random attempt." Virginia's voice was weary and her hands shook. Her face was glazed with a sleepless pallor, and she'd come directly to Bobbie's office from the boat train. "Still, I don't give a fig what he says. We were followed because of Anna. Someone's trying to stop me from asking questions."

"How do you know?"

"The book I told you about? The one Anna sent her sister? Someone's stolen it."

"Or Giraud had his man take it when he packed!"

"Quite. When I told Giraud about the book, he wanted to see it. Also, he seemed upset to hear that Marie Ickx was missing."

"Not any more. She's been ringing you all weekend."

Virginia felt herself shaken out of her mind-numbing fatigue as Bobbie described the encounter with Clive. "When he mentioned Marie Ickx, Sam stormed out of the pub. I haven't heard from him since. It proves he's still on the story, but I'd like to know why Clive's so interested. He called me this morning, asking me to dinner. But then he tried to pump me for what we knew about Anna's death, and whether you'd spoken to Lord and Lady Ladbrooke again. I tell you, he's up to something."

"Probably he's using me to meet Cranford or to cultivate Ladbrooke." She paused a moment. "But if Marie Ickx was trying to reach me, she may know something important. Can you come with me to the hotel this morning? I don't want to go alone."

Bobbie seemed to flinch.

"What is it?"

"I'm not sure how to say it."

"Go on."

"Well, last night Sam told me something. About you, that is. I wouldn't bring it up ordinarily. . . ."

Virginia knew what was coming. Sam must have told Bobbie about her nervous breakdown. Those frightening words, the threat of madness, they must have loomed before Bobbie, making her rethink everything. Virginia felt as if she were in a crowded room being laughed at. Bobbie would never trust her; never would this spirited woman put any faith in her sanity.

Bobbie was still groping for words, refusing to look her in the eye.

"Why don't you just say it," snapped Virginia.

Bobbie took a deep breath. "I'm sure it's a trick to keep me away from the story. But Sam said—he said you were a Sapphist."

Virginia burst out laughing. "Is that all?" she asked, her voice filled with relief.

"Well?"

"Oh, Bobbie!" she exclaimed. "Does he really think that would put you off?"

She nodded, now looking at her directly.

"And what if I tell you I've sometimes succumbed to the beauty of women?" She watched Bobbie for a reaction.

The young woman's bright blue eyes did not slide away

in embarrassment. Instead, mild curiosity seemed to light them from within. "So it's true?"

"Oh, yes, sometimes I suppose I do feel what others might call a masculine attraction." She laughed again, this time nervously. "Does that shock you?"

"Not really. I knew women in New York City who told me the same thing. Only then they'd try to take me to bed with them."

Virginia smiled. "That's hardly my style. I'm not trying to seduce you. I've had only one love affair. Her name was Violet, and the affair was more maternal than erotic. She comforted me and encouraged me to write. She took care of me during my sickness." Virginia stopped. She'd stumbled into secret territory.

"But now that you're married, you don't feel that?" asked Bobbie, perplexed.

"Marriage has nothing to do with it," said Virginia, glad that Bobbie hadn't noticed her slip. "Besides, it's not so unusual. Here in England boys and girls of the middle and upper classes are separated, the sons away at public school, the daughters usually at home. We inhabit such different worlds we naturally feel more comfortable with our own sex. It's as if men and women are strangers."

She paused. Bobbie was listening attentively. "Women's friendships take a sexual turn because many women, myself included, find it more pleasurable to be with each other than with men. I was tired of struggling—first with my father's notions of what a lady should be; then with my male acquaintances' vision of the perfect union. Even Leonard has his own expectations of how I should act. With Violet, I could be myself, and that meant I had the freedom to write. I didn't have to shape my feelings to suit what men wanted. I love Leonard—but I loved Violet, too."

"Is that what you feel about me? I mean, the same sort of thing?"

"Love? Not at all," Virginia replied, a little too quickly. "I want us to be friends. But most of all I want us to solve Anna Michaux's murder. That's what's important to you, isn't it? Not whether you or I have sexual feelings for each other."

Bobbie grinned, plainly relieved. "Right! And damn Sam, anyway." She crossed the room and opened the office door. "Come on, then. Marie Ickx awaits us."

⤙ 12 ⤗

Once a pastoral part of London, Soho was now a warren of restaurants and public houses, of market stalls and gambling clubs.

The two of them threaded their way through the crowds of soldiers looking for forbidden pleasures, Bobbie spontaneously taking Virginia's arm as they crossed Dean Street to the Litchfield Arms Hotel.

Men were sitting in the lobby as if they hadn't moved since Virginia's previous visit, although, Virginia noticed, the man who'd told her about Marie Ickx wasn't among them. But the same sallow-faced clerk slouched at the reception desk.

"You again?" He stared rudely at Virginia. "Thought you might be back, now that your Belgian lady has turned up."

"Would you ring her, please? Tell her Mrs. Woolf is here."

"You wants to see her, you climbs the stairs yourself."

"I'd be glad to. Just tell me her room number."

The clerk shuffled his cards. "Sometimes I have a terrible time with numbers. Have to jog my memory, know what I mean?"

Bobbie grabbed the cards out of his hand.

"Hey! Whatcha doin'?"

"Jogging your memory," she said. "Unless you want the police checking into a few missing immigration numbers."

"No need to get like that, Miss. It's Room 308. It just come to me."

"Yeah, I'll bet." She flung the pack of cards down on the counter.

"I learned that kind of talk in New York," she said on the way up the stairs. "Tough guy talk, you know."

"Yeah, I'll bet," mimicked Virginia with a smile.

At the top of the stairs they entered a narrow corridor. Number 308 was the last door on the right. From one of the rooms a wireless was blaring, "It's a Long Way to Tipperary." The first door opened a few inches as they passed. Two eyes peered from the darkened room within, then the door slammed shut.

Virginia stopped. The sinister eyes, the sour-smelling corridor reminded her all too forcefully of Le Havre. Once more she felt nauseated; the walls seemed to be pressing toward her.

As if she understood, Bobbie took her arm. "We've got to see Marie Ickx. Ignore the rest."

As they approached number 308, the song from the wireless grew louder. "At least she's in," said Bobbie, rapping on the door. There was no answer. She knocked again, calling Marie's name. Still she heard nothing except the music. She tried the knob, which turned easily in her hand. Inside, they could see a woman on a narrow bed.

"She must be sleeping," said Virginia.

"With the radio that loud?" Bobbie opened the door wider. The room was strewn with clothes and books. Drawers were turned out; a bookshelf had been overturned. She ran to the bed. "Oh, my God," she cried. Virginia rushed to her side.

The skin of the face was purplish blue; brown eyes bulged up at them in a gruesome stare. The mouth gaped open as if she'd been gulping for air or crying for help. Her hands were knotted into fists around clumps of blanket as if she'd tried to hold on for her life.

"No!" wailed Virginia, reeling backward. Bobbie braced her, then pulled her outside into the hallway.

"Don't faint." Bobbie took her by the shoulders and shook her gently. "Can you hear me? Concentrate."

Virginia forced herself to stare at a mark on the opposite wall. Bobbie ran back into the room and turned off the wireless, then closed the door on the brutal scene.

"Listen to me," she said. "Go downstairs and call the police. But don't let those men in the lobby know what's happened."

"But Bobbie, I—"

"Don't argue. I'll stay here and make sure no one goes into the room."

"But Bobbie, listen. I know that woman!"

"Of course, it's Marie Ickx. Now go."

"I mean I've seen her before. She worked at a tea shop near my house. The Belgian delicatessen. . . ."

"Later. But first get the police here. Go!"

Footsteps pounded up the stairs. Three uniformed policemen appeared on the landing. Virginia followed them, her face white.

"In here!" shouted Bobbie. She threw open the door of number 308. The policemen gathered round the bed, then one of them came to the door.

"You found the body?" he asked Virginia, who stood back against the wall, her face averted.

Virginia nodded. She closed her eyes, willing herself not to collapse. Voices sounded dimly in her ears. She was vaguely aware of Bobbie giving their names and identifying the dead woman as Marie Ickx. Then she felt Bobbie's arm around her waist. "I think Mrs. Woolf had better sit down."

Virginia opened her eyes. The bobby who'd taken command said, "You can go downstairs, Mrs. Woolf. But you'll have to stay. The Yard will want to question both of you."

Bobbie helped her to a chair in the office behind the reception desk. The clerk was no longer playing solitaire but was being interrogated by another policeman.

"That woman served me tea any number of times," said Virginia. "All this while looking for Marie Ickx—"

"Shh," said Bobbie. "Save your strength."

Virginia closed her eyes once more. She felt as if her breath had been pummeled out of her. Her head hurt yet she knew she had to convince the Yard that Marie Ickx was murdered because she had information about Anna Michaux's death. She was sure of it, even as she felt darkness closing in on her again, her heart beating faster, and once more she told herself to be calm. She could not appear hysterical or erratic; she must not be dismissed as mad.

"Well, well. Mrs. Woolf."

She jerked her head up. A man was standing in front of her, cleaning his glasses with a large handkerchief.

"Commissioner Allington!" she cried. "I didn't realize Special Branch—"

"Quite so. This is our investigation." He put on his glasses, refolded his handkerchief into his lapel pocket and took out a notebook. Angus Clarke, the short, sturdy MI$_5$ officer newly assigned to Special Branch, stood in the office doorway. Then, coming forward, he introduced himself as "Inspector Clarke."

"All right, Clarke. Question the clerk," Allington said. "Tell Grenfell to do fingerprints. And don't let anyone move the body until the medical men get here."

"Yes, sir," said Clarke with a pronounced burr.

"Why is this Special Branch's case?" asked Bobbie.

Allington ignored the question. "You are?"

"Bobbie Waters, *New York Tribune,* London Bureau." She held up her press credential.

"Put it away," he said with a scowl. "No press for now. I understand the two of you discovered the body. Tell me what happened. You first, Miss Waters."

Bobbie told him quickly. He wrote in his notebook, then looked at Virginia. "Anything to add, Mrs. Woolf?"

She shook her head.

"I gather you knew the woman?" he said.

"I know who she is . . . was," stammered Virginia. "Don't you remember? I told you about her. She was a friend of Anna Michaux—"

"Yes, Sir Henry's governess. The one who drowned herself."

"She didn't. Don't you see? Marie Ickx was missing. And now she's been killed because she knew something. She was trying to reach me."

"Trying to reach you, yes. And what did she tell you?" he asked, once more repeating her words.

"I didn't speak to her. That's why we came this morning." Virginia sat up straighter in her chair, her voice gathering strength. "Actually, I *had* spoken to her. She was a waitress at a tea room—a Belgian delicatessen—near my home in Richmond. I didn't realize that Marie Ickx and the waitress were the same until I saw her this morning." She paused for breath. Allington waited, his pencil poised. "What I'm trying to say is that Marie Ickx had something to tell me. She'd been ringing me at home, but I was away."

"Away?"

"In Paris, to see Anna Michaux's sister and—"

"Look here, Commissioner," said Bobbie. "Mrs. Woolf is exhausted. She's just returned from Le Havre, where she saw a man killed. She was almost killed herself."

"Hold on. Start at the beginning. A man killed? Le Havre?"

"I went to see the publisher Anna Michaux worked for. Henri Giraud. Now he works for the Belgian government-in-exile." She described the shooting. "Giraud says the man was a German agent, but I think it has something to do with Anna Michaux's death."

She stopped. Clarke had returned to the office, several sheets of blue notepaper in his hand. "Henri Giraud?" he said to Virginia. "Did you see him here or in Paris?"

"In Le Havre," she replied. "Why? Do you know him?"

"By reputation," he muttered. He turned to Allington, waving the papers in his hand. "These were tacked to the back of the mirror in the bath."

Allington took them. "Numbers?" he said. "Columns of numbers."

"So that's why someone was searching her room," Bobbie exclaimed.

"I wonder," Virginia murmured. "It must have been important . . . a code, perhaps?"

"What are you talking about?" said Allington. "We don't even know these belonged to the woman."

Virginia was conscious of Clarke's stare as she replied, "Because of the book Anna sent her sister. There was a lot of strange underlining, and an Inspector Brown from the Yard asked about it particularly. And then it was stolen from my hotel room."

Virginia caught Allington's puzzled look. "That's what I thought," she said. "The Yard didn't send anyone to Paris, did they?"

"I'll check into it," said Allington. "You've no idea who stole the book?"

Virginia felt herself flush. She shook her head.

Allington handed the sheets of notepaper back to Clarke. "Those are to be kept in Branch's files."

"Miss Ickx had a visitor last night," he said, for the moment ignoring Allington's directive. "Quite late, I'm told. Sam Josephs, a reporter for *The Mail.* Apparently he called here often."

Bobbie bit her lip, but her eyes betrayed her surprise.

"Friend of yours, Miss Waters?" asked Allington. "Come now. What business did your friend have with this woman?"

She only shrugged.

"What do you know about it then, Mrs. Woolf? Josephs gave you the coroner's report, didn't he? What are the three of you up to?"

A vein in Virginia's forehead was throbbing. "If we're up to anything," she replied, her voice rising, "it's because you refuse to move. Doesn't it matter that Anna didn't write the suicide note? That she was cremated but there's no record of the order?"

Her words came tumbling too fast for him to say anything. "No, you just brushed all that aside," she went on. "But if you'd investigated Anna's death, Marie might still be alive. Now you scold us like children. I have nothing more to say."

"Then we'll have to take a trip to the Yard. You're obstructing a criminal investigation."

His voice came as a physical assault, stripping away Virginia's last reserves of strength. "You don't care about these women at all," she sobbed. "You simply don't care. I'm not obstructing your investigation—you aren't investigating."

"Really, Nigel, you've gone too far," said a voice from the doorway. Virginia looked up in surprise. Lord Ladbrooke stood near Clarke, leaning on his umbrella.

"There's no need to be upset," he said, going to Virginia's side. After introducing himself to Bobbie, he turned back to Allington. "I gather Mrs. Woolf found the body. She's hardly a suspect, why are you detaining her?"

"No, but—"

"Well, then, don't waste time here. As Head of the Belgian Relief Committee, I want a thorough investigation. There's not a Belgian woman in London who feels safe with this butcher of yours still on the loose."

"But, my Lord, I think Mrs. Woolf knows more than she's telling," said Allington.

"Raising your voice isn't going to help."

"I'm simply trying to find out what information they have. Miss Waters knows the man who called on Miss Ickx last night. He's our prime suspect."

"Don't be ridiculous," said Bobbie. "He was with me."

"All evening?"

She nodded.

"We've told him all we know anyway," said Virginia to Lord Ladbrooke. "Marie Ickx was missing last week, but she tried to reach me over the weekend. That's all there is to it."

"I'm sure," he said, giving her a smile. "As a matter of fact, I came round this morning because Miss Ickx's employer, Mrs. Ottlinger, rang the committee to report her missing. She wanted us to send a new waitress. I told her I'd check on Miss Ickx."

"I know you take a personal interest," said Allington with an edge of sarcasm, "but Branch requires full cooperation of all witnesses." He shot an angry look at Virginia and Bobbie.

"Oh, please!" Ladbrooke said. "If you can't take Mrs. Woolf's word, whom can you trust? Our families have known each other for some time and I can certainly vouch for her. She shares my concern for the refugees. Isn't that right, Mrs. Woolf?"

Virginia could only nod. Whatever his assumption about the deaths, at least he seemed willing to press for a further investigation.

"And now," he said to her, "I have my motor outside. Let me give you and Miss Waters a lift."

Lord Ladbrooke helped Virginia from her chair. "If you have other questions, Nigel, tread more lightly," he said. "Mrs. Woolf isn't one of your Suffragettes out in Holloway Prison."

He smiled at his own joke and pointed his umbrella toward the lobby. "Shall we, ladies?"

⭢⚡ 13 ⚡⭠

"Why does he refuse to see it?" moaned Virginia. She sat on one side of Ladbrooke, Bobbie on the other, in the spacious interior of the Daimler.

"I'd still like to know why Special Branch is involved," said Bobbie.

"Because random murders lower public morale," said Ladbrooke. "In a time of war, it may be part of an enemy ploy to provoke panic among the citizens. But I'm not satisfied with the way Allington's handling this. I may go to the Home Office about it, even to Lloyd George if necessary."

"So you do see a connection between Anna Michaux's death and these other murders?" Virginia looked at Ladbrooke eagerly.

"Any reasonable man would," he replied. "Why don't the two of you come to luncheon, assuming you're up to it? You can tell me everything you've discovered."

They readily agreed. Ladbrooke rolled down the glass separating them from the chauffeur and instructed the man to drive home.

With a glance over his shoulder the driver nodded. His face was marred by a scar running down the side of his beak-like nose, ending in a knot of skin on his upper lip.

"War wound," commented Ladbrooke, rolling up the window. "Ugly, but he knows his motors."

Ladbrooke's townhouse was a narrow white-stone building in a Knightsbridge mews. While their host went to instruct his cook, the butler showed Bobbie and Virginia to the library on the second floor. The room was elegantly furnished. Books lined the wall on either side of the fireplace; on the other walls hung three Cézanne still-lifes and several small Turner watercolors.

Bobbie seemed unaware of the surroundings. She paced in front of the bookshelves. "I'm worried about Sam," she said. "Maybe he did go to see Marie Ickx, but I want to find out why before I tell Allington anything. Even if Sam is furious at me, I don't—."

"Sam Josephs the reporter?" asked Ladbrooke as he came through the door.

"Actually the city editor at *The Mail*," said Bobbie.

"Right. Sir Henry mentioned he wrote the story about his governess." Ladbrooke poured glasses of sherry. "Can't imagine he's a suspect either." He leaned against the chimney piece and gave Bobbie a reassuring smile. "My wife won't be joining us, but it's probably just as well. I'd like to hear the whole story and the details might upset her. Now, Mrs. Woolf, what led you to question Anna Michaux's suicide?"

Virginia began to relax. She spoke calmly, narrating clearly. Ladbrooke nodded in agreement as she listed the inconsistencies in the case.

When she came to Henri Giraud, Bobbie interrupted. "You have several of his books," she said, gesturing toward the shelves. *"Editions du Nord."*

"I hadn't realized he was one and the same," he said. "Fine firm in its day. But you say he now works for the Belgian government?"

"As the Minister of Information," said Virginia. She summarized their conversation about Anna, then described the shooting incident.

It was the only time Virginia saw emotion in the man's angular face. "Now I'll definitely speak to the Home Office. We can't have you threatened like that."

"I think someone was trying to warn me off." Virginia's voice was strong. She went on to describe her suspicions about the stolen volume of Michelet and its underlined words, as well as the list of numbers found in the hotel bathroom. "I know it's a wild guess, but the underlining and the numbers may be a hidden message. . . ."

"Did Allington like your theory?"

"Not really, though Inspector Clarke seemed to. And one more thing, Clarke thought he knew Giraud."

Ladbrooke nodded but he said nothing as the butler came in to announce luncheon.

Over a perfectly browned roast chicken, Ladbrooke turned the conversation to art.

"Maynard Keynes is doing a splendid job for the government but after meeting Fry the other night I thought he'd be a great help with the Degas purchases. Of course, there's Clive Bell, too. Your brother-in-law, isn't he, Mrs. Woolf? He's been after me to put him on the Committee. But frankly, I find him rather too insistent."

"Can't we get back to the murder investigation," Bobbie interrupted in exasperation. "What do you think of Sir Henry Cranford?"

Virginia flinched at her abruptness, but Ladbrooke seemed unperturbed.

"He certainly doesn't question the suicide. Of course, I don't know what Allington's told him. . . ." He paused. "But really, Henry's just trying to avoid public attention. He'll want to get to the bottom of this once I've spoken with him. He's at his factory today. I'll have a chat with him tomorrow."

After luncheon the car was brought round for them and as Virginia settled into the back seat, she felt reassured. Their new ally would do everything he could to have Allington reopen the case. Bobbie, however, looked troubled. As the Daimler started toward *The Tribune* office, she rolled down the separating window. "Take us to Sir Henry Cranford's," she commanded. "In Chester Square."

The driver gave her a wary glance over his shoulder. "But his Lordship said—"

"I'm sure he won't mind."

"But Cranford's not there," objected Virginia.

"It's Mrs. Murphy I want to see. Perhaps she can tell us something about Marie."

When they drew up in front of Cranford's townhouse, Bobbie asked the chauffeur to wait. A look of annoyance accompanied his nod, but Bobbie ignored him and led Virginia to the basement level service entrance.

The housekeeper answered the bell.

"Hello, Mrs. Murphy," said Virginia. "I'm Mrs. Woolf. Remember? I came round the other day to see Sir Henry."

The housekeeper's look of surprise gave way to recognition. "But himself is away in the north, mum. His train isn't due till teatime."

"Actually, we wanted to see you," said Bobbie. "I'm Miss Waters, a friend of Mrs. Woolf."

"Me?" She led them inside, moving awkwardly.

The kitchen was filled with the warm smell of bread baking. Mrs. Murphy sat them at a table and poured out cups of tea. Then she went back to kneading a ball of dough. Two loaves were cooling on the sideboard.

"We used to make bread on our farm," said Bobbie. Her tone was forced. Mrs. Murphy gave her a sidelong glance.

"Miss Waters is an American," Virginia said with a sharp look at Bobbie. "Over here on holiday."

Mrs. Murphy wiped the back of her hand across her forehead. "Wouldn't mind a holiday myself."

"I can imagine," said Virginia. "Anna Michaux's death must have been terribly difficult. . . ."

"I still can't believe it. A good Catholic, went to church every Sunday. The next thing I hear she's gone and jumped into the Serpentine."

"It's terrible when someone is that sad," said Bobbie.

"Don't know about that, Miss. She was happy 'nough when she left here that night."

"I understand she was meeting someone," said Bobbie. "Was it her friend, Mademoiselle Ickx?"

"I think it was a gentleman." She gave a little smirk looking up from the doughboard. "She was worried she was late. I heard her say she 'hoped *he'd* wait.' "

"She had a special gentleman friend?"

"Mind you, Mrs. Woolf, I'm not one to gossip. But every once in a while she'd get herself prettied up. Never told where she was going, but you could tell she was excited. Like she couldn't wait to see him."

"She never mentioned his name? The man never came here?"

She shook her head. "The only caller she ever had was Miss Ickx. Like a fortnight ago, it was. Miss Ickx popped in. Anna was out with the children and Miss Ickx waited in her room." Mrs. Murphy thought for a moment. "But, now I remember, she didn't stay. All of a sudden she rushed down the stairs again. Anna seemed a bit riled when I told her. I suppose they patched things up because Miss Ickx rang her up that Friday."

"The night before she died?" asked Virginia.

"That's right. The same night Anna asked for paper and twine to wrap a book to send to her sister." Virginia and Bobbie looked at each other.

"Did you see it?" asked Virginia.

"Yes. I thought it was funny, an old book like that. But then Anna was peculiar about her books, never wanted them disturbed. She always had her nose stuck in one, sometimes two at a time." She laughed, shaking her head. "Either reading or doing figures, that one. I told her she'd wear out her eyes."

Mrs. Murphy put the two new loaves into the oven and sat down at the table. "Still, I don't like it, Mrs. Woolf. Why would Anna ask me to leave the service door off the latch if she didn't mean to come back? She even told me to expect her 'bout midnight."

Bobbie pointed at the door. "It was still unlatched in the morning?"

Mrs. Murphy furrowed her brows. "Come to think of it, I unlatched it myself Sunday morning. Sir Henry must have bolted it when he came home." She shrugged. "Expect he didn't see the note I left, or he forgot. Anyway, the children came running to me when they found her bed empty."

Once more Cranford's story didn't square. He'd told Virginia he had no idea that Anna was out. But his housekeeper had left a note for him. Had he really not seen it? Or had he latched the door because—Virginia gave an involuntary wince—because he knew that Anna wasn't coming home at all.

"What's the matter?" Mrs. Murphy asked.

I was thinking of Anna's sister," Virginia said. "I saw her in Paris. She's terribly upset."

"I don't wonder. She used to write Anna every week."

"You saw the letters?"

"Mrs. Woolf! Maybe other servants—"

"I meant the envelopes. You're sure they were from her sister?"

"It was thin blue paper, like the French use, with foreign stamps. Anna would say, 'Oh, good, from my sister,' when she'd see one on the hall table."

Virginia took another sip of tea trying to hide her excitement. After what Elise Robert had said, the letters couldn't have been from her. She thought for a moment, glancing at Bobbie. Suddenly an idea occurred to her. It was a risk, but worth taking.

"Anna's sister asked me to collect her belongings," she said. "She wants me to ship them to her."

"I don't understand," said Mrs. Murphy. "I packed her books and clothes in her suitcase, just like Sir Henry told me. This morning a man came round for it. Said he was from the agency."

"You mean the Belgian Relief Committee?"

She shook her head. "Something called Piccadilly Employment. A Mr. Smith, it was. He wanted to know if all of Anna's things were in the case. Said Anna's sister wanted them, especially the books. Friendly sort. He reminded me of my own son with his curly red hair."

"About six feet tall with green eyes?" interrupted Bobbie.

"That's him. Face like a map of Ireland. How he came by a name like Smith, I don't know. I asked him and he said, 'Blame it on the English'." She laughed, but then stopped, aware of Bobbie's frown. "I didn't do anything wrong, did I?"

"No, no, Mrs. Murphy," Virginia assured her. "Everything's quite in order."

14

"That bastard," muttered Bobbie as they came up the basement steps. "It must have been Sam."

"What do you suppose he was after?"

"Her books. He must know something about them. Come on."

As they reached the top step, they saw Ladbrooke's chauffeur talking to a heavy, square-jawed man whose large ears stuck out from his uniformed cap. He stole a look in their direction and then strode back to the second Daimler where he busied himself wiping the windscreen.

"Crane Court," Bobbie instructed Ladbrooke's driver as he held the door for them.

It was no surprise to Virginia that Bobbie had a key to Sam's flat. But when Bobbie turned on a table lamp inside, Virginia grimaced. The furniture was dusty. There was a pile of unwashed china in the alcove that served as a kitchen. "Doesn't he spend time here?"

There was no reply. She turned to find Bobbie rummaging through the bedroom wardrobe.

"What *are* you doing?"

"What do you think?" Her voice was muffled.

"Wouldn't it be tidier if you waited for him?"

"Tidier?" She wheeled from the closet. "Please, I'm not about to worry about decorum." She dropped to her knees and lifted up the folds of the heavy quilt covering the bed.

"Here it is. For heaven's sake, give me a hand," Bobbie said, poking her head out from under the bed. "Push it from the far side."

Anna's suitcase was heavy for its size but together they managed to slide it out into the sitting room. Its sides were battered and covered with border-control stickers. From the handle hung a tag on which Anna had written her name.

Discarding the few clothes piled on top, Bobbie went directly to the books, quickly thumbing pages.

"What are we looking for?" Virginia asked as she began to do the same.

"Whatever Sam thought he'd find."

Most of the books were French classics—Corneille, Molière, Racine. "She must have brought these from Brussels," Virginia said. "Most of them were published by *Editions du Nord.*"

She turned to the inside cover of one. The bookplate read: "J. G. Marcus, Booksmith, Charing Cross Road." The volumes Bobbie had already discarded bore the same plate. "I was wrong. She got them here. Evidently Marcus is the English agent for *Editions du Nord*—" She stopped, recognizing the book in Bobbie's hand. It was James Joyce's *Portrait of the Artist as a Young Man.*

"This was published only last year," Virginia said, taking it from her. "Very scarce. I spent months trying to find a copy." She opened it to the bookplate. "It's from Marcus's bookshop too."

"So?" said Bobbie.

"You'd hardly expect such a place to stock it. All his other books are French classics." She flipped through the first pages of the Joyce novel. "And look at this!" she exclaimed. "Underlining. Just like the book Anna sent her sister."

Bobbie peered over her shoulder. "For her translation work?"

"I doubt it." She read the first few underlined words aloud: "Time, story, glass, smell, Uncle, older, he—"

"An experienced translator shouldn't have trouble translating 'he' or 'time'!" She paused, turning a few pages. "It's what struck me when I saw the underlining in Michelet's *Louis XV et Louis XVI*. The words are too elementary for a translator to worry about."

"Maybe she was just marking her progress," said Bobbie. She began to sort through the clothes from the suitcase.

"But think a minute. We guessed those lists of numbers the Yard found in the hotel were a code. Maybe the numbers have some connection to the pages of this book or to the Michelet. The other books aren't underlined, are they?"

"Not that I noticed."

"Then the Joyce and the Michelet are special. Mrs. Murphy said that Anna was always reading or doing figures. Maybe she was writing in code. Or maybe there are messages in invisible ink. You know, like Mata Hari writing between the lines of books."

"Isn't that a little much?"

"There's got to be something or why would Sam steal Anna's books?"

Bobbie didn't reply. She was running her fingertips along the flowered fabric which lined the bottom of the case. As she reached the right rearmost corner, there was a hollow and the cloth gave way with a rip.

"Well, well." She grinned at Virginia and withdrew a packet of blue notepaper. Separating the sheets, she placed several in front of them on the floor. Each page was filled with numbers, set off in columns of three.

"Don't they look like the lists of numbers that the detective found at the hotel?" asked Bobbie.

Virginia agreed the form seemed identical. She scanned the first page:

15	8	3
120	2	8
17	1	1
32	12	5
85	16	7
1	8	2
30	5	3
10	2	10

The numbers seemed to have been written with a fine-nibbed pen. "It's Anna's handwriting!" said Virginia. "I'm sure. And look, the last number is never higher than twelve. Perhaps these are dates?" She paused. "No, that can't be right." She groped behind her for the Joyce novel. "I wonder," she muttered. She consulted the list of numbers, then turned to the fifteenth page and counted eight lines down. She found the third word in the line, but it was not underlined. "Damn," she said aloud. "Still, the numbers must be a code, don't you think?"

There was no reply.

"Bobbie?"

She looked up from the page. Bobbie was staring at the door of the flat. "Sh-h-h, Sam's coming," she whispered. She thrust the pile of blue notepaper behind her. "Put that book somewhere."

As Virginia hid it under one of Anna's blouses she heard a gruff voice call, " 'Allo."

She whirled. Two men were standing inside the door. One was tall and balding. The other was fat with a birthmark like a smear of plum jam across his right cheek.

The balding man stepped toward Bobbie. "Don't want no trouble now. Just hand over what you've got there."

"I don't know what you're talking about."

The man lunged for her arm.

"Don't touch her!" screamed Virginia.

"Take care of the schoolmarm, Mick," said the balding one.

The fat man came at Virginia, who took several steps backward, tripping over the books on the floor. Another scream rose in her throat but she managed to stifle it. She cowered against the wall. "Stay away from me!"

Suddenly the man pinned her against him. The sour smell of old beer filled her nostrils. She felt his hot breath on her neck.

"Thought I told you to shut your bloody lip."

It was the man of her childhood, the man with the fumbling fingers under the streetlamp; the animal who appeared in her recurrent nightmare. The room spun as she struggled in his grasp. She screamed again and kicked at his shins, but the man clamped a fleshy hand over her mouth. She bit hard. He yelped but still held fast. Her knees started to buckle. It had come at last: The body in Le Havre, Marie's grotesque face, both flashed before her, and she was sure this man was going to kill her. She groaned, the room starting to go black. She was flung back onto the bed. She heard Bobbie shout, "Stop it! Here, take them."

Virginia opened her eyes. The fat man was leering down at her. Beyond him, the other man held the packet of blue notepaper in one hand, Bobbie's wrist in the other. "All right, Mick, enough," he called to the fat man. "Take care of the suitcase."

The fat man raised it above his head, then slammed it to the floor. The flimsy wood broke into several pieces. "Nothin' more 'ere," he said.

The bald man released Bobbie. She stood to one side, rubbing her wrist.

"Are you finished?" she said. Her face was white, her eyes dark with anger.

He reached down and patted her on the head. "That's

what I like in me ladies," he laughed. "A little spirit. But I don't want one peep outta you now. No calling the coppers. Understand?"

He reached out and wrenched her arm backwards.

Dumbly, she nodded, watching him stroll to the door and tuck the sheaf of notepapers into his pocket. The fat man followed him, but at the door he turned back to Bobbie.

"Blimey, Miss Waters, I nearly forgot. You tell your Irish chum we're sorry we missed him. Next time we'll tip a pint. You and Mrs. Woolf, too."

❧ 15 ❧

"Here, drink this."

Virginia took a sip of the whiskey and began to cough.
Bobbie thumped her on the back. "More?"

Virginia shook her head. Her face was pale and her hands
were trembling.

Bobbie sat beside her on the bed. "Are you hurt?"

"Not really." She glanced over at Bobbie. The young
woman's face was white, her cheekbones bright with two red
patches. "What about you?"

Bobbie rubbed her wrist. "I'm okay. But my God, that
fat one was hideous." She spoke lightly but Virginia sensed
the fear behind her words. "I wonder if they were the ones
who tore up Marie's room?"

And strangled her, too, Virginia thought to herself. During her breakdown she'd had terrifying visions of laughing
men following her, squeezing her, suffocating her. Now it was
all real. She had been stalked by a grotesque man, touched by
his sweaty flesh, sickened by his hot breath. Someone had
obviously known about the lists of numbers and wanted them
badly enough to murder. She and Bobbie could have been
killed. They'd known their names, they'd obviously been following them.

She rubbed the back of her neck. The throbbing was still there, a voice ringing in the back of her head, "You're going mad, you're going mad." She closed her eyes. There was the monster's face, the birthmark spreading across his cheek. He was panting, his throat gurgling with laughter again. Spittle ran out of the side of his mouth.

Bobbie said something but she barely heard her. It was all too real. She forced her eyes open. "Sorry, what?"

"Are you all right?"

"Yes . . . yes," she made herself say.

"Then let's get out of here. I want to find Sam. . . ." She stopped. "What's the matter?"

"I can't do it," said Virginia in a whisper.

"Of course you can," said Bobbie. "Drink some more of this."

"I mean, I can't go on with it. We might have been killed. I was shot at yesterday. It's too much."

Bobbie's eyes shone with her excitement. "But doesn't it prove we were right? They weren't going to hurt us, they just wanted to scare us."

Virginia looked at her. There was a fundamental difference. A difference of age, of experience. And of strength, too.

"Can't we just leave it to Lord Ladbrooke? Allington will reopen the case and—"

"You don't know that. Besides, Lord Ladbrooke thinks a lunatic is murdering Belgian women. Those numbers mean it's more than that. We have to find out what Anna and Marie were writing." Her voice became more insistent. "We started this, we've got to finish it."

Virginia stared into her lap. There was so much she couldn't explain, at least not yet. She felt ashamed. She was weak and fragile, just as Leonard and Dr. Wright had been telling her all along. Even worse, she felt a coward. This healthy, robust young woman would never understand her hallucinations, her fear of being watched and followed, much less her fear of going mad.

"I know you're tired," said Bobbie. "You go home, I'll try to find Sam."

Virginia nodded, not trusting her voice.

"And take the book with you." Bobbie found the Joyce volume on the floor among the scattered clothes. "See if you can figure out anything. Tomorrow, go see Mrs. Ottlinger. Perhaps she can tell you more about Marie."

At the end of Crane Court Bobbie put Virginia in a taxi and with a wave set off on foot down Fleet Street. At Hector Lane she started to cross to the entrance of *The Mail* but Fleet Street was jammed with horsedrawn carts, motor cars and lorries, and she had to wait for a gap in the traffic.

She took one step forward and then stopped. The pedestrians on the opposite side parted and she caught a glimpse of Sam. His back was to her and he was talking to a man partially hidden by his large frame.

Bobbie dodged between two stalled lorries. She was about to call out when she recognized the clerk from the hotel. Sam was passing him a roll of pound notes.

Virginia eased her key into the lock of the front door of Hogarth House and tiptoed into the foyer. Through the closed door of the sitting room she could hear Leonard talking. She put her ear to the door.

"Kerensky's finally turned up here. And Ramsay Mac-Donald's arranged for a speech at the '17 Club next Monday. I'll introduce him."

"Not the best of timing." The voice was deeper and more languid than Leonard's, and Virginia recognized it as Keynes. "You know Lloyd George doesn't want to stir up trouble."

"We want to hear what Kerensky has to say about the

Bolsheviks. It's important for us socialists. You should realize that even if you've deserted the cause."

She sighed, grateful that at least their politics would keep them busy, and quietly she turned, starting up the stairs. The third step creaked.

"Virginia?" called Leonard, throwing open the door. "Virginia! Come in here!"

She fixed him with a stare. "You needn't use that tone. Besides, if I don't change my clothes, I'll catch a chill."

"You weren't worried about that this morning. Come down now. You'd better hear what Maynard has to say."

The economist was short and slim with a tidy fringe of mustache above his full lips. He remained standing even when Virginia sat down on the sofa. Leonard rested one arm on the chimney piece and continued staring at her.

"Well?" she said, glancing from one man to the other.

Keynes cleared his throat. "This afternoon I was at my club. Returned from Paris only this morning, you know...."

"For God's sakes, get on with it."

He exchanged a look with Leonard. "And while I was at my club, Sir Henry asked me to have a word with you."

"About his governess?" asked Virginia, forgetting herself.

"Oh God," said Leonard in exasperation. "So there's reason for his complaint. He's threatened legal action."

"Nonsense. What exactly did Sir Henry say, Maynard?"

"That you've been badgering his housekeeper. And that his governess' suitcase was stolen."

"I had nothing to do with that."

"Sir Henry thinks you did. After all, doesn't your American friend—" he turned to Leonard—"a Miss Waters. Doesn't she know Sam Josephs?"

"What is this? Guilt by association?"

"More than that, Virginia. Sir Henry found out that Josephs convinced his housekeeper to give him the suitcase."

"Sir Henry, the detective," said Virginia tartly.

"The Yard's been following Josephs ever since this morning," Maynard went on. "They saw you and Miss Waters arrive at his flat. Since you also asked Mrs. Murphy about Anna's suitcase, it's no wonder Sir Henry believes you're involved."

Virginia felt backed into a corner. Not wanting Leonard to know about the two men in Josephs' flat, she counterattacked: "I don't see how it concerns you, and I resent your coming round to tell tales. You might have spoken to me about Sir Henry, you didn't need to involve Leonard. Besides, there are others interested in Anna Michaux. In point of fact, Lord Ladbrooke's—"

Maynard's eyes widened. "Alex is involved?"

"He's calling for a full investigation of the Belgian women's murders. So you and Clive can stop upsetting Leonard."

"It wasn't their doing!" exclaimed Leonard. "What am I supposed to think when Roger tells me you've been shot at, actually *shot at* in Le Havre!"

"He rang you?"

"Thank God for that. He was worried when you rushed out of the station. Told me all about your meeting with this fellow Giraud."

"Damn him," muttered Virginia. "Of course, he didn't bother to tell you that I said I was going to Bobbie's office."

"Yes, he did, but when I rang *The Tribune* her employer said neither of you was there."

"I suppose," Maynard cut in, "that's when the two of you were busy with Sir Henry's housekeeper."

"Maynard, please," said Leonard. "Sir Henry's housekeeper is the least of our worries."

"That's not the point. Sir Henry wants no more trouble. It's especially important to me because I'm bringing him to Garsington this weekend. We have a crucial meeting in Oxford on Sunday, and we'll motor there from Ottoline's. Needless to say, I don't want him bothered."

"Oh, Pozzo!" Virginia couldn't restrain a laugh. "You're bringing Sir Henry to meet Huxley and Russell and the other conscientious objectors and Oxford socialists Ottoline has out there, and you think *I'll* be the problem?"

"Sir Henry may teach them a few things about politics," said Maynard. "That's not my concern, anyway. All I'm asking is tact on your part."

She smiled. "I'll behave, I promise." She looked back at Leonard. "As for this morning, I'm sorry you were upset. I had to do it, and I was quite right." She paused. Somehow Leonard's scolding had dispelled her reservations. As it had so often in the past, anger overruled pain and depression; the echoing voices were banished.

"I understand I had a telephone message from a Marie Ickx," she said, suddenly businesslike.

"Several times. She didn't ring today, though."

"What did she say?"

Leonard waved his hand impatiently. "She wants to meet you. You can reach her at a bookstore. Marcus's was the name. Two men from the Yard came round asking for you, too."

"Two men?" Her stomach knotted. "When?"

"Half an hour ago."

She felt her pulse racing. Were they really Yard men? Or had the brutes in Sam's flat discovered she'd taken the book? Had they hurried after her to frighten her?

"Are you sure they were from the Yard? What did they look like?"

"They said they were," replied Leonard, giving her a quizzical glance. "They were wearing tan macs, that's all I noticed."

She clenched her hands into fists to hide their trembling. "I'd better ring the police now," she said, forcing her voice into a calm monotone and hurrying to the hall telephone before Leonard could stop her.

Reaching Allington, she kept her voice low. Five minutes later, her face even paler and her hands still shaking, she put through another call.

"Bobbie? Virginia. No, I can't speak up," she said. "The Yard's looking for Sam. They've been following him, and you know very well what they found at the flat. Cranford wants to bring charges for the theft of the suitcase." She paused, then lowered her voice even more. "But listen, two men came here looking for me. Said they were from the Yard, only Allington didn't send them. And I was right about that other chap, the one calling himself Inspector Brown. He was an imposter too. That's correct," she said. "I think someone's after Anna's book and they're posing as Yard men to find out what *we're* up to."

She paused to catch her breath. It seemed as if Bobbie's voice was fading into the distance as the laugh of the man in Sam's flat echoed in her ears. She forced herself to speak slowly.

"I'm sorry, Bobbie, but I told Allington about Anna's papers. He agrees the notes may be connected to the ones found in the hotel. We're to go in tomorrow and have a look. But I didn't tell him about the Joyce—"

Suddenly Virginia was aware of someone behind her. She spun around. Maynard was standing there, pulling on his overcoat.

"I have to ring off now," she said into the phone. "But you were right this afternoon. I was just tired." She paused, adding in a stronger voice. "We *have to* go on."

"More secrets?" asked Maynard as she hung up.

She shook her head. "Really, Pozzo! For all your fine friends, you still haven't learned any manners."

16

Leonard was mollified the following morning, not only because she was to see Allington later in the day but also by Lord Ladbrooke's letter in *The Times* calling for an investigation of the Belgian murders. It reassured him that Anna Michaux wasn't Virginia's private obsession.

Virginia posted a letter to Elise Robert for more information about the so-called Inspector Brown before setting off for Mrs. Ottlinger's delicatessen, only two blocks away from Hogarth House. There she took a table by the window. A new waitress brought her croissants and coffee. Across the room Mrs. Ottlinger stood by the cash register. A short woman, her ample figure and the gray hair twisted into a bun befitted the motherly role she'd adopted toward Virginia. Usually Mrs. Ottlinger rushed to her table to ask after her health and ply her with pastries and hot chocolate. This morning, however, she turned away when Virginia waved. Later, when the new, young waitress brought her bill, Virginia asked if she'd known Marie Ickx.

The woman shook her head.

"Not even through the Belgian Relief Committee?"

"No!" The waitress hurried through the curtained door to the kitchen.

Virginia went to pay. "You're working hard today," she said to Mrs. Ottlinger, putting a shilling on the counter.

Mrs. Ottlinger scooped the money into the till.

"Could you take a moment? I'd like to talk to you about Marie Ickx."

Mrs. Ottlinger glanced at her, frightened. "The police told me not to talk to anyone. Especially you, the man from Scotland Yard said."

"Who? Tell me his name."

She didn't reply. Allington might have threatened her with deportation, Virginia thought. Allington or one of his men, guessing that she might come to the tearoom. Or was it another imposter? Perhaps the man calling himself "Inspector Brown," or the two men who'd been at Hogarth House yesterday? But the woman either didn't know or chose not to say.

"Just one thing, Mrs. Ottlinger," Virginia persisted. "Did Anna Michaux ever come here? Did Marie ever mention her?"

The Belgian shook her head. Tears stood in her eyes, but she turned away without another word.

Whoever it was had frightened her, clearly, thought Virginia as she left. Still, if it was the Commissioner himself, he didn't yet know about Marcus's bookstore. She was carrying the book from Anna's suitcase in her handbag and now, deciding to visit the booksmith, she hurried to the Richmond tube station.

She hadn't noticed the man in the tearoom, though. He'd been sitting with his back to her, a burly workman taking his morning tea. Mrs. Ottlinger nodded to him and he had hurried out the front door, keeping Virginia in sight.

Across the street and several doors down, still another man was watching. He had a hat pulled low over his face and he wore the frayed, mismatched clothes of a refugee. He, too, waited as Virginia passed, followed by the workman, and then fell into step behind them, skillfully keeping out of sight even aboard the tube to Charing Cross Road.

On the lookout for Marcus's shop, Virginia pushed through the morning browsers strolling by the carts of volumes lining the store fronts. She went past Foyles and past the smaller, more specialized dealers. Suddenly she felt chilled, sure she was being watched. She wheeled around. Her fear changed to anger as she spotted Roger, waving from across the street. In his old French broadbrim, wht she called his "wide-awake" hat, he struggled through the crowds to her side.

"Leonard's let you out, I see," he said with a grin.

She didn't smile.

"I'm sorry, Virginia, really I am. But I could hardly *not* tell him what happened. I'm concerned."

He took her arm as if to remind her of his affection. "What are you doing here? Hunting out more of Thomas Browne's sermons?"

She ignored the tease about one of her literary obsessions. "I'm looking for a Mr. Marcus."

"He's in the next block. Lovely chap. He's been here only—" He peered over his glasses at her. "So that's it—another Belgian!"

He hurried to keep up with her. "I can introduce you. Smooth the way."

She kept walking at a rapid pace.

"Call it my act of contrition."

Finally she slowed with a shrug. It was impossible to stay angry with him. "But you mustn't tell anyone, not Leonard, not even Vanessa."

He nodded and pointed at a door, which read J. G. Marcus, Booksmith. They had to pass through the door sideways, so precariously were books piled in the entry. Inside was a jumble of shelves holding books stacked every which way. Like a garden gone to seed, books had taken over the shop, run wild without any strong hand to keep them down. Throughout there was the redolent odor of aged varnish, leather and dust.

The shop seemed deserted. "M'sieur Marcus?" Roger called.

The bookseller ambled out.

"Ah, *c'est vous,* M'sieur Fry," he said, extending his hand.

"Jean, good morning. May I introduce Virginia Woolf?" The man bowed ceremoniously. With his tonsured hair and bent figure, he could have been a medieval abbé. He gazed piercingly at Virginia and she had the odd feeling that he might have been expecting her.

But before he could speak there was a knock at the shop's rear door, muffled yet insistent. The bookdealer turned back through the curtains.

In the rear office, his visitor sounded heated, but Virginia couldn't be certain. Roger settled into the chair at Marcus's desk to inspect a Daumier lithograph. Virginia was drawn to the glass case behind the desk. Assuming it to be the cabinet for Marcus's more valuable books, she bent closer. While there were several leather-bound volumes showing the distinctive marking of Louis Elzevir, the Dutch master of six-teenth-century printing, she was surprised to see two shelves filled with modern French fiction and poetry, all carrying the insignia of *Editions du Nord.* Virginia wondered why Marcus had included these among his antiquities. She was about to comment when the bookseller reappeared.

"You've discovered my Elzevir's!"

"It's a fine collection. But actually it's the others, the *Editions—*"

"The Gallimards, excellent, yes," he interrupted her, un-locking the cabinet and handing her several of the Giraud editions. "These are the ones you want to see." It was a statement, not a question. Virginia was puzzled.

"Those aren't—" Roger began, but Marcus went right

on: "They don't come in very often. When they do, they're locked up immediately. The war has made them very valuable. I have only a few sources left."

"Yes, I've heard how rare they've become."

She was sure he was testing her. "If you still have business to attend to. . . ." She gestured toward the back of the shop.

"All so secretive. In this country it is strange work, this. *Se recueillir*—how do you say? To collect? No one should know what you're after."

"*Oui, oui, je comprends,*" she replied. Familiar with the language she understood that the man was using a pun to advise her to collect herself, to hide what she was really after.

"Now," he said, dropping his voice, "was there a particular volume you were seeking?"

"Michelet's *Louis XV et XVI,*" she said, looking at him directly. "Then there's this too." She withdrew the Joyce volume from her handbag and placed it on the desk.

"What in the—" exclaimed Roger.

Virginia nudged him quiet. Marcus nodded, looked through the pages of Joyce, then thrust it back into her open bag.

"That's not something for me. But this—" he opened his desk drawer and withdrew a book wrapped in brown paper. "You take this." He wrote something on the front of the parcel and handed it to her. "There is your receipt."

She looked down. Scrawled across the wrapping paper was the note: "From M.I. Leave immediately."

She looked up at him. "Come, Roger, we must be off," she said, keeping her voice calm.

"But I have a few things to discuss with Jean."

"*Mais non,* M'sieur Fry, we do that another time." Marcus waved them toward the door.

Outside, Virginia didn't reply as Roger demanded an explanation. The door to the shop was still ajar and the same angry voice could be heard from the rear. She quickly let herself back in.

"You imbecile!" There was the sound of a hard slap. "I know you have it. Give it to me!"

She heard a groan. Suddenly someone seized her arm and spun her around. She was staring into the unshaven face of Henri Giraud.

⊰ 17 ⊱

Giraud still gripped Virginia's arm as Roger ran into the shop.

"What the bloody hell?" he bellowed at Giraud.

Before Giraud could reply they heard the shop's rear door slam. Giraud rushed through the curtains. In a moment he returned with Marcus leaning on his arm. They spoke in low murmurs, then Giraud asked:

"Do you need a doctor?"

Marcus rubbed his inflamed cheek but shook his head. "No, no, I'm all right. You take care of Madame Woolf."

"I'm calling the police," said Roger, turning toward the door.

"No!" said Giraud sharply. "We don't need any questions about immigration papers."

"This isn't Le Havre!" said Roger.

"There's no time to explain. I must speak to Mrs. Woolf. Alone."

Alerted by the coldness and urgency in his voice, Virginia said, "Of course, but you're sure we can leave M'sieur Marcus?"

"Really, I'm fine," said the bookseller. He turned to Roger. "Come, M'sieur Fry, I'll show you my new order of prints."

"Please, Roger," said Virginia when her friend began to object again. "Do as they say. It must be important."

Giraud and Virginia found a tea shop two corners down. Virginia stared at his moth-eaten cardigan and blue serge trousers shiny with wear, but he seemed unaware of her puzzlement. His face was lined with fatigue, grizzled, his eyes red-rimmed. He removed the oil stained cap he'd worn low on his forehead and rubbed the scar on his unshaven cheek. He said nothing until they had been served, the waitress leaving the table.

"What's this all about?" Virginia asked impatiently. "Why are you here? And dressed like that?"

"Marie Ickx. . . ."

"But you said you didn't know her."

"Keep your voice down." He glanced at the waitress. Under Giraud's gaze, she ducked her head and went back to her tabloid. "There's a lot I didn't tell you. Marie's death forces me to."

"You mean you made up the story about Anna's moods? You didn't really think it was suicide?" Her mouth fell open. Her thoughts hurtled ahead of her words. All her doubts, her suspicions were justified.

"But why?" she burst out. "Especially when I was trying to convince the Yard to reopen the case. You deliberately misled me!"

"There was a reason. Just as there's a reason for my being in London now."

"In disguise?" she scoffed.

Giraud smiled. "It's effective. You didn't see me this morning, nor did the other man who was following you."

"What man?" Virginia stared at him. Was he deliberately trying to frighten her? There he sat with his damned attractive smile, casually telling her she'd been followed. "You'd better explain," she said. "Otherwise I'm going to the police."

"I want you to promise that you'll keep this to yourself."

"I can't. If you know something about Anna Michaux's murder, then—"

"Damn it all, of course I do. But I don't have proof." He dropped his voice. "Will you promise?"

The pleading note convinced her, that or something she couldn't yet fully acknowledge. She bit her lip and nodded.

"Anna worked for me. Marie too. They were both agents for our organization."

"Organization? The Belgian government?"

"In a way. As you know, my official title is Minister of Information. But actually I'm directing Intelligence. You have MI_5 and MI_6, we have our own group. Anna and Marie were two of our people in London. What they were doing was crucial to our investigation."

Virginia was stunned: The governess, an agent, the publisher, head of an intelligence organization? For all the talk in London about MI_5 and German espionage, Mata Hari and coded messages, she would never have taken a leap into this shadowy reality. She felt as if she'd just awakened from a drugged sleep. The blurry shapes and slanted walls, the half-heard voices and mumbled words suddenly came into focus. She made herself speak, brought up sharp by his one frightening phrase:

"Your investigation?"

"The British are about to try to break through the Hindenburg Line. The Prime Minister himself is behind the new strategy. The Germans may have gotten wind of it, to what extent we're not sure. All we know is that someone has been supplying information, someone with access to government plans. Anna and Marie were trying to uncover who—"

"Cranford! He's the one, isn't he? That's why Anna was killed, Marie too. . . ." She stopped. He was smiling at her ruefully.

"Anna obviously took the job with Cranford for a reason,

yes, but as far as we know she hadn't any proof. Besides, we're sure more than one man is involved."

The blandness of his tone annoyed her. "But Anna must have had enough information to tell Marie Ickx. That's why they were both murdered—because Cranford knew they'd expose him." She started to rise from her chair. "We'll go to Special Branch. The man must be stopped."

"For God's sake, sit down and lower your voice."

She obeyed, but looked over at the waitress who was watching them. "What are you waiting for then?" she asked in a strained whisper. "Two women have been murdered, I've been threatened, and you say the Germans are receiving military secrets! I can take you to Commissioner Allington—"

"Whom you expect to investigate Sir Henry Cranford as a traitor? You really think men like that are so easily swayed without proof? Professionals, careerists? He'd laugh me out of his office. Too, there's a problem with Special Branch and MI$_5$. I've seen it happen. Crucial information is lost, not acted upon because Allington and Vernon Kell are trying to outsmart each other. Allington worries about his loss of authority. He'd try to keep the investigation out of Kell's hands."

"You know these people?"

"Of course."

"But how?" she asked.

He shrugged. "It's necessary, given our own group."

"But you're saying it's because he's so defensive, Allington, that you can't go to him?" She thought a moment. "Still, mightn't it be to his advantage? I mean, perhaps he hasn't really closed Anna's case but just wants Kell to think so." She paused again. "Why else would he insist he's in charge of the Marie Ickx investigation? He was furious when we asked why Special Branch was involved."

"We?" Giraud narrowed his eyes, and Virginia quickly told him about Bobbie. "She was convinced from the beginning that Anna was murdered. Yesterday she enraged Allington by refusing to answer his questions. We both did. Then Lord Ladbrooke intervened. . . ."

"Ladbrooke?"

"A Conservative peer. He's also head of the Belgian Relief Committee. If you did go to the Yard, I'm sure he'd back you."

His rueful smile returned. "We'd still need more evidence. Besides, I want the informers to think they're safe now that Anna and Marie are dead. They may show themselves if we let them think they've gone undetected. And that, Mrs. Woolf, could be crucial for the Allied cause."

Virginia was surprised to find him so convincing. Usually she dismissed such talk with its drum beating and appeal to false loyalties as so much schoolboy drivel. Now, she realized, she was moved. Giraud had pulled at the web of her cynicism and unraveled her defenses against an emotion she distrusted: the primitive feeling of patriotism. She hated it in herself, only this time, it wasn't spurious. Oddly, almost too easily, she heard it as a call to action; it stirred her blood.

"Then we must stop them," she said finally.

He fixed her with his large brown eyes. "I hoped you might feel this way. The war's at a pivotal stage. President Wilson will soon decide how many American troops to send to the Front. Until then the Allies must come up with a strong attack along the Hindenburg Line. If the Germans learn what the British are planning, the Western Front may collapse." He paused. "I mean totally, which is why I need your help."

She took in a sharp breath. Here was one of those moments of which she had been acutely aware throughout her life. There was a globe hanging between them. Once it fell, the stream of time would ripple with infinite change. And she had the strangest sensation that he knew it. He'd led her to this point skillfully, step by step; if she agreed now there would be no turning back. He was filling the globe with such intensity that it would hang heavier and heavier. It would have to fall.

"What can I possibly do? You don't want to involve the police or MI₅, yet you're asking *me* to hunt spies and murderers. I'm not trained for that. My God, the last three days I've been followed, assaulted, shot at. Last night I almost collapsed."

"But you didn't, did you? Besides, none of us was trained. I'm a publisher." His voice was bitter. "But the Germans killed my wife and child. I had to do something. I agreed to join Intelligence. We learn when we have to. Just as you and Miss Waters went on when you realized Anna's death wasn't a suicide. You've done a good job of making people uncomfortable. That's exactly what I want you to continue doing. Let the Yard know you're not going to drop it. Make a pest of yourself. Question Mrs. Ottlinger, stop by the Relief Committee. Use your friends, your social connections, Mr. Keynes, Mr. Bell and Mr. Fry, even your sister and your husband. Miss Waters's friendship with Sam Josephs will be helpful, too. Let everyone know you've adopted Anna as a case of your own. If they think you're going to write about her, even better."

She lit a cigarette, thinking. On the one hand, he was telling her she was needed. On the other, that she would become a target, possibly a decoy. It was to invite paranoia; but this time it wouldn't be her imagination. The line between reality and fantasy would be frighteningly blurred.

Her head came up with a jolt. He had talked of her friends and Nessa and Leonard, her family's social connections, and Bobbie's friendship with Sam. She jabbed the half-smoked cigarette into the ashtray.

"You've really been quite thorough, haven't you? How do you know all of this? How long have *you* been watching me? Miss Waters, too, though a few minutes ago you pretended not to know who she was." She felt a tingling sensation at the back of her neck. However attractive, however compelling, Giraud was also a liar. "If you want my help, you'd better start telling the truth."

"I was only trying to protect you. We have other people working for us, naturally, and they told me you went to see Sir Henry. I wondered if it was about Anna. Still, when you came to Le Havre, you didn't know who she was. That's why I wanted to convince you of the suicide. But the shooting changed things."

"So it *was* connected to my questions about Anna?"

He didn't reply directly. "The fact that you and Miss Waters discovered Marie's body—" To her startled look, he added, "Yes, I know about that. It means you're deeply involved, like it or not. I wish you weren't, but you are. And I'm afraid the collaborators realize it too. The man who followed you from the delicatessen this morning is the one who threatened Marcus."

She stiffened, as if through force of will she could keep her fear at bay. She pointed to the parcel Marcus had given her. "He must have thought Marcus still had it." She tore off the wrapper.

"Look! It's the same book Anna's sister gave to me." She stared at him. "Michelet's *Louis XV et XVI.*" Her voice rose with excitement as she flipped through the first pages. "There's the same underlining, too."

"It's not Anna's, it's Marie's."

"Of course!" She knew why he was sure. "So you did take the copy from my hotel room, then?" He nodded. While she'd already guessed as much, her throat now went dry. More terror. She felt assaulted as he calmly continued. Every word he uttered was driving her deeper into the reality of his secret, lawless world.

"I was afraid you'd guess it was a code. We used Michelet to encode our messages. The message was spelled out by the first letter of words indicated by the lists of page, line and word numbers. That's why we had to take it."

"Oh God! Do the collaborators know that? Because they stole Anna's messages!" She recounted the theft of the lists of numbers from Sam's flat. "But they didn't find Marie's notes. She'd hidden them in the bath at the hotel. Inspector Clarke from the Yard discovered them behind the mirror." She felt numb, imagining for a moment the physical pain of Marie's suffocation, of Anna's drowning. Involuntarily, she gulped for air as if she were being held under water herself.

Giraud seemed unaware of her agitation. "I doubt they've broken our code, though now they must realize it's based on a book." He paused, outwardly calm. "Inspector Clarke," he mused more to himself, as though he recognized the name. Then: "Still, I don't want you to say anything about our codes yet. Or the Michelet volume. Let the Yard muddle along for the time being."

"But what about the other—"

He waved her quiet and pushed his chair back from the window.

"What's the matter?"

"The man who slapped Marcus—the one who was following you this morning. He's coming this way." He thought a moment, then stood up and beckoned the waitress. "Is there a rear entrance?" he asked.

She pointed to the kitchen and was about to object when he abruptly turned to Virginia: "I'll leave messages for you with Marcus. If you need me, do the same. Now I'm leading him off. Stay here, but keep away from the window."

"But what about this?" She held up the Joyce volume, but he'd already gone. She shrank back into the corner. Within minutes she saw the man's large head above the café curtain. He didn't give the shop a second glance as he stopped and stared down the street. Then he broke into a run.

Virginia recognized him immediately. Yesterday he'd been dressed in livery and polishing a motor's windscreen. It was Sir Henry Cranford's chauffeur.

18

The two o'clock appointment with Mrs. Woolf and the American reporter was the least of Allington's worries. His superior, C.I.D. head Sir Basil Thomson, had again upbraided him for his "lack of cooperation" with the MI5 liaison officer. All files, memoranda, surveillance and interrogation notes were to be made available, Thomson ordered, so that Clarke could get on with his investigation of the Swan and Edgar's department store bombing.

Allington had complied by commanding his men to bring all material, "and I mean every last scrap," to the office adjoining his own where Clarke was installed. Barely managing to suppress a smile, the Deputy Commissioner watched as Clarke's irritation grew along with the piles of folders.

Allington found the MI5 officer especially irksome. He seemed to make a point of slouching, as if he were practicing a disappearing act. Flickering from brown to green, his eyes were oddly inexpressive. Covertness, even a certain reptilian slyness seemed to lie at the base of the man's personality. The unkempt hair and mustache, the wrinkled tweeds, all, Allington suspected, were a pointed insult to Branch's code of dress and bearing.

Now, marching into the Deputy Commissioner's office,

Clarke gave Allington a knowing smile. "A nice little ploy, Commissioner. But really, there's nothing at all in those reports you so kindly made available."

"Nothing?" repeated Allington without looking up. "I thought MI$_5$ thrived on desk work."

"Not in that rag and bone shop."

"Perhaps you'll find Bomb Division more to your liking. They're testing the bomb wrappings from yesterday's attack on Swan and Edgar's. We're sure it's the Irish again but you can have a go off your own bat."

Clarke reached for the matches on Allington's desk. He took his time tamping his pipe and lighting it.

"You're not going down yourself?" he asked.

"Not just yet. I have things to do here."

"Ah, yes, Mrs. Woolf at two."

"Now you're reading my appointment book?" he looked up.

Clarke shrugged. "Since she found the Ickx woman, I'd like to sit in."

"Surely Sir Vernon doesn't give a fig about that case. Haven't you enough with the bombings?"

"Whither thou goest . . . Commissioner." Clarke rolled out his "r's" as if to irritate Allington further. "Besides, you can't be altogether happy with the Belgian Butcher theory, not after we found those notes at the hotel."

Allington waved his hands in two small arcs as if he could make Clarke disappear. "Do as you like. But let me do the talking."

Bobbie was already downstairs at the duty counter when Virginia came rushing in, flushed and out of breath, carrying the parcel she'd hastily rewrapped at the shop.

"I thought you weren't coming," said Bobbie.

"I'm late, I know. . . but for a good reason." Two bobbies passed, wrestling a Punjabi toward a rear office. Virginia waited until they'd passed. "You should know about this before we see Allington." She gestured at the sergeant behind the desk. "Did he say how long it would be?"

"He said the Commissioner would ring down."

Her words coming fast, Virginia described the incident at Marcus's and her conversation with Giraud. Then she showed Bobbie the book. "It *is* the basis for a code," she whispered, "we were right. Giraud told me Anna and Marie used it to send information to him."

Bobbie let out a low whistle. "So that's why he wouldn't talk about Anna! Are you going to tell Allington?"

"Not yet. Giraud's afraid Special Branch and MI₅ will botch things if they know too much about his organization. Apparently—" she glanced over her shoulder at the duty sergeant—"he thinks Allington's a fool."

"As I do too. He'd never question Cranford."

"But Cranford must be involved. Why else would his chauffeur follow me all morning?"

"You're sure?"

"Giraud and I saw him from the tea shop."

Bobbie frowned. "If Giraud doesn't want us to tell any of this to the Yard, what do we do now?"

"First we find out what the Yard's doing about Anna and Marie's deaths. Then we're to make Cranford uncomfortable with more questions, really stir him up. This weekend Keynes is bringing Sir Henry to Ottoline Morrell's house party because they have a meeting Sunday morning. So I want you to come with Leonard and me."

"I'm not sure, Virginia." Bobbie's voice was weary. "Maybe I should stay in town. Sam might want to reach me. I'm worried about him."

"What are you going to tell Allington? He's bound to ask about him."

"I like Giraud's plan. Let Allington do the talking." The

duty officer beckoned to them. "Put the book away," she said. "They're ready for us."

"So good of you both to come," said the Commissioner.

Angus Clarke, Virginia noted, was standing by the windows.

"Leonard rang me this morning," said Allington. "He wanted to confirm your appointment."

"Hardly necessary. I told him I was coming in."

"Apparently he's very worried."

"He tends to exaggerate."

"Tends to exaggerate? But you haven't been straightforward, have you?"

Virginia knew the Commissioner's tone quite well. The angry father, the scolding stentorian voice. Little girls were spoken to this way; so were some grown women. She forced herself to give him a smile.

"But Commissioner, I'll give you any information you want, now that you're reopening the Anna Michaux investigation."

"Reopening, no. We're doing nothing of the sort. You're here for two reasons and two reasons only. One, I want you to look at the papers from the hotel. And, two, I want to know where Josephs is, and why he stole that suitcase."

"He didn't. Besides, we were assaulted!" exclaimed Bobbie. "Why aren't you going after those two thieves instead of Josephs?"

Allington rubbed the bridge of his nose. Virginia gave Bobbie a warning look. "Look here, Commissioner, what's important are the notes in Anna's suitcase. As I told you on the telephone, I think they looked like the ones found in the hotel."

"Yes, the ones in the hotel. . . . We'll come to that. What were you doing in Josephs' flat in the first place?"

"Mr. Josephs and I often have newspaper business," replied Bobbie.

"Newspaper business. I suppose Mr. Josephs writes about garden parties?"

"We often cooperate on stories. . . ."

"Stories about Miss Michaux's suitcase, it would seem," he said. "You should know Sir Henry's filed an informal complaint against both of you, as well as Josephs."

Silence, broken by Clarke. "You seem upset, Mrs. Woolf."

"I am," she said. "Rather, I'm puzzled. Isn't that excessive on Sir Henry's part?"

The Scotsman sucked on his pipe and watched her. She turned back to Allington.

"Hasn't it occurred to you, Commissioner, that Sir Henry's trying to prevent an investigation? Why else would he raise such a fuss about a suitcase?"

"He's answered our questions to our complete satisfaction," said Allington.

"Including the fact that Anna Michaux was meeting someone that night? That the housekeeper told him to leave the door off the latch for her return, but he locked it anyway?"

"Sir Henry locked it because he didn't realize that Miss Michaux was still out. As for her meeting someone, there's no proof of that whatever."

"But she told the housekeeper she was. That's why she was dressed up. She was meeting a man, not setting out to drown herself."

"And another thing," put in Bobbie, "Sir Henry denies that Marie Ickx visited Anna, yet—"

"We've been through all of this," said Allington. "The suggestion that Sir Henry's hiding something is preposterous. Josephs is the man who's not talking, and I mean to find him."

Bobbie gripped the arms of her chair. Virginia touched her arm to calm her, realizing that Clarke was staring at them.

"We don't want to cause trouble," said Virginia. "But do hear us out. Sir Henry must have been surprised to hear about those hidden lists of numbers." Her eyes narrowed as she scrutinized Allington's face. "Does he have any idea what they might be?"

"Any idea? Not at all. He'd never seen anything like them. Did the thieves take anything else?"

Virginia shook her head. "They knew exactly what they wanted. They didn't bother with the clothes and books."

"What sort of books?" asked Clarke abruptly.

"French classics. I expect for her work as a translator."

"You didn't take any of them?" He pointed with the stem of his pipe at the bulging handbag.

"What? Oh, no, these are just review copies." Feeling her face go hot, she stared down at her bag, relieved to hear Allington's scolding voice. "Clarke! Do you mind? Now, Miss Waters, I'd like a description of those two men."

Bobbie adopted an impersonal tone. As an afterthought, she added that the fat one with the birthmark might have been Irish. " 'Mick,' he was called, and he might have had a slight brogue."

"Ah, now we're getting somewhere. Right, Clarke?"

"Might explain some things," he replied doubtfully. "Tell me, Miss Waters, did either of them seem to know Josephs?"

"Why?"

"Mrs. Woolf?" he persisted.

"They did say something about having a pint together."

"That was just rubbing our noses in it," Bobbie objected. "Besides, Sam knows a lot of underworld sorts, contacts he uses in his work." Allington permitted himself a slight smile. "Look," she added lamely, "he's had a byline for fifteen years. A lot of people know him."

"Fifteen years, we're aware of that," said Allington. "But

you're a special friend, aren't you?" He glared at her. "So we think you can tell us where he is."

"You had him followed, you find him." She was barely controlled, her upper lip quivering.

"Our man lost him."

"That's my fault? I haven't seen or heard from him since Sunday night."

"Indeed, Sunday night, the night he was seen with Marie Ickx—the night she was murdered."

"Impossible. We were at the Cock Tavern."

"But you didn't spend the night together, did you?" he paused, watching her expression. "In fact, Josephs left you and then called on Miss Ickx. The clerk said he went roaring up to her room. Mad as a hornet, he said."

"That clerk's a damned liar!" She gave a defiant toss of her head.

"I'm warning you, Miss Waters. If you've any idea where Josephs is you'd better tell us. His Sinn Fein sympathies are well known. We're looking into Miss Ickx's connections with the Irish as well."

"That's right. Blame it on the Irish."

"Blame it on the Irish," repeated Allington, slamming his palm on the desk. The noise startled Virginia from her thoughts. Special Branch was more interested in the Irish than the Germans. If their investigation of Marie's death was going in this direction, they were bungling it, just as Giraud had predicted.

"Mrs. Woolf?" Clarke said. "Would you explain why you went to see Giraud in Le Havre?"

"He was Anna's employer in Brussels before the war. I hoped he could tell me more about her."

"Did he think suicide likely, given her work for him?"

She glanced at him, struck by the ambiguity of his reference to her work. She suspected he knew more than he was saying and she had to be careful. "He told me she was moody, yes," she said.

The Scotsman's pipe had gone out and he crossed to Allington's desk to pick up a box of matches. "You haven't spoken to him since?" He concentrated on the flame over the pipe bowl, then suddenly his eyes shifted and met hers.

She knew she was blushing again. "How could I?"

"That's not the point," Allington interrupted. "Here are the notes from Marie Ickx's room." He took several sheets of blue paper from a file. "Are these like the ones you saw in Anna Michaux's suitcase?"

Virginia leafed through them slowly. "The list of numbers seems similar."

"Just one minute," interrupted Clarke. "Has Mr. Josephs had any contact with Henri Giraud?"

"What a ridiculous question!" exclaimed Bobbie.

"I'm not so sure. Marie Ickx belonged to a refugee group. They publish a newspaper. Since Josephs knew Marie Ickx, he may also have met Giraud on one of his trips to London. You do realize he often comes here—"

"I told you, Clarke, I'll do the questioning."

Virginia looked from the Commissioner back to Clarke. Perhaps it was Allington's habit to dismiss his underlings with contempt, even though Clarke's questions were more astute than his own. Nevertheless, she felt she couldn't reveal Giraud's presence or purpose in London.

"I suppose Giraud comes here to keep his hand in," she said, "so he can return to publishing after the war." She knew it sounded forced; Clarke was again staring at her with a curious glint in his eye.

Allington, however, seemed to accept her explanation. "Keeping his hand in, quite so," he repeated, then, as a clear dismissal: "I think that's all for today. But I'm warning both of you, don't play detective. Understood?"

Virginia didn't move. Giraud had told her to make a pest

of herself. Certainly, it wasn't difficult; Allington's abruptness grated on her, rasping her like a file with rusted edges.

"How can you expect that?" she demanded, her voice rising in indignation. "No, I won't stay out of it. Especially when Sir Henry's chauffeur is following me."

There was a loud rap at the door. "Yes?" Allington called out, obviously rattled.

Lord Ladbrooke marched into the room. "Look here, Nigel, I wanted to be here when you interviewed Mrs. Woolf. Then I hear from her husband you've called her in. Why haven't you let me know? Mrs. Woolf's recovering from a serious illness." He placed his gloved hand gently on her shoulder.

"*Really!* I'm quite all right," she said. "My husband worries too much." She glanced at Bobbie, then at Clarke who was watching the aristocrat. "I'm simply trying to convince the Commissioner that Sir Henry's involved in this. To prove it—" she looked up into Ladbrooke's concerned face—"I've just informed him that Sir Henry's chauffeur is following me."

"What!" exclaimed Ladbrooke. "Did you know this, Nigel?"

"No. But I'm not surprised. Sir Henry asked the Yard to do something about Mrs. Woolf. Evidently he decided to look after you himself. A bit excessive, I grant you. I'll ask him to call off his chauffeur on the condition that you promise not to bother him anymore."

Virginia swallowed hard. "No. I want to know what Sir Henry's hiding. You can issue all the damned orders you want, Commissioner, but I'm going to find out who killed Anna Michaux and Marie Ickx and why!"

She was staring at him, still holding the note papers from the hotel on her lap. Seemingly dazed and upset, she began to fumble with the folds of her cape, plucking at them, pulling them around her midsection. For a moment she looked like a great bird readying itself for flight. Then she rose, suddenly letting the pages fall from her lap to the floor. With one hand hugging her cape tight against herself, she reached down with the other and retrieved the slightly crumpled pages.

"If you'll excuse us, Miss Waters and I are leaving," she said. She put the papers on Allington's desk, then stalked to the door, bending slightly at the waist as if her indignation were propelling her forward. Bobbie gave her a peculiar look, but followed quickly.

"I'm advising you, ladies." Allington's tone was bland as he addressed their backs. "Don't interfere or I'll have you up on charges. Clarke, you take them down." Allington turned to Ladbrooke. "Now, sir, since you're so worried about my investigation, I'll be glad to fill you in."

Clarke was silent as he took them down to the duty desk. But as they turned to leave, he stopped Virginia with a pointed stare at the folds of cape she still held clutched around her waist. "And Mrs. Woolf, if you make any sense of that code, do let me know."

19

On the train back to Richmond, Virginia worried about Clarke. He'd obviously seen her slip the uppermost code page under her cape, but he'd chosen to let her carry it away from the Yard. Why she herself had done it she couldn't say, except that she was curious about the kind of messages Marie had sent to Giraud. But why hadn't Clarke told Allington? Why was the detective keeping things from his superior, letting suspicions fall on Sam Josephs and the Sinn Fein?

All these questions still gnawed at her when she reached Hogarth House, but she mustered a look of calm as Leonard greeted her with a kiss. His animosity was gone. He'd been reassured by Lord Ladbrooke's telephone call, he said, for after all, it seemed that the man really did have the welfare of the refugees at heart. Virginia, it followed, had been acting out of generous impulse.

"Though I'm glad you've put all these murders in the hands of Scotland Yard," he added later over supper.

She didn't bother to correct him. "My difficulties aren't something to serve up in public. Ladbrooke even mentioned my illness to Commissioner Allington."

"He was genuinely worried about you. Policemen can be bullies. Ladbrooke told me the Yard was especially hard on you."

She nodded, letting it pass.

For the next two days London was shrouded in mist. Nothing seemed to distinguish the fourteenth and fifteenth of November: the press put a bold face on the stalled Western offensive; Parliament debated General Haig's war strategy, Irish Home Rule, workers' strikes and the Bolshevik Revolution. By and by someone thought to remember Votes for Women, but it was like a vaguely recalled tune whistled with neither enthusiasm nor consequence.

Sir Henry Cranford was verifying shipments to the Western Front. Allington and Clarke were questioning Irishmen about Sam Josephs. Bobbie dutifully completed a story about Tommies on leave in London, although her thoughts were on Sam, whose whereabouts were still unknown. Leonard, meanwhile, fairly hummed to see Virginia returned to her desk. She even helped him set type for the first press run for a Katherine Mansfield story. The crisis, it seemed, was past.

But, aware of her own deception, Virginia found herself musing that there was always more to the ordinariness of a Monday or Tuesday, or in this case, a Wednesday and Thursday, than meets the eye. What on the surface seemed a part of the daily round was, in fact, one of those small private acts that propel history forward, or at least, now, revitalized her intentions.

The private act in question had happened totally by chance. She wasn't working on her novel or a review. She had instead decoded the page of numbers she'd stolen from Allington's office. Marie's code was really quite simple. The column of three numbers indicated, precisely as Giraud had explained, pages, lines and words in Michelet's *Louis XV et Louis XVI,* and yielded first letters which when transcribed read:

"Dbl Shfts Cran Shef Mtg PM Tues Suede Amb Wed"

With breath quickening, she read the obvious shorthand aloud, finally settling on a translation: "Double shifts, Cranford Sheffield." Yes, that had to be the meaning of "Shef"—she knew that one of his munitions factories was located in

Sheffield. Was Marie reporting increased production there, perhaps for the military offensive Giraud had mentioned? "Mtg PM Tues"—that was easy, she thought: "Meeting with the Prime Minister Tuesday." But "Suede Amb Wed" gave her a momentary pause. "Amb" equalled ambassador, "Wed" was Wednesday but "Suede"? Her mind leaping ahead, she guessed Marie had used the French word for "Swedish." "That's it," she exclaimed aloud. Cranford was also meeting with the Swedish ambassador. Sweden was neutral. Did Cranford have holdings there? Or was he sending information to the Germans through Sweden? There had been rumors in the press about Swedish espionage, and now she was convinced: here was Marie's proof that Cranford was a traitor. She would take this to Giraud, take this to Allington—

Suddenly she stopped. "You silly fool," she scolded herself. This was an old message, one that Giraud had presumably already received. And yet he still didn't consider it proof enough for Allington. Her mood of triumph deflated, she lit a cigarette and began to thumb idly through the Michelet volume.

Then it happened. One of the pages felt heavy, and thinking it hadn't been cut, she looked more closely. At the top and bottom, the signature had already been sliced, but then pasted back together. With growing excitement she jabbed out the cigarette and with her ivory knife separated the leaves. Several pieces of thin blue note paper dropped into her lap. They'd been flattened between the book's pages, which had been glued together to form an envelope.

The globe of her desk lamp burned brighter; the handwriting leapt off the page. There it was—Anna's spidery scrawl. At the top of the first sheet she had written:

"These are the lines you wanted translated from Michelet's *Louis XV et Louis XVI* (*Editions du Nord,* 1916). We will rejoice with their completion."

The first line read, "One of Voltaire's grand moments

was summer." It was preceded by a page number, as were the following short sentences which filled the four other sheets.

Her face was flushed, her hair falling around her face as she studied the sentences. They were all quite simple, she thought. No translator should have had a problem with them. And why was Anna translating for Marie? Why had Marie hidden the sheets in this book? Why leave this book with Marcus? Why had had he given it to her? For safekeeping? Because someone—presumably Cranford's chauffeur—was in the back of the bookshop? Her thoughts raced forward to one explanation: this was another code, one which Anna had invented because—she hesitated—of course, because the other code had been broken. Her mood of triumph returned. That was it: Anna had written a final message for Marie. Knowing that she'd been discovered, knowing that their old code wasn't safe, she'd managed to send this to Marie. It was the information needed to expose Cranford.

Leonard called her away from her desk. "Enough work for today," he said. But the following morning she was still convinced she was right. This was Anna's last message; the courageous woman, her life in danger, had made sure Giraud would have his proof. Virginia wanted it, too. She was resolved to decipher this new code and thus she announced she was off for the British Museum Reading Room to work on a review. Leonard suspected nothing. He gave her a parting kiss and reiterated their arrangement to meet in town for the concert they were to attend that afternoon.

With its high-domed ceiling and circular expanse of white wall, the Reading Room had often reminded Virginia of an underwater cavern whose denizens moved slowly but effortlessly among rock and coral. She could still imitate her father's hoarse, theatrical whisper when he had first taken her here and announced, "This is where you'll do your best work." Today, recalling this, she could scarcely agree. After two hours Anna's sentences still hadn't yielded their secret.

She'd begun with the first line translated by Anna herself: "p. 39, One of Voltaire's grand moments was summer." She scanned page 39 of Michelet. Nothing fit the sentence. But the chapter opened with the phrase, *"Un des grands moments de Voltaire avait été justement ce triste retour d'Allemagne. . . ."*

There was the equivalent of "one of the grand moments." But there was no mention of summer. Then, after a moment, she saw it: *"Été"* meant summer as well as being the past participle of the verb *être,* to be. Anna had made a mistake. But why? Surely an experienced translator wouldn't make such a blunder.

The next line, translated from page 163, read: "He succeeded at Brest, he armed a fleet." This time she found the line quite easily, there being only one sentence on page 163 containing the phrase *"à Brest":* *"Il réunit à Brest, il arma une flotte."* There it was again. *Réunit* had been mistranslated as "succeeded" rather than as "reunited" or "mustered." Anna had deliberately mistranslated, Virginia was sure of it. She checked the remaining 30 lines of translation: every one contained an obvious error.

Virginia wrote out the first letters of all the mistranslated words. The result was a confusing jumble. There was certainly no message, even allowing for the most obscure form of abbreviation or shorthand. She thought for a moment. Since Anna had been so assiduous in her mistranslation, then the proper translations might provide the solution.

She began to make her way down the list of 30 translated lines, listing the page, line and word numbers next to the original French word in Michelet, followed by the mistranslation, then the correct translation. Where several meanings might be indicated, she added them in parentheses. She was careful as well to retain the original capitalization:

Page, line, word	Michelet	Anna's Translation	Correct Translation
39/3/1	été	summer	was (had been)
163/15/7	réunit	succeeded	reunited

She'd listed seven more of the mistranslations when the next line in Anna's notes brought her up sharp. On page 95, she'd mistranslated the word, "suicide" as "murder."

"Good lord," Virginia muttered as she entered the words in her list. She was stunned. Had this been Anna's warning to Marie? Had she known all along that she was to be killed, that her death would be made to look like suicide?

Virginia stared up at the domed ceiling, her eyes moist. The poor woman, she thought. If Anna had felt she needed to devise a new code, then she must have been desperate. Despite her fear, though, she'd been disciplined enough to make this gallant attempt to alert her comrades. But no, it still didn't make sense. Why mistranslate 30 lines to hide one word? There had to be more to it. She pushed herself onward, finally completing the list of 30 words. Then she wrote out the first letters of the correct translations horizontally. She peered at it: it was gibberish. In the first place, only four stops were indicated by capital letters; in between was a hodgepodge of letters meaning nothing. While Marie's code had yielded the message so easily, neither the mistranslations nor the original French words in Anna's code revealed anything; not even a clue, much less a message. Nothing.

She sighed, gazing up at the names of great men engraved in gilt around the lip of the dome overhead. For the moment she gave in to her habit of reading the names in a bitter litany, lamenting that they hadn't included Jane Austen or Charlotte Brontë. Once more she reminded herself that Macaulay, Sterne and Dickens had never been any use to her. Or, as she now told herself, "No woman swings her words like dumbbells."

Somehow the private joke helped. She went back to her diary but rather than juggling letters, she began to doodle aimlessly, drawing tongues of flame swirling in circles at the bottom of the page. No, she didn't feel defeated or depressed —she was sure of it when she realized what she'd been drawing. After all, the famous Zimmermann telegram—the details of which she only barely recalled from her earlier months of convalescence—had required experts from the Admiralty and the Foreign Office working for months. Here she'd taken only a few hours, and she'd accomplished the first step—she was convinced of it—toward breaking Anna's code: the mistranslations were the key. And with enough time and perseverance, with what she realized was a burning need, she'd penetrate the meaning. She was damned if she'd let Anna's courage turn to dust.

When Leonard escorted her to their seats for the concert in the Aeolian Hall, he noticed her heightened color and ebullient mood. "Your morning go well?" he asked.

She nodded with an eager smile. He couldn't suspect that her exhilaration was any different from her pleasure at finding the perfect phrase to fit her meaning. Indeed, as she realized while listening to the music, it was quite similar: she was sure it would come to her, just as a line or phrase would suddenly spring to her mind to give substance to an echo or faintly heard rhythm. She leaned back in her chair and closed her eyes. There before her were the faces of Bobbie and Giraud, appearing like promises of success. She smiled to herself; soon she would have something to show them.

When the musicians struck the blaring notes of the final piece—a contemporary appeal to patriotism—she and Leonard exited quickly through the side door.

"They ought to ban trumpets until the war is over," said Virginia. "You'd think we were all to stand up and march . . ." She stopped. In the midst of the chauffeurs loitering about she caught sight of Lord Ladbrooke's driver. It made sense that the aristocrat would attend the concert but she hadn't seen him inside. And when she stared at the chauffeur, pointedly as though to test him, he puffed on his cigarette as if he didn't recognize her.

At the tube station, Leonard asked if she wouldn't change her mind and come along to see their old friend, Margaret Llewelyn Davies, at a Women's Co-operative Guild meeting in Hampstead.

"After that musical show of jingoism, it might clear my head," she said. "I found myself thinking that if one energetic young woman mustered us all and rode roughshod over all our self-satisfied generals, the war would be over in a day."

Leonard laughed. "You may be right. . . ."

Again Bobbie's face flashed before her and reminded her of her own vigorous promise to succeed. "But I think not. I must buy stockings for our Garsington weekend. Then I'll go directly home," she said finally by way of excuse.

Swan and Edgar's windows were still covered with planks and sacking, yet, as a shopgirl explained, "business went on as usual." Outside Virginia skirted the large hole in Piccadilly left by the blast, then stopped, staring fixedly into the open pit, mesmerized by the tangible reminder of violence. A wound in the earth, the destruction of civilization, and this was what men called the glories of war. Whether it was the Germans, the Irish or the British, it made no difference. She flinched, roused herself, and then instead of taking the tube to Richmond as she'd promised Leonard, she hurried to keep the date she'd secretly made with Bobbie by telephone that morning.

Before the war, the Café Royal was known for its devil-may-care atmosphere, and even in the bleakness of wartime London, the red velvet draperies, gleaming mirrors and gilt moldings seemed to insist that life could hold more than rationing queues. Whether because of the left-wing politics of its habitués or because the police, too, enjoyed the old luxuries, Yard men often mingled among the patrons. Their identities were well known. It was a fashionable game for the regulars to call out, "Good evening, Inspector," as one of them strolled by.

Virginia had already taken a corner banquette and ordered a glass of sherry when she saw Bobbie enter.

"Damn that boss of mine." Bobbie slammed her bag on the table and gestured to the waiter for another glass of sherry. "Kept me late to go on about my absences, then loaded me with a raft of nonsense assignments."

"Still no word from Sam?" asked Virginia, guessing at the real reason for Bobbie's mood.

She shook her head. "The police have been following me all day." She pointed toward the entranceway. Two plainclothes detectives lounged just beyond the glass doors. "They might as well be wearing sandwich boards."

Virginia laughed, too confident to worry about the Yard now. "I've some frightfully good news, proof that we're on the right track." She took out the diary and gave Bobbie Marie's page of numbers.

The American recognized it immediately. "Where did you—?" She gave Virginia a sly smile. "Right under Allington's nose!"

"But look here," Virginia said, pointing in her diary where she'd decoded the message. "You see what it says...."

Bobbie looked at the shorthand, then her face lit up. " 'Cran'—Why, that's Cranford. It has to be."

"I read it, 'Double shift Cranford, Sheffield, Meeting Prime Minister Tuesday, Swedish Ambassador Wednesday'."

"Right. And it makes perfect sense, too." She lowered her voice, glancing once over her shoulder. "Someone told me that the Swedes've been passing information to the Germans—under the guise of neutrality, of course. But MI₅'s been watching them after a Belgian group uncovered it. Which ... lord, it could well have been Giraud," she added, suddenly making the connection to the gossip she'd heard at the Cock Tavern.

"He surely got this message," Virginia said. "But there's more." Now she removed the pages of translation she'd tucked into the back of her diary and spread them in front of Bobbie, explaining how she'd found them. "I'm convinced it's another code." She showed Bobbie the obvious errors in translation. "It may be Anna's last message to Marie. I doubt it was ever sent to Giraud. It must have been what Marie's killer was looking for—"

"Quick! Put it away," interrupted Bobbie. "It's Sam. Jesus, look at him!"

Josephs was rushing across the dining room: his hair was tumbled and sweat glistened on his forehead, and he hadn't shaved for at least two days. He sidestepped waiters, oblivious to stares.

"Where have you been?" Bobbie jumped to her feet. "The police're looking for you!"

"There's no time, I want the book."

"What are you—"

"I know you have it." He took her arm roughly.

"Sam! You're hurting me."

"What about you, Mrs. Woolf?" he growled. "The two of you took that Joyce novel from my flat. I need it!"

Virginia paled as she looked at him. "Why? What's it got to do—" She stopped, staring past him to the front door. "Oh, my God," she gasped.

Sam turned. Inside the entry stood two men partially blocked by the maître d'.

"Look," Virginia whispered, recognizing the fat man with the strange birthmark, the man who had grabbed her in Sam's flat, as well as his bald companion. Bobbie recognized them too; she clutched Virginia's arm.

Sam stumbled backward and started to run for the rear of the restaurant.

"Wait!" Bobbie called after him as he knocked over two unoccupied chairs, then dashed through the doors to the kitchen. The two men were now pushing past the maître 'd.

"Don't you two move," snarled the fat one as he rushed by, disappearing through the still swinging kitchen doors.

"They'll be back when they find he doesn't have the book," said Virginia, reaching down to grab her handbag. "Hurry." The two of them rose from the table but were stopped by the Scotland Yard detectives who'd been following Bobbie. Virginia gestured toward the kitchen. "You want Sam Josephs? He went out the back."

The two policemen broke into a run, but another man loitered a few more seconds in the restaurant's foyer. The brim of his hat only partially hid the scar on his cheek. He took one last look at Virginia's strained expression, then went outside and hailed a taxi.

❧ 20 ❧

The pony cart bringing the Woolfs and Bobbie from the railway station rounded the bend in the narrow lane, and Garsington came into view. Rising above the ploughed fields and
brown-tinged downs, the estate's grey limestone seemed two-
dimensional in the opaque light of late afternoon. The high
roof and the spiked tops of the surrounding yew trees pressed
flat against the lowering clouds.

The driver helped them down from the cart. A few feet
away a golden peacock spread its broad tail and let out a cry
of welcome to its sequestered world.

Millie Grayson, the Morrells' housekeeper, took their
wraps. She'd been with Lady Ottoline for years and now
adopted her mistress' expansive gestures and melodic lilt of
voice to explain that the hallway's gray-pink walls were "to
remind you of a sunset." She hung Virginia's cape next to a
fur-trimmed overcoat.

"Has Sir Henry Cranford arrived?" asked Virginia.

"Yes, mum. He and Mr. Keynes both. Mr. Morrell's
takin' 'em over the farm."

Virginia ignored Leonard's disapproving look as they
followed the woman upstairs. As requested, Ottoline had
given Leonard and Virginia adjoining quarters. Bobbie was

across the hall, "next to Mr. Keynes," Millie told her. She brought pitchers of hot water. A half hour later Virginia was feeling less dusty, even refreshed. On the lace-covered bed lay her new apricot dress. She'd already set out her comb, brush and hairpins as well as her diary and the two books on the dressing table. Still in her robe, her hair falling over her shoulders, she stood at the window looking out beyond the ilex tree and formal hedges to the beech-crowned Wittenham Clumps, long ago the hilltop site of a Roman camp.

She was glad for the solitary time before dinner. Leonard had taken Bobbie to find Philip Morrell for a tour of the farm. He had been attentive to the young woman since Virginia had brought her home last night distraught and in tears, sure that Josephs was in danger. Rather than scold them, Leonard had risen to the occasion by calling Allington to demand that Josephs be given protection.

"He isn't a common criminal, you know," he had shouted into the phone. Virginia, pouring Bobbie a brandy, had added in a quiet voice: "I'm sure Sam can take care of himself. We needn't tell Leonard everything, but perhaps he'll talk some sense into Allington. Have dinner here, spend the night, and we'll take the train out to Garsington together."

Now Virginia stood at the window watching the two of them cross the far field. Last night she'd been the calm, competent one; Bobbie had collapsed. For all of Leonard's and Dr. Wright's predictions, she'd been able to take command, escorting the American upstairs, repeating her reassurances that Sam would be fine.

Still watching Bobbie and Leonard, Virginia flushed with pleasure at the memory of the impulsive kiss she'd given Bobbie last night as they stood at the guest room door. She knew it had made the young woman uncomfortable. So she'd lied, muttering that her maternal feelings had gotten the better of her. Bobbie had looked upset, as if a promise had been broken. But today she was cheerful, even seeming to forget her worries about Sam as she charmed Leonard during their hour-long train ride from London.

Virginia turned from the window and went to the dressing table where she began to brush her hair. Yes, she mused, the kiss had made her feel pretty and confident. It had been tentative, as delicate as a butterfly brushing past Bobbie's cheek. But it sealed their affection. It was a gift of identity, like a diamond wrapped up; the radiance burnt through. She saw in Bobbie the energetic, brave woman she wanted to be; she'd felt this with other women before, even with her own sister years ago. She and Vanessa had been united from nursery days; they'd been allies against the masculine world of their father and brothers, yet inextricably connected was a sexual attraction to women too. What she felt for Bobbie was not unlike what she had sensed when she'd been with Henri Giraud. It was an illumination—one was perceived and understood, one's self reflected, even recreated by a mirroring soul.

She stopped brushing her hair and stared at her face in the mirror. It seemed defined, pointed, sharp like an arrow. Not blurry or out of focus. Life with Leonard had seemed so stalled these last two years. He had forgotten who she was; fixed on her illness and ignored the many selves that passion coalesces into one identity. Too many people thought of love as simply taking off one's clothes. But what she felt for Bobbie was a flash of recognition, a confirmation. What was the image, she asked herself, pausing. Like a burning ember? No, that didn't convey the speed and spontaneity. It was more like a flame. That was it, a flame burning in a flower. She repeated the phrase aloud, "A flame burning in a flower," and opened her diary to the page opposite the code and her impatient doodlings. Across the white page she wrote in bold letters:

Rejoice when love is like a flame burning in a flower!

She looked at the line and smiled; for the moment it was an inner meaning almost expressed: a flame lighting the flower from within, much as love gives a woman's face a glow. Yes, rejoice, she told herself.

She paused, feeling a momentary fatigue as her thought veered back on itself, like a sudden turning of a path in the woods, unexpected yet beckoning. An idea that had flickered through her mind but had later been forgotten in the heat of the incident at the Café Royal was now clear: When Sam had demanded "the Joyce novel," she'd thought of Anna's pages of translation, and now she unfolded the pages from her diary to reread Anna's words: "These are the lines. . . . Michelet. . . . *Editions du Nord,* 1916. We will rejoice with their completion." "Re—joice," she said, drawing out the syllables.

There it was! How could she have missed it? Her breath came rapidly. The clue had been so simple. Not only the word "rejoice," but the date Anna had listed for the *Editions du Nord* publication of Michelet—1916, not the correct date, 1906. Joyce's novel was indeed published in 1916. So it must be part of the code, somehow keyed to the mistranslations!

She let out a small whoop of triumph. At the same instant, there came a knock on her door. Without waiting, Ottoline Morrell swooped into the room.

"My dear!" her voice went yodelling. "What are you crowing about?" She advanced on the dressing table like a ship under full sail, her red and blue silk scarves floating behind her.

"Oh, I see," she said, glancing down at Virginia's diary. "Already writing your impressions of Garsington? And this," she added, pointing at the page filled with numbers and flaming circles. "You write in symbols now, do you?"

Virginia smiled, closing her diary. "They're just notes to myself."

"A diary's so necessary," Ottoline said. "The only way we artists can express our deepest thoughts."

Virginia picked up her hairbrush and gave her hair a few

brisk strokes. "I doubt my thoughts are especially deep," she smiled.

"Oh, come now, I know you better than that." Ottoline turned, glancing at herself in the mirror. Her artificially bright red-gold hair was piled in ringlets, which accentuated the sloping forehead, long nose and receding chin.

"I really must do something about myself before dinner," she murmured, touching at the wisps of hair falling round her face. Then, as her eyes wandered to the books on the dressing table, she picked them up and scrutinized the spine of each. *Portrait of the Artist* and Michelet's history—you do have eclectic taste."

Virginia went on brushing.

"Well, to each his own." She put down the books and flounced to the bed, propping herself up against the headboard like a schoolgirl. Virginia turned on the dressing table bench. There was no stopping Ottoline when she began a litany of complaints: Everyone was deserting her; Katherine Mansfield had written to say she'd no longer play the cook to her countess; D. H. Lawrence was threatening to turn her into a homicidal Sapphist in his new book—"it's to be about Garsington, my dear, and simply slanderous"—and Bertie Russell was flaunting his new love to make her jealous.

It was standard fare, though, as Virginia reminded herself, what she called "Ottoline's vapors" often gave way to penetrating insights. Ottoline had made her life a continual experiment, trying youthful religious fanaticism, then love affairs in Italy, and finally marriage to the Liberal MP Philip Morrell. She'd turned Garsington into a haven for conscientious objectors—Clive Bell and David Garnett were both here, doing farm work to satisfy their national service requirements—as well as for artists and socialists. Demanding intensity, she was often mocked behind her back, yet the mockers never refused her generosity.

"Now, what do you have to tell me?" she asked.

"I'm afraid my life is rather dull, tucked away in Richmond."

"What about Miss Waters? Very pretty, I hear. Your new conquest?"

"Don't be silly," Virginia said, heading off the inevitable question. "Anyway, she likes men better than women. But I enjoy her immensely."

"I hear you've been making mischief."

"What do you mean?"

"Maynard tells me he's awfully concerned. Asked me to look out for you. He says there'd been 'difficulties' between you and Cranford."

"Maynard's making a lot out of nothing."

Ottoline gave her a sulky look. "Really, I don't keep secrets from you."

There was a knock on the door. "Ah, good, now I'll meet Miss Waters. Come in," she trilled.

It wasn't Bobbie, but Millie, flushed and excited. "Lord Ladbrooke's downstairs," she blurted. "Lord Alex Ladbrooke."

"My word," said Ottoline. "Did we invite him?"

Millie shook her head. "He wants to see Mrs. Woolf. Says it's important!"

Ignoring Ottoline's questioning look, Virginia threw on her dress, slipped into her shoes and hurried downstairs. Ladbrooke was pacing in the front of the great fireplace in the green sitting room, yet before she could say anything Ottoline had already pushed herself forward and taken his hand.

"Alex! How lovely to see you. What a *nice* surprise!"

"I'm sorry to interrupt your party," he said in a steely voice, "but I must speak to Mrs. Woolf."

"You know you're always welcome. But whatever's going on? Has this to do with Sir Henry too?"

"I'm afraid it's confidential. Do you mind?" Skillfully, he

took Ottoline by the arm and led her to the door, promising a few words before leaving.

Virginia, relieved to see him, was alarmed as well. "What's happened? Tell me," she cried once he'd shut the door.

"I don't mean to upset you." He sat down in one of the brocade armchairs and gestured her to the one opposite. "But I need information from you."

She felt his gray-blue eyes on her. "The assumption is there's a maniac loose, someone with an irrational hatred for Belgian women. That's what I've managed to convince the Yard. Finally they're prepared to reopen the case—"

"I'm glad to hear that!" interrupted Virginia.

"Nevertheless, I gather you've learned there's more to it. You must tell me, especially if it bears on this person, Henri Giraud. He's told you something? Something about Cranford?"

Virginia paused, trying to decide what to do. Lord Ladbrooke had helped her, even defended her against Allington's bullying questions, but there was Giraud too.

Studying her face, Ladbrooke spoke in a gentle tone. "Please. I can go directly to Sir Vernon Kell. He'll act promptly."

"Even if it involves Sir Henry?" she asked.

"Of course. What matters is the defense of the realm. . . ."

Virginia stood up. "If I were to tell you he's a German collaborator?"

He said nothing. His eyes, however, were wide with alarm.

"I know it sounds incredible. But I may have proof."

"Proof?"

"Anna was watching Cranford. That's why she got herself hired as his governess. A few weeks ago she sent a message to Giraud—"

"You mean she worked for him? Who is this man?"

"She and Marie were both agents. Giraud's some sort of director of Belgian intelligence."

Ladbrooke scowled, but his voice was calm. "And I take it her message implicates Cranford?"

"Anna must have supplied the information to Marie who sent the coded message. It refers to Cranford's talks with the Prime Minister as well as a meeting with the Swedish Ambassador and double shifts at the Cranford firm in Sheffield. Miss Waters guesses that Cranford is passing munitions orders to the Germans through the Swedish."

Ladbrooke rubbed his chin. "Good God, I can't believe it," he murmured after a moment. "Still, Cranford did order double shifts a fortnight ago, and Sweden may not be as neutral as she claims." He shook his head. "But Sir Henry a collaborator? He's proven himself the most loyal, the most devoted. . . . Have you told the Yard any of this?"

"Giraud feels we need more evidence. Especially since Allington is bound to have the same reaction as you."

"I'm ready to be convinced. What kind of evidence?"

She chose not to mention the new code keyed to the Joyce novel, what she assumed was Anna's last message. Why she wasn't sure. But it was one act of loyalty to Giraud after she'd betrayed his presence in London. Instead, she said, "Bobbie and I are going to badger Cranford with questions, make him realize we know his story doesn't hold together."

Ladbrooke scowled again. "I wouldn't, Mrs. Woolf."

On the verge of losing her temper, she sat down. For all his help, the man now assumed he was in charge. Once again she and Bobbie were being brushed aside, their suspicions of Cranford easily dismissed.

"And why not?" she asked, her annoyance evident.

"In the first place," he explained patiently, "if what you say about Sir Henry is true, then you and Miss Waters are terribly vulnerable. Didn't you tell me that Sir Henry's chauffeur has been following you? Of course, there may be another explanation. . . . But what you really *should* know is there's a fellow named Bayard. This is what I've found out. Have you heard the name?" When she shook her head, he said, "He's been threatening Mrs. Ottlinger—the delicatessen owner. She's frantic. He may be the maniac we're looking for, or he may even be involved in the sort of thing you're talking about." He paused to let her feel the full force of his words. "So, please, allow me to handle this. *I'll* tell Henry the Yard plans to reopen the case."

"Here? Tonight?" Her voice was pitched high. For all her confidence upstairs, she now felt herself pulling back. Ladbrooke had frightened her. If he alarmed Cranford, there was no telling what the munitions maker might do. The face of his chauffeur flashed before her, then the image of the terrifying fat man—was he this fellow called Bayard? She felt a weight on her chest, remembering the man's powerful grip in Sam's flat, remembering Marie's face after she'd been strangled. Too, there was Giraud: Ladbrooke might be upsetting the Belgian's plans. Alerting Cranford prematurely might send the other collaborators back into hiding.

Ladbrooke failed to notice her strained expression and darkened eyes. "After dinner I'll have a chat with Henry—"

"I do wish you would," exclaimed Ottoline, suddenly bursting back into the room. "He and Maynard have shut themselves up in the library to prepare for their meeting tomorrow. All very hush-hush, and Sir Henry fairly snapped my head off when I went in to tell him you were here. I thought the two of you were friends?"

Ladbrooke gave Virginia a pointed look as Ottoline, without waiting for a reply, swirled out of the room.

⤙ **21** ⤚

When Virginia came downstairs at the sound of the dinner gong, Ladbrooke was waiting to escort her into the dining room. He had been talking to Leonard and Bobbie about his art collection. Clive, typically, hovered nearby.

Virginia took Ladbrooke's arm. He appeared relaxed, she thought, as if he had nothing on his mind. She would follow his example, watch Sir Henry calmly, wait for any false gesture, any revealing word. She smiled over her shoulder at Bobbie, now being attended to by Bertrand Russell; the philosopher had evidently taken a fancy to her.

The wainscoting of Ottoline's dining room was a deep, enamel red, with fine lines of gilt edging the upper wood panels. Virginia knew that D. H. Lawrence had helped with the decoration, and as she took her seat she admired the result: it reminded her of the color of sealing wax. She had been seated toward the end of the refectory table, with Philip Morrell at the head and Lord Ladbrooke on her right. Bobbie was seated directly opposite her, beside Russell.

Among the other dinner guests were Clive and Mary Hutchinson, Lytton Strachey and Carrington and Aldous Huxley, as well as several young men, the gaggle of Oxford undergraduates whom Ottoline often invited to Garsington.

They were all seated when Maynard, Sir Henry and Ottoline made their entrance. Ottoline was wearing a cobalt blue tunic over orange harem trousers stuffed into high boots of red Moroccan leather, but Sir Henry, immaculate in a formal dinner jacket, seemed unaware of either her exaggerated costume or her flamboyant gestures as she introduced him around the table.

"And you already know Mrs. Woolf," she said when she reached Virginia. "Can't wait to hear the plot the two of you are hatching."

Virginia bowed her head, blushing. She cast a glance at Lord Ladbrooke who sat straight in his chair, evidently unruffled by Ottoline's remark.

Soon separate conversations started, but Virginia found herself only half listening. She sat up when she heard Ottoline call to Philip from her end of the table.

"Our cowman, dear. It was dreadful, wasn't it? I was just telling Sir Henry."

"Terrible sight, Sir Henry," Philip replied. "Never, ever, want to go through that again."

Philip leaned toward Virginia to explain: "Our cowman drowned himself in the bathing pool. Took the constabulary several weeks to finish with the whole depressing business. I actually had to attend the inquest."

"He left a note?"

"Good heavens, the man couldn't read or write. All we had to go on was his wife's saying he'd been unhappy."

"You had some sort of trouble like that too, didn't you, Sir Henry? Your governess, wasn't it?" Clive's tone was inappropriately cheerful. He winked at Virginia.

"Please," Sir Henry said. "It's hardly a welcome topic. My family was so upset I sent them away to the country. It's been a tragic time for all of us."

Virginia looked down at her plate, aware that Leonard was watching her. Ladbrooke cleared his throat.

"I suppose they'll stay in the north for a while, now that the Yard is reopening the investigation?"

Cranford paled. "What do you mean, Alex?"

"You haven't been told? Allington's decided to take another look. He thinks your governess' death may be connected to the murders of those other Belgian women."

"Ridiculous," Sir Henry said. "Nigel said nothing of the sort. We're all quite satisfied." He paused, evidently still stunned by the news. "So, if you don't mind, Alex, we'll discuss this after dinner."

"Oh, I think we'd all like to hear the story, Sir Henry," Clive said.

"Drop it, Clive," growled Maynard.

"Of course, Pozzo, whatever you say. Though perhaps we can discuss your trip to Paris instead. Those new paintings you purchased, all the little bargains discovered on the sly? Or is that not appropriate either?"

There was embarrassed silence around the table. Maynard pursed his lips and turned away. They'd finished dessert and Ottoline tried to come to the rescue. "We'll have coffee in the green room," she announced, rising from the table.

The deep blue-green of the sitting room walls seemed as translucent as the eye of a peacock feather, the air heady with Ottoline's perfume mixed with the pungent odor of the clove-studded oranges sitting along the chimney piece. In the grate a large log fire cast a reddish glow across the cream-colored and mauve brocade furniture.

Maynard and Philip stood in the corner, Leonard sat in an armchair facing them. Lytton, semi-recumbent on the settee, was holding forth for the young men from Oxford. Carrington sat on the floor, her head leaning against Lytton's knee. Huxley fiddled with some of Ottoline's marble figurines as Mary Hutchinson tried to engage him in conversation. Ottoline herself served the coffee, keeping an eye on Bobbie and Russell, who had settled themselves near the hearth. But neither Sir Henry nor Ladbrooke was to be seen.

He must be putting Cranford through the hoops, Virginia thought as she joined Bobbie and Russell, though several minutes later Sir Henry marched across the room to join Maynard on the sofa. His face looked pinched, unhappy.

Virginia nudged Bobbie. "Ladbrooke must have really had a go at him."

"Would someone mind telling me what's going on?"

"Later, Bertie," Virginia whispered. Ladbrooke himself was just entering. Clive was at his side, talking continuously, like a dog yipping at his master's heels.

"The aesthetic emotion is what you look for," he announced for the benefit of the room.

"I'm fascinated, Bell, really I am," drawled Ladbrooke. "Perhaps you'll come to tea and bring me a copy of your book."

"Say tomorrow, at four?"

"Fine, fine," Ladbrooke answered. "And now, I really must be off. Mrs. Woolf, may I have a word with you?"

Withdrawing to the corner where the coffee tray was placed, she was aware that Clive, Bobbie and Russell were all staring. Cranford was watching them too.

"My driver has the motor waiting," Ladbrooke said. "But I did want to tell you, Sir Henry's sufficiently uneasy. I'm not convinced you're right, you understand, but I'll tell Allington when I get back to town. There's a meeting tomorrow which I gather is very important. If any information trickles out, we'll know the source. You might tell Giraud—when will you see him?"

"Monday, probably. I'm to leave a message at Marcus's book shop."

Ladbrooke took her arm. "Be careful, though. Remember, Kell's first-rate and altogether willing to take it from here."

As Ladbrooke left the room, Clive called out, "Tomorrow at four, Alex," causing Maynard to turn, his face a mixture of curiosity and irritation. Cranford himself, however, seemed quite unperturbed. Leonard and Maynard listened as his baritone grew louder to praise Lloyd George's control of General Haig and military strategy.

Suddenly Cranford's words were drowned by the singing from the far side of the room. "Pack up your troubles in your old kit bag," blared from the pianola where Philip sat treading the pedals, gesturing like a conductor at Lytton, who was spiraling across the room in a pair of Ottoline's high heeled pumps. Russell caught Bobbie up in his arms and they too began to dance as Virginia moved toward the sofa.

"Sorry, Sir Henry, Lady Ottoline likes her dancing," she overheard Maynard say.

"All in good fun, I'm sure," Cranford replied. "But it's time for work. Shall we, Keynes?" He gestured to the door. "I want to review a few things before tomorrow."

Maynard flushed with annoyance but fell in behind the industrialist. For all his boasting, Cranford treats him like an underling, Virginia mused, but won't old Pozzo be surprised when he learns the truth?

She moved to Leonard's side. "Weren't you thrilled by the great Sir Henry?"

"No worse than any other politician."

"His clichés are ridiculous, and that's the least of it."

"He's only spouting the Government line. One has to be polite, if only for Pozzo's sake—"

A door slammed in the hall. "Call the police!" The voice was Maynard's. He appeared in the doorway, shouting. "Philip! Stop your damned music! Sir Henry's been robbed."

Philip hurried from the pianola.

The guests crowded round.

"From the library—" Maynard gasped, but before he

could go on Sir Henry pushed past him. "It's my valise. It's been stolen. My papers, government documents, gone! Call the police!"

Philip went to the telephone.

"We can all sit down at least," said Ottoline lightly.

"I suppose we're going to be accused of the theft," Bobbie murmured to Virginia.

"No doubt," she said, already sure she knew what Cranford was doing.

Twenty minutes later Philip reappeared with a policeman from the local constabulary. As if he didn't know what to make of the scene, Sergeant Edwards darted a look from one guest to another.

"I want everyone's room searched," Cranford ordered, obviously unimpressed by the local man. "There were important papers in that case, highly confidential. You've got to find them."

"Sir Henry! You can't think—"

"I'm sorry, Lady Ottoline. Who else could have taken them?"

"Look here!" exclaimed Philip. "There's no need to accuse our guests."

"I'm not accusing anyone. But I've got to have those papers."

"Please, Philip." Keynes' tone was conciliatory. "Try to understand." Cranford eyed Morrell who turned to his wife:

"I'm afraid he may be right, Ottoline. And the rest of you understand, don't you? Does anyone object?"

Virginia heard some grumbling, but Philip had already led the sergeant and Sir Henry out to the stairs. Keynes followed.

When they returned to the hall, they went directly past the green room into the study. Then they came back to the assembled guests.

Sir Henry cleared his throat. "It appears the thief entered

through the French doors. They were left unlocked, apparently—"

"They always are," said Ottoline.

"We found footprints in the flower bed beyond," the sergeant said. "Someone must have entered while you were at dinner. Probably some bloke after money."

"You might have thought of that before searching our rooms," Clive said.

"My apologies, Bell," said Sir Henry as he scribbled a card and gave it to the sergeant.

"Here. Use my name at that number. Call them immediately."

Edwards glanced down at the card. "But that's Special Branch, sir. I don't think—"

"Of course it is." Sir Henry cut him off. "Get on with it."

"Yes, sir," said Edwards, practically clicking his heels and going to the telephone in the hallway. He was gone for less than a minute, and returning, announced that Allington's assistant had said the Commissioner would be up in the morning. With a sharp salute to Cranford, he then went off to search the grounds.

Sir Henry and Maynard stood to one side, aware of the angry glances in their direction. Finally Sir Henry muttered he was going to bed, Keynes escorting him out. A few minutes later, Virginia and Leonard bid everyone goodnight. When they reached the landing he turned to her.

"You and Miss Waters aren't involved in this, are you?"

" 'Involved'?" she snapped. "Hardly. That robbery happens to be a hoax."

Virginia sat up in bed, her diary propped open against her knees. The two books—Michelet and Joyce—lay beside her. Despite the hour, she wasn't tired. Just as Giraud had predicted, Cranford had overplayed his hand. The "theft" of the valise was too frantic a ploy; any information now going to the Germans would appear to come from the thief, not Cranford. And the search of the bedrooms, that was a trick, too. Cranford might easily have looked in her diary, seen her efforts at decoding. Which given the rate at which things seemed to be accelerating, was even more reason for her to get on with it.

Midnight. Virginia had taken every mistranslation she'd listed from Michelet and tried to find its underlined equivalent in Joyce's novel. It wasn't difficult. *"Été,"* mistranslated as "summer," meant "was": "was" appeared as the eleventh word in the first line of the first page of *Portrait of the Artist.* She'd recorded "was" in her diary, indicating its position: page 1, line 1, word 11. But she was disappointed to see that Anna had not underlined "was" in the Joyce text.

The second word, *"réunit,"* correctly translated as "reunited," was harder to find. She read several pages; the language washed over her and she found herself enjoying the prose. Perhaps she'd misjudged Joyce, she thought, too quickly dismissed him as a showman. The sentences had lovely cadences, the power to lull one into a peaceful pool of rhythm. She started to doze off. Suddenly a word on page nineteen jolted her awake: "reunited," there it was in the tenth line.

She noted it in her diary as 19/10/3, but was again disappointed to see it wasn't underlined. The pattern didn't make sense. She couldn't even be sure her translation was the one that Anna had meant to suggest. No code works like this, she told herself: the receiver of a code has to decipher quickly, hence it must be precise. She stared at the numbers on the diary page: 1/1/11; 19/10/3—yes, they were all in the same form. Then she turned to the list she'd made indicating the locations of Anna's "mistranslations." In front of each word copied from Michelet she'd written page, line and word numbers in the same way. The first word listed was *"été,"* appearing in Michelet on page 29, line 3, the first word in the line. With her breath coming quickly now, she opened Joyce's novel to page 29, counted down three lines and found the first word in the line: "Mr."

She knew she was on the right track. Not only was the word underlined in the Joyce text, but, indeed, the capitalization suggested it was the beginning of a message.

Rapidly she continued down the list of mistranslations, writing the page, line and word numbers from Michelet in one column, then the indicated word in the Joyce novel next to it. With each word, she was even more convinced. Every one in the Joyce text was underlined; every third or fourth word began with a capital. She raced ahead, completing the list in fifteen minutes. Then she began to write out the first letters of each word horizontally: "M" from "Mr."; "t" from "table"; "n" from "nicer"; "g" from "garments."

"M-t-n-g," she read out the letters. "Meeting!" she exclaimed. It was the same abbreviated form of the word used in the other coded message. She'd broken the code! She wrote out the rest of the letters, using the capitals to indicate the separate words. And there it was:

"Mtng Sun Tnk Atk Tues Flndrs Dtls Flw"

She had it right, she knew it. She threw on her robe, grabbed up the diary and hurried across the hall. Light showed under Bobbie's door and she entered without knocking, holding up the diary in triumph.

"I've done it. Anna's last message. Look!" She put the diary down on the bed. Bobbie leaned over to study it. "I'm not sure what it all means but it seems to be about Cranford. See? 'Mtng Sun.' " She pointed out the letters.

"Of course," Bobbie murmured. "That meeting tomorrow, the one they're so secretive about."

"But what about the rest of it?" said Virginia. "T-n-k—"

"Tank!" Bobbie burst out. "A tank attack! Cranford would know about a tank offensive since the munitions orders would be sent to him in advance."

"And 'Flndrs' has to be Flanders, doesn't it? Anna must have discovered that Cranford was relaying information about a tank attack in Flanders—"

"And that he'll be sending details after the meeting." She pointed to the last two abbreviations. "See, 'Details follow'."

Virginia sat down on the bed with a sigh. "Maybe he's already alerted the Germans," she said. " 'Tuesday Flanders' —they must know that much already. Too, there must have been information in his case meant for the Germans; that's why he arranged to have the papers stolen."

Bobbie sat down beside Virginia. "So what do we do now? Just march into his room and confront him? Show him your diary?"

"My hunch is he's already seen it—when he demanded a search of our rooms. There isn't much we can do except wait for Allington. Even if he is a friend of Cranford's, he's still a policeman. We show him this," she pointed to the decoded message. "He'll have to believe us."

⇥ 22 ⇤

Virginia and Bobbie stood at the dining room window watching for Commissioner Allington's arrival. Maynard and Sir Henry were already outside on the gravel sweep, and Cranford's chauffeur had started up the Daimler whose exhaust was puffing clouds into the cold morning air.

"He means to get away quickly." Virginia tapped her diary which she held clutched to her chest. "But our dear Sir Henry is in for a shock." Her voice was bitter. The thought of what he was doing, what he'd done to Anna and Marie, filled her with revulsion.

A small black roadster drew up beside the Daimler. Sergeant Edwards stepped out of the passenger side. But when the driver emerged they saw it was not Commissioner Allington but rather Clarke. The Scotsman sauntered directly over to Cranford.

The two women ran through the hallway and out the front door.

"Inspector Clarke!" Virginia called out. "He's lying. You can't let him leave!" Clarke looked up from his notebook, his face betraying no response. "Here." She thrust her diary at him. "This is the proof. From Anna, his governess."

"What the bloody hell?" Cranford exploded. "I'm talking about a robbery and you're still carrying on about my governess."

"I warned you, Virginia," said Maynard.

"Stay out of this, Mr. Keynes," said Bobbie. "Inspector Clarke, listen to us. There's a meeting this morning. . . ."

"Of course there's a meeting," Cranford said. "That's why Keynes and I must leave immediately, Clarke. I'd hoped that Nigel would attend to this personally, but I assume you'll do everything to find the thief."

"I'm Commissioner Allington's assistant, Sir Henry, quite correct."

"There was no robbery." Virginia looked from Cranford to Clarke. "He staged it to make it look like one."

"Really, Inspector! This woman has a history of mental illness. She runs around telling people I've murdered my governess. Now she claims I've stolen my own case." He grimaced. "Keep her away, will you!"

Clarke had been watching without any change of expression and now he took his pipe from his mouth and beckoned with it to Sergeant Edwards.

"Take Mrs. Woolf and Miss Waters inside," he said. "Have Lady Ottoline call the other guests. I'll be in shortly."

"You're not going to stop him?"

"Mrs. Woolf, please. Edwards?"

While the sergeant led Virginia and Bobbie toward the house, Cranford answered Clarke's questions, his face still rigid with anger. Virginia cast a look over her shoulder; she was sure Cranford's chauffeur was peering at her through the limousine's windscreen.

Inside she reached out for the wall of the foyer. Her head was reeling, she needed solidity. Time and again people had looked right through her, condemning her as mad. All Cranford had had to do was say she was crazy and this idiot Clarke would send him on his way. Her words had no meaning; she knew if she looked in the mirror she'd see no reflection. She heard the rush of a great millstone inside her head, its shrillness roaring in her ears.

Suddenly she felt someone take her hand. She turned and looked down into Bobbie's face. The young woman's eyes blazed. She fixed on them. No, she was not crazy. Bobbie felt the same way. Here was something to fix on, to bring her back from the abyss.

"That bloody bastard," Virginia shouted, her anger pouring out of her.

"What are you doing?" Bobbie said, seeing that she was going to the telephone.

"Ringing Lord Ladbrooke. He said he'd speak to Kell. He'll have to do it immediately. Now!"

Virginia was already in the hall where the telephone was on a table against the wall. She clicked the hook. "Operator, this is a trunk call to London. For Lord Alex Ladbrooke."

She heard Clarke's voice behind her. "Put that down, Mrs. Woolf," he ordered, taking the earpiece.

"Listen to me very carefully," he went on. "I don't want any more scenes. It won't help. You're going to wait until I question everyone else. Then we'll have our own talk." Virginia was tight with anger, but something in his voice made her acquiesce.

He escorted them into the green drawing room where the other guests had been assembled. Some had been outside for morning walks. Others, like Lytton and Clive, had just arisen and were still in their robes. No one was happy with Clarke's presence.

"This is outrageous," someone said. "He gets on his high horse and accuses us of stealing. Now he's not even here to stand behind his charges."

"Your name?" Clarke asked.

"Lytton Strachey. S-T-R-A-C-H-E-Y," he spelled it out. "One of those infamous CO's Cranford suspects of espionage."

"Thank you, Mr. Strachey. I'll ask each of you where you were at the time of the robbery." He withdrew a small memo pad. "Please be as precise as possible. Try to remember if you noticed anything unusual. According to Sir Henry, he left his valise in the library at seven-thirty when he went in to dinner."

"Correct, Inspector," Ottoline volunteered. "Sir Henry and Maynard didn't hear the dinner bell and I went in to get them. Sir Henry escorted me, Maynard followed. Everyone else was already seated."

"And Sir Henry did not take the case up to his room?"

"No, I hurried him along," said Ottoline. "We were late going in. I didn't want to upset my cook any further."

"Everyone was at table? And no one left during dinner?"

Their nods confirmed this. "Would you all agree, then, that it was approximately nine-thirty when you came in here for coffee?"

Again there were nods.

"Did you all come in together?"

Ottoline thought a bit. "No. Sir Henry was out in the hallway. I think he stayed behind to talk to Lord Ladbrooke."

"Lord Ladbrooke? He was here last night?"

"Yes. A surprise visit. He drove back to London after dinner."

Clarke looked over at Virginia as if he expected her to say something. When she didn't, he went on: "So you all came in here, except for Sir Henry and Lord Ladbrooke?"

"Yes. We left the table in the order we were seated," said Russell. "The others first, then Miss Waters and I, and finally Virginia and Pipsy, that is, Mrs. Woolf and Mr. Morrell."

In rapid order Clarke confirmed whether each person had come directly to the green room. Clive was the last to be questioned.

"And Mr. Bell, you left with Mrs. Hutchinson?"

"Yes." He reached over and took Mary's hand. Virginia

wondered if Clarke had noticed the quick glance Lytton shot Clive.

Clarke shut his notebook, dismissing them. "Please remain on the grounds."

When Bobbie and Virginia came to the door, he kept them back.

"You seem to have Sir Henry convinced you're the thief," he said with a slight smile.

"Really, Inspector! I don't steal government papers."

There was amusement in his eyes. "That's not entirely accurate, as both of us well know." He watched her. "I assume you've deciphered it. And that that's your evidence against Cranford."

She opened her diary. "Here's the message from Allington's office. Giraud explained the code he and Marie Ickx and Anna used. Based on numbers referring to the first letters of words in Michelet—"

"Giraud's in London?"

Virginia ignored this. "Anna and Marie were keeping track of Cranford's activities. 'Double shifts Cranford Sheffield Meeting Tuesday Suede,' " she read out. "That means Swedish. 'Swedish Ambassador Wednesday.' But there's more." She turned a few pages. "Last night I broke the second code, the one Anna used for a last message. Here—" she read the message aloud, and looked up into Clarke's face, her eyes bright. "That's why I wanted you to stop him. This obviously refers to their meeting this morning. 'Meeting Sunday.' So Cranford will be able to tell the Germans what went on."

"And I'll bet anything they're arranging the final details of the attack." It was Bobbie, impatient to have Clarke's reaction.

The inspector's face still registered no expression. "Hold on. There's no indication in either of those messages that Cranford's collaborating. Giraud may have had his suspicions, granted, but all we know from this information is that he was watching Cranford closely." He sighed. "It doesn't get us much further, does it? If Cranford's been passing government secrets, we need to know to whom and how. Who the other collaborators are, how their operation works."

Virginia stared at him. She'd worked so hard to get this far, and again the man was dismissing her evidence. She could see why Giraud had been so impatient, so reluctant to go to the police. "What do you want?" she burst out. "Cranford's name on a plaque? Any reasonable person would see it—Cranford attracted Giraud's attention because he was using the Swedish Ambassador as a conduit to the Germans. If you're not convinced, I'll call Lord Ladbrooke. He'll take the information to MI5."

She marched across the room.

"You'll do no such thing," Clarke bellowed.

"How dare you?" Virginia wheeled to face him. She stopped. Clarke was holding up a small, rectangular blue card. "Whom do you think I work for?" he said.

"You?" Bobbie said, going over to look at his identification, recognizing the crest of Britain's MI5. "But you're Allington's assistant."

"So that's how you knew about Giraud," Virginia murmured.

"Yes, I'm on special assignment from Sir Vernon Kell's office. Branch has been getting nowhere. I'm assigned to oversee a coordinated effort."

"And do you suspect Cranford?"

"We're sure more than one man's involved, Mrs. Woolf. But we need solid evidence."

"There isn't much time," Virginia said. "If the attack is scheduled for Tuesday—"

"I know that," he interrupted her. "That's why it's imperative I see Giraud."

"Sam could help too," added Bobbie. "I mean, you don't agree with Allington, do you?"

"That he's a suspect? Yes and no. He knows more than he's told us. But for the moment I'm more concerned about Giraud. Mrs. Woolf, do you know where he is?"

Sweat broke out on her brow. Certainly Clarke was not dismissing Giraud's suspicions now. "He told me," she said softly, "to leave messages at Marcus's bookshop in Charing Cross Road. I can go there tomorrow and arrange a meeting."

Clarke smiled. "Thank you. I know it has been difficult. Ring me at the Yard as soon as you hear—"

There was a knock on the door, Millie the housekeeper. "Sir? There's a telephone call for you."

Clarke was gone only a minute. When he returned, he seemed troubled. "A known German agent was seen boarding a train for Coventry yesterday morning."

"That's where one of Cranford's works is."

"Right, Miss Waters. It's also less than two hours from here. This fellow uses the name Bayard—we can't ignore the possibility that he has something to do with all of this, perhaps even the theft of Cranford's papers." He paused, noticing Virginia's expression. "You know the name?"

"Ladbrooke mentioned him. Someone named Bayard has been threatening the woman who owns the Belgian delicatessen where Marie Ickx worked, a Mrs. Ottlinger."

His face was impassive. "We'll check into that. Meanwhile, I'd better talk to the servants—before I drive to Coventry." He gave Virginia and Bobbie a thin smile. "You've done a splendid job. Indeed, just your decoding, Mrs. Woolf. At any rate, I'll expect your call tomorrow. And Miss Waters, if there's any news from Josephs, you'll let me know?" He paused at the door. "Remember, all this is confidential."

They saw him off twenty minutes later. Virginia returned to the house and wandered down to the basement kitchen.

"Mrs. Woolf," Millie greeted her. "Can I get you something?"

"Thank you, no. I just wondered if you'd seen Mr. Bell, I mean after the policeman left?"

"He's dressing to leave. Said he and Mrs. Hutchinson wanted an early start. Shall I check?"

"Don't trouble yourself."

"It's not you who's makin' me busy."

"Yes, the Inspector did rather complicate things, coming so early and needing to talk to all of us."

Millie gestured with her knife for emphasis. "It's a wonder a Yard man hasn't learned his manners. Our own Sergeant Edwards, he knows a pleasant word'll get you more'n vinegar. Not that one, though. Coming into my kitchen and saying we stole Sir 'enry's things."

"I'm sure he knows you didn't. You were serving and clearing dinner. You couldn't have."

The housekeeper laughed. "That's the truth. But it wasn't me he went after. It was Doris. That silly little goose. She's only sixteen, and that officer got her all upset. She's supposed to be doing the bedrooms, but I expect she's having a good cry up there."

"What did he say to her?"

"She thinks he's going to tattle on her. Shut her mouth like a prune an' just burst into tears. Don't think the Yard man knew what to do."

" 'Tattle on her'—for what?"

Millie glanced over her shoulder into the pantry. "Well," she said, dropping her voice to a whisper. "Doris had a gentleman caller last night. Sir Henry's driver it was, dressed up in his uniform to give her a ride in the motor. Collins—that was the name—he pops into the kitchen for a cuppa. I wouldn't wonder if Doris turned his head. He came round again while dinner was being served and waited for her to be done."

"I didn't see her in the dining room."

"I let her go early. She was all fidgety, excited about her ride. Never rode in a motor before. Him so big and military."

"I'm surprised I didn't hear the car on the drive."

"Oh, well, that's the secret right there. Collins didn't want his master to know, so he left the motor in the lane beyond the hedge."

"And Doris was afraid to tell the Inspector?" asked Virginia.

"Collins told her not to. He came to the kitchen this mornin' to ask directions for Blenheim. When he saw Doris he told her it had to be a secret. Otherwise, he said, he might lose his position. She gave him her word."

"You say the chauffeur was going to Blenheim?" Virginia asked.

She nodded. "Doris don't know the route, so I came in from the pantry to give the proper turnings."

Strange, Virginia thought to herself. Why had Sir Henry and Maynard made such a point about a meeting in Oxford. Were they going to Blenheim because the meeting was so secret, so important? Did it have anything to do with the fact that Blenheim Palace was Winston Churchill's family seat and he was the recently appointed Minister of Munitions? That must be it, she thought with growing excitement. And she was also right about Cranford staging the robbery: His chauffeur *had* been in the house last night and could have removed the case during dinner.

Her thoughts were interrupted by the sound of a motor car starting up outside. When Virginia reached the door, Clive and Mary were already perched on the high seat of her bright red roadster. Several of the others had gathered to see them off. Virginia tried to shout to Clive but the motor drowned her out. He pulled his motoring cap down on his forehead, lowered the goggles over his eyes, and with a cheerful wave, hunched forward over the steering wheel and wove the car out through the gates.

Lytton was with Carrington, laughing. Virginia pulled him to one side.

"I know Clive lied," she said. "Last night, he didn't come in with you for coffee, did he?"

Strachey tugged at his beard. "I don't want to get him into a spot."

"I won't breathe a word." Lytton gave her a sidelong look; she knew very well they'd all received such promises before, only to hear the secret repeated in public. "Please," she coaxed. "It's very important."

He lowered his voice. "I don't know what he was up to. But I'm sure he wasn't in the sitting room right after dinner. Best I can recall, Mary came in with Huxley, then sat with us. When Clive strolled in about ten minutes later, he gave her a kiss. He seemed very nervous."

"How so?"

"His face was flushed, and you know his giggle when he's excited." Lytton narrowed his eyes. "He whispered to Mary —something like, 'Won't his lordship be surprised!' " He paused, noting Virginia's eager expression. "You don't think he stole Sir Henry's valise, do you? I mean, that doesn't seem Clive's style."

"I don't know. But he may—"

"Look," Strachey interrupted, his voice suddenly high with concern, "please, don't say anything to the police. They'd love to arrest a CO."

"I won't. At least not for the time being," she added as she turned back toward the house.

But she certainly intended to find out what her brother-in-law was up to.

✣ 23 ✣

With Cranford dozing beside him, Keynes saw Tom Tower rising above the Oxford college spires on the horizon. It was a welcome sight. Although he'd studied at Cambridge, he was more at home in any university setting than in the purlieus of government and now felt a pang of regret as he thought of all the Oxbridge men losing their lives at the Front.

He expected the motor to swing into one of the narrow sidestreets behind the walls of New College. Instead the chauffeur drove straight on.

"I say, Sir Henry!" he exclaimed. "We missed the turning."

The industrialist yawned. "That's part of my surprise. Our meeting's at Blenheim."

"Blenheim?"

Cranford laughed. "You'll be pleased to hear the PM's finally going to take care of Haig. You know what Lloyd George thinks of him—that the good General's nerves have always been stronger than his imagination?"

"The meeting's to oust him?"

"Lloyd George's convinced the Allied Conference at Rapallo to establish a Supreme War Council," said Cranford. "And he's appointed Sir Henry Wilson his representative.

The military rightly takes it as a public humiliation of Haig. The PM couldn't be happier—'the squealing of so many stuck pigs,' he calls it. And if, after our meeting today, the tide of the war turns then he'll have proved his point. Call it history in the making. That's why Churchill's arranged for us to come to Blenheim. All of it's top secret and must remain so until we bring it off."

Keynes knew that Blenheim Palace was the Marlborough family seat and that Winston Churchill, the younger son of Lord Randolph, had recently returned to Lloyd George's good graces. What was more intriguing was that, as Minister of Munitions, Churchill was in a crucial position to influence military strategy. Indeed, he'd heard Churchill disparage Haig's ineffective maneuvers along the Hindenburg Line in Flanders. Coupled with "Winnie's" boyish fascination with tanks and howitzers and the latest in mortars, Sir Henry's secrecy and hints of a turn in the war could only mean a dramatic change in the use of weaponry. And that, Keynes thought to himself, would explain why he'd been called upon to square things in the Treasury Accounts; why Sir Henry had had him checking and rechecking contracts and budget figures. And, of course, why Sir Henry had been so upset about the theft of his valise.

It wasn't long before the limousine glided up the hill toward Blenheim Palace. At the gatehouse a guard waved them to a halt, took their names, checked them off on his list.

Churchill himself greeted them in the vaulted hallway. His eyes were sparkling, his round face alive with anticipation as he directed them to the library. Inside, the mood was tense. Keynes took his designated seat next to Sir Henry. At the head of the table the Prime Minister stood beside an easel that held charts and diagrams. He called out good morning but then turned to study a file of papers. While having had dealings with the PM in the past, Keynes now watched him, fascinated, as if seeing him for the first time. With white hair, twinkling blue eyes and a mischievous smile, Lloyd George had such seductive charm that many called him the Welsh wizard. Others, however, considered him a circus acrobat who used government policy and party loyalty like trapezes, leaping from one to the next according to whim or the urgings of the crowd below. In the fiery, crusading oratory for which he had become famous, his rhetorical flourishes often appealed more to the emotions than to reason.

Now, none of the other men at the table ventured to speak to him directly, and even their murmurings to each other had ceased. The assembled group was neither the entire cabinet nor Lloyd George's full cadre of loyal friends. But each man knew that he was at Blenheim for a reason: Lord Alfred Milner, a member of the War Cabinet without portfolio; Andrew Bonar Law, Chancellor of the Exchequer and Leader of the House of Commons; Stanley Baldwin, from the Treasury Office; Lord Rothermere, the press magnate recently appointed Air Minister; to Keynes' right, Colonel Edward House, the Texan sent as personal representative of Woodrow Wilson; and finally, next to Cranford, the Shipping Controller, Sir Joseph Maclay, the wealthy Scotsman to whom, along with Cranford, people most often pointed when criticizing the "businessmen's war."

All of them looked up as Churchill now ushered in a young army officer. A thick roll of charts under one arm, the man stood at parade salute at the end of the table.

"Ah, splendid, Colonel Fuller," Lloyd George boomed. "Join me here by the easel and we'll begin."

Further north, another meeting was under way, this one in a dank basement flat on the outskirts of Coventry. Six men sat round a rickety kitchen table, but only the man with a hacking cough knew that their visitor was not the out-of-work refugee he claimed to be.

"A month ago you might have found something," consoled one of the workers. "They were scraping up every able-bodied soul they could lay their hands on."

"But no more?"

"Impossible," replied another in French. "Every machine is fully manned."

The heavyset man at the end of the table shook his head from side to side. "Always the same. You work your balls off, but when times are slow it's us they turn on, and then—" he snapped his fingers—*"alors,* no work!"

Giraud still wore his blue serge trousers and patched coat. His beard had grown darker, his hands were grimy, and he spoke in a rough, tired voice, as if overcome by fatigue and disappointment. One of the men, taking pity on a fellow refugee, offered him a cigarette. Giraud lit it. "So no more double shifts? Aren't the English still short of shells?"

The heavyset man shook his head. "Haven't you heard? Last month, a new contract. The Lewis gun had to be redesigned for a special mount. With special cases, too."

"For shipping, you mean?"

"No. On the gun itself. The case holds four, five hundred rounds. An amazing machine. Blow the Jerries right into the sky, it would."

"Mon Dieu," said Giraud. "It must be huge. No one could carry it alone."

"Wasn't meant to be carried. For tanks, the foreman said. Thought he was General Haig himself, going on about the new tank and us finishing in time to ship last week. Supposed to make sure they were packed watertight. Get it wrong, and he came down hard. 'Bloody Belge,' he was always shouting."

"They've already sent them to the front?" asked Giraud.

"Right. To Le Havre. Sir Henry himself came and gave us a sermon about the destiny of Belgium. Bastard! Came during tea-break, not a tick before."

Giraud joined the others' laughter. "That must have been a job," he said, "the fitting and the gun both. How many did they have you doing, anyway?" He stabbed out the cigarette and looked around the table.

"New borings is what it came down to," said a young, hawk-faced man who had been silent. "Jigs weren't right so we were off schedule right from the start. Two weeks it was to catch up but we finished all thirty under the wire. The Sheffield plant did the others, I hear. You could try over there, you know. They had double shifts, too."

Giraud nodded, thanking them, and headed back to the station. With him was the thin, coughing man. It was cold and neither of them spoke until the train arrived.

"You get what you need?" asked the worker.

"It confirms our last message, yes."

The other man looked sad. "Too bad about—"

Giraud interrupted him. "Just keep me informed of Cranford's orders, but be careful. And for God's sake, let me know if anyone comes round with questions."

The library had grown stuffy with smoke during the hour and a half of Fuller's presentation. As Chief General Staff Officer at Tank Corps, he had introduced the Mark IV tank design as well as the Corps' newly devised "Battle Drill." Keynes was keenly aware of the significance of the innovations. Beyond the discussion of details there was an implied criticism of how tanks had been used in the past: an entrenched infantryman and thus a cynic about technological warfare, Sir Douglas Haig had grudgingly ordered tanks into the line of attack in ones and twos, and then only after lengthy artillery barrages. Keynes had heard enough of the details of an assault on the Hindenburg Line in the Ypres Salient to know that the soldiers who called Haig an idiot were right. The advance bombardment not only announced the presence of the tanks but churned the already sodden soil into a swamp. All along the line tanks had been mired, like so many flies caught in sticky honey; in front of them thousands of troops had been trapped and slaughtered, helpless in the water-filled shell holes. Keynes shuddered to think of it; Haig now refused to reconsider tanks, pointing to this tragic failure to justify his original skepticism. But the tankmen, evidently, had gone back to their blueprints and, like Fuller, they were set on proving their machine's efficiency.

Keynes glanced down the table at Lloyd George. The PM listened intently as Fuller announced the improvements to the Mark IV design: the tank would be equipped with heavy fascines, bundles of slates which could be unrolled as bridges across the Hindenburg Line's double trenches; individual tanks would be designed with "grapnels" to tear large gaps in the barbed wire; and the machine's chassis would be heavier and armed with a longer-range rotating gun, capable of carrying more rounds of ammunition.

"It's a brilliant design," Sir Henry whispered to Keynes, barely controlling his excitement.

Keynes gave him a sidelong glance. Cranford was beaming. So that was it, Keynes thought: this was the secret weapon Lloyd George had concocted with his closest advisors. He was going to take over the military High Command and order the use of tanks in Flanders—despite the previous bloodbath in Passchendaele. He groaned inwardly. Lloyd George was going to sacrifice more lives in his pursuit of power over Haig.

Fuller flipped through the charts on the easel until he came to a map. "We've made two crucial changes in maneuvers," he said. "We're not sending battalions in front of the tanks. Instead they're going in *with* the tanks. In file, two by two. Infantry and armor will move in unison, attack in parallel waves. Furthermore, we've taken them out of the mud and brought them to higher ground. The key is terra firma—" he turned and pointed to the map. "And here we've found it. In Flanders, thirty-seven kilometers north of St. Quentin on the Cambrai plain. Our sixty tanks are moving Tuesday in preparation; two battalions of infantry will position themselves in anticipation of zero hour at 0620 Thursday." He paused. "The key element is surprise. By the time the enemy realizes we've altered our position and mode of attack, we ought to have torn a magnificent hole in their line."

There was a moment of stunned silence. Then Churchill burst into applause. "Bravo, Colonel. It's stunning, altogether splendid!"

Others joined in the applause. Keynes clapped too, but sensed several of the men around the table had their private doubts, not so much about the attack plan itself, but about the irregular method of planning. It was Lloyd George's genius at work—proving Haig's ineptitude with action rather than words. The PM had obviously cut a good many corners and as a result there was bound to be protest, a Parliamentary Debate. Keynes found himself wondering if he wouldn't be called on the carpet at Treasury for his own small part in it.

No one took exception to the Prime Minister's maneuvering, however. Bonar Law wore a distinctly glum expression, but said nothing, and Keynes quickly reassured himself that he was hardly the one to object. He was the low man on the ladder here. Sir Henry had invited him as a gesture of thanks for loosening up funds in Treasury; in return Cranford had allowed him to witness an historic occasion.

And Lloyd George certainly thought it one. He now stood before the group, his eyes sparkling. "I do want to remind you of the need for secrecy. No one knows we're meeting here, Churchill's seen to that, and I want you all to keep it that way. It's quite extraordinary to discuss such details but you're my most trusted men, and I wanted you to have the full picture." He winked at them. "I suppose you realized something was coming to a boil. I've asked Rothermere to arrange air support over Cambrai, and Churchill's fought for the necessary supplies and munitions; Maclay's put his ships at our disposal, and Cranford, you've done an astonishing job manufacturing the new parts and gun fittings. Keynes and Baldwin, you too. You've seen to the money end of it, though I should add that Lord Ladbrooke, at a somewhat greater remove, has been most helpful with the banks. And Bonar," he laughed, "you've kept up your usual good temper, reminding me that I'm only mortal. All in all, I owe you men a debt of gratitude. When we ring the bells of victory, it will be as much for you as for the Tank Corps!"

There were smiles around the room. The Prime Minister had already started to button his overcoat and Cranford rose, waiting at the door as the others filed past talking among themselves.

"Enjoy that, did you, Sir Henry?" Lloyd George called out, still in good humor.

"Quite. But I'd like a word with you. There may be a problem." Keynes, standing nearby, watched a scowl cross the PM's face as Cranford reported the theft of his valise.

"The contracts and orders won't reveal much," he added. "And perhaps it was just someone's mad idea of a joke." Keynes grimaced, knowing full well that he was referring to Virginia.

"I don't like it," said Lloyd George.

"There's no indication of a date in those papers. Someone might be able to put two and two together but he'd have to be fairly clever."

"Still, you called the Yard immediately?"

"Went right to Allington. His assistant was investigating at Garsington early this morning."

"I see," Lloyd George said as he checked his pocket watch. "But Special Branch has had its problems lately. I'd best get on to Kell at MI$_5$."

"Of course, yes." There was a hint of annoyance in Cranford's voice. "But we don't want to stir up a mare's nest, do we? Besides, Nigel's always been most cooperative."

"I'm sorry, Henry. We can't take the chance. I want to make absolutely sure no one knows about this. That goes for Parliament as well as the Germans!"

⇢ 24 ⇠

Sir Vernon Kell, a slight, almost delicate man, sat in Commissioner Allington's chair and tapped his fingers on the desk blotter. He wore a well-tailored gray suit and starched white collar, and with his pencil thin mustache, he appeared more a fussy banker than the Head of Military Intelligence.

It was 9:30 when Allington walked in, whistling under his breath.

"Good morning, Nigel," Kell called out. "In a cheerful mood?"

Allington's resentment of Kell was evident in his glare. "Was," he muttered. Kell smiled, making no move to relinguish his seat at Allington's desk.

"What brings you here so early?" the Yard man said.

"Hardly early. I've been awake since the PM rang me at five-thirty this morning!"

Allington's head came up. "The PM? Five-thirty?"

"Thought that might get your attention," said Kell. "He's put MI₅ in charge of this Garsington business. He feels it must be handled with the utmost discretion. So he's turned it over to us—"

"Utmost discretion?" he repeated. "The Garsington business? What the hell are you talking about?"

Kell smiled ominously. "You haven't heard? Sir Henry

Cranford's valise was stolen Saturday night from the Morrell estate. Clarke was up there yesterday. Sir Henry wanted you personally but apparently you weren't on duty." He stood up. "There's no sense troubling you with details. It was a major breach of security. The Prime Minister's concerned, especially as you've managed to lose both Henri Giraud and Sam Josephs." He smiled again. "I'm sure you'll give Clarke your utmost cooperation. He's a good man. You're lucky to have him, as I told the PM this morning."

Allington waited for five minutes after Kell left. Then he hurried to the door and shouted for Clarke.

Clarke sauntered in.

"Put a bit of wood in it, man." Allington gestured to the open door.

Clarke closed it as ordered. "What can I do for you?" he asked.

"What the bloody hell are you up to? Kell's just been here. Apparently you intercepted a phone call from Sir Henry and traipsed off to Garsington on your own. You let everyone think I ordered it and then turn it into a bloody incident. Your head man's gloating that the Prime Minister assigned the case to MI₅ because Branch didn't take it seriously enough. I want to know exactly what's going on."

"There's nothing to tell. The leads go nowhere."

"The leads go nowhere? That's not what Kell says. And now the Prime Minister has intervened."

"Sorry, that's not my doing. Undoubtedly Sir Henry told the PM about the robbery."

"I know that, thank you. But apparently you told Kell there's some connection to this Giraud. I should have been informed. Not a day late, and not by Sir Vernon at the request of the Prime Minister. I'm asking *you*: what's MI₅ doing about Giraud and Josephs?"

"Waiting. They're bound to pop up. When they do, we'll have them."

Before Allington could object there was a knock on the

door. "Who is it?" barked the Commissioner. A uniformed bobby stepped into the office. He nodded at Allington but turned to Clarke. "A message for you, sir." Clarke took the folded sheet and read it, ignoring Allington's glare.

"When did this come in?" he asked.

"Just now. You left word—"

"Yes, of course," Clarke cut him short. He put the note in his pocket and turned to leave. "Hold on," said Allington. "Is this something I should know about?"

"No, just a summons from my superior." Clarke emphasized the word. "And Sir Vernon's wish is my command."

"Damn his bloody command anyway," Allington muttered as Clarke closed the office door.

Virginia slept fitfully, dreaming of a face which loomed before her, a woman with large dark eyes and dark hair who cried, "Help me, help me."

It was Anna who haunted her, she realized, as if she had become a symbol of betrayal, a reminder of what men like Cranford with all their power were capable of. The industrialist's face flashed before her. It was he she hated, not an anonymous group of conspirators. Clarke could talk about needing enough evidence to arrest the whole group. He could chase down the mysterious Bayard. What mattered for her was Cranford; she'd like to see him hanged, she thought, surprising herself with her vehemence.

She heard Leonard rise and go into the bath; she dressed quickly and slipped downstairs and out the front door.

Mrs. Ottlinger's delicatessen was just opening. The Belgian woman seemed wary as she served her, then quickly went to other tables. Virginia found herself staring. The woman's dark, sad eyes were disturbing, forlorn, with a tragic cast that was somehow familiar.

When she had finished and paid for her coffee, she approached Mrs. Ottlinger. "You know," she said, "the police are reopening the investigation of Anna Michaux's death." She paused. The woman's hand went to her mouth. "Also," Virginia went on, "they want to find the man named Bayard, the man who threatened you."

The woman's head jerked up in dismay. "No, that can't be. . . ." She stammered. "It has nothing to do with me." Her eyes were brimming with tears. "I know nothing about Anna or Bayard. So please, leave me alone!" She ran through the doorway to the kitchen. Virginia could hear her sobbing heavily.

Why would Mrs. Ottlinger grieve for Anna? Virginia wondered, especially when she'd claimed she hadn't known her. Or was she crying for Marie? She'd seemed cold and distant when she'd heard about her waitress' death. And why had she seemed upset that the Yard had reopened the investigation when she'd made it clear that neither Belgian woman meant anything to her?

Here was something else to tell Giraud. He'd instructed her to watch Mrs. Ottlinger. Now it was clear that the delicatessen owner was somehow involved. Too, she'd obviously recognized the name Bayard. Who was he? Why was he threatening her, as Ladbrooke had claimed?

When Virginia reached Marcus's bookstore, the shades were still drawn even though it was going on ten. She tried the front door, expecting it to be locked. It swung open, the lock broken. She took a few steps and stumbled in the dark, hitting her shin. Her eyes adjusting to the dimness, she realized books had toppled from the shelves and lay strewn about the floor. Tables were overturned, too. She groped her way to the front windows to raise the shades.

The shop had been ransacked. Lithographs were torn into pieces. Marcus's desk lay pitched forward; the glass panes of the valuable book cabinet shattered. She could see that the shelf which had held the *Editions du Nord* volumes was now empty. Her stomach knotted, and she was about to run into the street for help when she heard a groan from the rear office. She paused, then clambered over the fallen furniture and books, and pushed through the curtains of the doorway.

The back room was darker than the front. Hoarse, muted gasps came from the far corner. She fumbled in her bag for matches, still moving toward the moans.

Suddenly someone grabbed her from behind, one arm round her middle, a hand clamped over her mouth.

"Don't make a sound," the voice commanded. She struggled in the man's grasp. "I'm warning you," he said.

She recognized the voice. "Giraud!" she tried to shout through his hand. "It's me, Virginia."

He released her. The light on Marcus's desk came on.

For a moment she stared, open-mouthed. His grip had betrayed him. She'd felt his strength, his roughness. He was perfectly willing to use force when he chose to, more than she'd thought him capable of. Then hearing another groan, she turned and seeing Marcus in the corner, she pushed past Giraud. The shop owner lay on the floor with his hands and legs bound, a gag in his mouth, a bloody gash parting his forehead. She knelt and removed the gag, and began to dab at the wound with her handkerchief.

"Have you called a doctor?" she asked over her shoulder.

"I'd just gotten here—"

"Well, do it. He needs help." She heard her own voice rise. "The informers must be desperate. I found another coded message from Anna, you see. Probably her last. She'd discovered that Cranford was sending details of some military plan to Germany. A tank attack in Flanders."

"My God! She couldn't—" He stopped abruptly as he cocked his head and waved her quiet.

"Someone's here," he whispered.

A voice called out from the front of the shop. "Bay—a-r-r-d! Bay—a-r-r-d!" Virginia recognized the Scottish burr immediately. Clarke shouted again: "Bay—a-r-r-d? We know you're in there."

She started to call out. Giraud clamped his hand over her mouth again. "Sh-h-h," he whispered in her ear. "Meet me tonight. Nine o'clock. The alley, Litchfield Arms."

He let her go and flung open the rear door.

"But wait," she cried. "It's Clarke, he's with—"

"Just do as I say. Meet me tonight."

"Wait. He's with MI$_5$!"

But Giraud was already gone. She ran outside and was about to shout after him when Clarke thrust her to one side. "Damn," he said, watching Giraud round the corner. A bobby rushed through the curtained doorway.

"Next time check if there's a back door," Clarke barked at him. "And call an ambulance." He turned back to Virginia. "You all right?" he asked. "You're lucky. Bayard's a dangerous man."

"Bayard? What are you talking about? It's Henry Giraud. He found Marcus just before I arrived."

Clarke shook his head. "Hardly. That's the man we've been following, Bayard."

"Impossible! Marcus works for Giraud. Why would Giraud hurt him?"

"Perhaps he'll be able to tell us."

The old man was moaning. Virginia went to him and bent down. "It's all right, M'sieur Marcus. You're safe now."

His eyes fluttered open. "Mrs. Woolf?" His eyes opened wider, taking in his surroundings. "Is that you?"

"Yes. Don't worry, you'll be taken to hospital."

"What's happened here, Marcus?" demanded Clarke, leaning close to the man's face.

His eyes fluttered a few more times. "Gir— Gir—," he tried to say.

"Giraud?" asked Virginia.

The old man nodded weakly. "Yesterday, the drawer...." he stammered. "A note. . . ."

The man's head seemed to roll back and forth. He groaned again.

"Marcus!" exclaimed Virginia as Clarke turned and went to the desk drawer. Two attendants now rushed through the door. Virginia moved aside as they examined the bookseller and gently moved him onto the litter.

"We'd better take him to hospital, sir," said one of them. "He's unconscious."

Clarke waited for the stretcher to be carried out. Then he read aloud the message he'd retrieved from the drawer. "Monday, twenty-one hundred, Litchfield Arms. Bring Joyce."

Her head came up sharply. It was all happening too quickly. Like a flickering kaleidoscope, Giraud's note changed what she thought she knew.

"What's the matter?" demanded Clarke, noticing her startled look.

"I didn't think Giraud was aware of Anna's last message or the new code key in Joyce. But if he was, why didn't he tell me?"

Clarke's mouth set in a grim line. "There's a lot you don't know about Bayard."

"Not Bayard! Giraud. And he didn't hurt Marcus. It had to be someone else. Giraud was only using Marcus as an intermediary. He must have come back this morning to see if I'd received his message—" Virginia stopped. She was confused, trying to convince herself she had no reason to doubt Giraud. Yet there was no satisfactory explanation for his presence here at the bookshop or his desperate flight either.

Clarke raked his hand through his hair. "Could still be a

trick," he said. "The man has been positively identified as Bayard, a German agent operating out of the Schaeffer Gallery in Paris. Still, meet him just as the note says. I'll be there, too. That's the only way we'll find out who he really is."

25

Clarke was wrong, Virginia told herself. Henri Giraud couldn't be an enemy agent, it was impossible. Perhaps the wrong person had been followed from the start, a bureaucratic mixup between MI$_5$'s agent abroad and Clarke here in London. And Giraud *had* to flee. There was too much at stake for him to answer questions officially; if Cranford was to be brought down there wasn't time for MI$_5$'s interminable procedures and accusations.

Still, as she walked back to Piccadilly Circus, doubt nagged at her. How much did she really know about Giraud? She'd caught him in several lies already. But everyone was lying. It was the coin of the realm. Coming from Allington, Clarke, Cranford, from Clive and Mrs. Ottlinger, and from Strachey and probably Leonard too. No longer was anything clear or straightforward. It was as though she were being sucked downward into chaos. She needed a lifeline—Bobbie. Bobbie would see through it all. In her cheerful, confident voice, she'd rescue her from this endless sea of doubt and mendacity.

Instead, the American hesitated after hearing Virginia's account from a nearby callbox. "That's damned weird behavior," she said. "MI$_5$ wouldn't make a mistake like that. . . .

Yard men perhaps, but Kell's people are supposed to know what they're up to."

"Then we've got to find Giraud."

"What'd he say this morning?" asked Bobbie, ignoring the pitch of Virginia's voice.

"Only that he'd see me tonight. But I don't want to wait. We ought to find him now. I'm only a few blocks away, can you meet me?"

"Sorry. I'm chained to my desk. Draper's furious. Besides—" she lowered her voice to a whisper "—I think Sam's trying to reach me. There were two phone calls before I came in this morning from someone who refused to leave his name. I ought to be here if he rings back." Now she raised her voice. "Well, my dear, I must go. Talk to you later. Mr. Draper has another assignment for me." Virginia heard the abrupt click as she hung up. "Damn," she said aloud. She left the call box and leaned against the marble wall of the post office.

Once more she felt a hot, prickly sensation at the back of her neck. Customers stood in line for their stamps and postal orders, and they were looking at her, or seemed to be. They must find me odd; they must see the glint in my eye, the redness in my cheek. "Humanity has no mercy," she muttered, hurrying out to the street.

A block away she stopped herself. She was doing what she knew she mustn't. Letting confusion get the better of her. Things are out of proportion, reality distorted, she told herself, and what she was feeling was deserted, alone on a rock, a victim exposed. Without Bobbie, without Giraud—the only two who had quickened her blood, renewed her confidence and, yes, even her passion; all that she thought had died over the past two years—yes, without them she'd be lost. Still, she felt more alive than she had in ages, and even fear could be good, seen as such in this new world of lies. No longer was she numbed, paralyzed. There was no reason to sink into inertia. Dr. Wright might interpret it as mania but so what? She was damned if she would sit home, shut up in her room. No, the only way to soothe herself was to act.

She checked her bag for money; she had plenty, and she set out for the nearby tube station, beginning an afternoon of search. First to the Relief Committee, then back to the Litchfield Arms. No one in either place knew Giraud nor could they say if a man of his description had been there.

Scotland Yard was next. Commissioner Allington was out, and no one had the slightest idea where he'd gone or when he'd return. Clarke, too, had left for the day and wasn't expected back.

What's the matter with them? fumed Virginia. They're letting Cranford slip through their fingers. She forced herself to slow her pace and turned in at a Lyons tea shop near the Yard. Undoubtedly Lloyd George himself was at this very moment handing vital information to Cranford, government secrets that would go instantly to the Germans. And none of these ordinary women, taking tea at Lyons during their afternoon shopping, would ever believe that a respected British magnate could be changing their lives so dramatically. A son or sweetheart or father might die in Flanders and here they sat eating their scones.

Virginia took a sip of tea, then, as she often did when needing an outlet for her feelings, she opened her diary. She did not want to dwell on her fears, that would accomplish nothing, and instead decided to describe Ottoline and the events of the weekend:

Her vitality seemed to me a credit to her & in private talk her vapours give way to some quite clear bursts of shrewdness.

She thought of all the petty jealousies she'd noticed among the guests and went on:

The horror of the Garsington situation is great of course; but to the outsider the obvious view is that O. & P. & Garsington house provide a good deal, which isn't accepted very graciously. However to deal blame rightly in such a situation is beyond the wit of a human being: they've brought themselves to such a pass of intrigue & general intricacy of relationship that they're hardly sane about each other. In such conditions I think Ott. deserves some credit for keeping her ship in full sail, as she certainly does.

Yes, it was true, she thought, lifting her pen from the page. Especially with Sir Henry shouting for the police and Ladbrooke showing up unannounced and—she paused. What was the matter with her? She'd been running all over the city and she hadn't even thought of Ladbrooke. Perhaps he would know what MI_5 was doing. Even better, she thought to herself as she put her diary back into her bag, she heard Clive make the date to have tea with him this afternoon. She would ask Bell what he'd actually seen in the hallway. He might have the one piece of evidence to prove that Cranford had staged the theft himself.

It was already 4:30. Back outside on King Charles Street she was lucky and hailed a taxi almost immediately. Ten minutes later the butler brought her up to the second floor library.

Ladbrooke and Clive had been deep in conversation and both started up from their chairs as she was announced and shown in. She went directly to Ladbrooke and shook his hand. "I'm sorry to barge in, but I must talk to you. To you, too, Clive," she said, aware of her brother-in-law's irritation. "There's something I have to ask you."

Clive looked at her warily, shifting in his seat.

"I know you lied to Inspector Clarke," she said. "Saturday night you didn't come directly into the green room with the others. Why?"

Clive shrugged and she saw a darted sidelong glance at Ladbrooke.

"Well? Where were you? You saw something. Tell me."

"Oh, for God's sake, 'Ginia." He held up his hands. "I was in the W.C. Am I supposed to go on about that to a bloody Yard man?"

"You didn't see Sir Henry Cranford's chauffeur?"

"Sorry, no." He clamped his mouth shut.

"Did you, Lord Ladbrooke?" she turned to ask. "I mean, when you and Sir Henry were out in the hallway?"

"No one else was there. But what are you getting at? Why would we have seen Henry's chauffeur?"

So Ladbrooke hadn't heard about the theft. That surprised her, but for the moment she simply recounted the story, along with her theory that Sir Henry had staged the robbery himself. "Ottoline's housekeeper told me that Collins, the chauffeur, *did* come to the house after dinner, so it would have been easy. He could have slipped into the library and just made off with the case."

"I'm not following. Why would Sir Henry have his own man do that?"

"Because of your warning. The valise contained secret documents." She stopped, glancing at Bell, then back at Ladbrooke. "Perhaps we'd better talk in private."

Clive stood, his eyes angry. She was going to hear about this, she was sure. Clive didn't take snubs lightly.

Ladbrooke escorted him to the door. "You've been most helpful, Bell. And I look forward to reading your book." He gestured to a dark blue volume lying on the end table. The title, *Art,* and beneath it, the author's name were etched in white letters across the front cover.

Clive cast a supercilious look at Virginia. "Always glad to be of service," he said. "Perhaps you'd like to read my essay, *Peace at Once,* too."

"Now there, I'd wager we'd disagree." Ladbrooke smiled and closed the door after him. "I hope I wasn't too rude," he said, returning to his chair. "But he does natter on. Now, why are you convinced Sir Henry arranged to have his papers stolen?"

Virginia repeated her theory. "He was desperate, the tank attack is scheduled to begin tomorrow—"

He sat up straight in his chair. "Good heavens, Mrs. Woolf, how do you have that information?"

She explained what she had chosen to withhold from him at Garsington: that Anna had tried to send a final message. She quoted it to him verbatim, watching his reaction.

Ladbrooke calmly crossed his long legs; still, his brow was creased as she complained, "And even with that evidence Clarke refuses to arrest him."

"I suppose they have to be careful. Nigel—Allington, that is—assured me—"

"Clarke doesn't work for Allington. He's MI5. The bizarre thing is that he's had his suspicions about Cranford all along."

"He's sure now?"

"I don't know. But he's certainly not doing much about it."

"I only wish I'd been told. . . . I think I'd best find out what progress Clarke's actually made."

"Progress!" exclaimed Virginia. "He doesn't care about Cranford. He has a different theory entirely. Remember, you mentioned this chap, Bayard?"

Ladbrooke gave a brief nod.

"Clarke thinks Giraud is Bayard."

"On what basis?"

Virginia narrated the episode at the bookshop. "Clarke saw him run out. He says that his people have identified him as Bayard, who's supposedly a German agent. It's ridiculous. But meanwhile Sir Henry's free. God knows what information he's got." Virginia's voice had risen and she tried to calm herself. "Giraud, I think, is the only one who can set him straight. Clarke, I mean. We're meeting Giraud tonight. I just hope Clarke isn't too stubborn to listen. There isn't that much time."

Without warning Ladbrooke stood up. "You're absolutely right, there isn't. I'll ring Clarke and find out what he's planned. If I can't talk any sense into him, I'll get on to Kell again."

He helped her on with her cape. "My driver will run you home."

Virginia could think of no way to refuse, and she had to admit she rather enjoyed the luxury as Ladbrooke helped her into the limousine. In the comfort of the rear seat she began to relax. Lord Ladbrooke would make Clarke realize how blind he'd been, Cranford would be brought in for questioning. She'd been right to make the detour, confront Clive, which had spurred Ladbrooke into action. It was power, influence, and however uncomfortable they made her, Ladbrooke had both.

The car had just passed the Richmond tube station when the driver rolled down the separating window. "Can you give me directions from here, m'um?"

Virginia craned her neck forward. "You see the tearoom? Take a left at that corner." She peered forward again through the mist. She could make out a man hurrying along the pavement. "Slow down," she ordered. Yes, it was the same hat, the same coat: Giraud.

"Stop the car," she said.

"But you said the next turning," the driver objected.

"Stop," she ordered.

Giraud glanced up and down the street. Then he opened the door of the delicatessen shop. In the rectangle of light Virginia saw the broad figure of Mrs. Ottlinger. She raised her hand and beckoned Giraud to follow her inside.

"I'm getting out, driver," said Virginia. "Don't wait for me, I can walk from here."

She didn't wait for his reply but hurried across the road. She could see customers at the small tables. Neither Giraud nor Mrs. Ottlinger, however, was in the room.

She hurried past the windows and round the corner to the narrow lane which she knew led to the rear of the High Street shops. The ground was muddy and littered with rusty tins. She stepped gingerly through the lot, making her way to the tearoom's kitchen door. Beside the door, set high in the wall, was a slightly open window through which wafted the smells of freshly baked bread. Virginia pushed herself flat against the wall and listened. Yes, they were in the kitchen. She could hear them quite clearly. Their words were like heavy stones, hurtling over her.

The Belgian delicatessen was the last stop Giraud had planned to make before setting off for the Litchfield Arms. He'd spent most of the day circling round London to lose the men following him. Yet when he'd dodged one tail, he was picked up by another, then another, and another. And it wasn't clear which of them were policemen. Crossing Regent's Park, for example, he had turned back at the top of a knoll and spotted someone loitering by the Hanover Gate entrance; as he continued to the footbridge in the park's interior, the man had clumsily hidden himself behind one of the bare chestnut trees lining the pathway. But once Giraud had rounded the park and come through the zoological gardens, the man was no longer in sight, raising the possibility he'd been picked up by another.

Thus at the delicatessen Giraud couldn't be sure he'd shaken himself free. He gave one last glance up and down the street, then followed Mrs. Ottlinger into the kitchen. He leaned against the counter, his arms folded across his chest, and watched her.

"We have business to discuss."

"You have brought a message from my husband?"

"*N'est pas important,*" he said quickly. "Schaeffer is not at all pleased with you."

"But we have handled everything!"

"Keep your voice down," he commanded. "Schaeffer is worried."

"There is nothing to worry about. The police are satisfied."

"Mrs. Woolf still asks questions?"

"She's only guessing. There is no proof, Bayard—"

He interrupted her with a jerk of his hand: "That's not our main concern. It was stupid to permit Marie Ickx here."

"That wasn't my doing, I had orders." The woman began to whine again. "I'm told there's no longer any difficulty. Schaeffer has been informed." When he did not reply she continued, her throaty whisper growing thinner.

"The messages will go through. Schaeffer will receive everything."

"It's been too slow. We must have it by tomorrow."

"He will have it—"

"He believes the source is no longer reliable."

"He's wrong, Bayard, believe me. Tell him to be patient. It's arranged."

"I have my orders, too. He wants a meeting to confirm it. Set it up for me tomorrow night."

"But I don't know who—"

"Use your contacts. Under the circumstances, you'll think of a way. And leave the reply with the clerk at the hotel."

"Wait," she said with panic in her voice. "My husband? You have brought me news?"

He shook his head. "When you've arranged the meeting, you'll get your letter."

⤜✸ 26 ✸⤛

Pressed beneath the window, Virginia had heard the threat in Giraud's voice. Mrs. Ottlinger let out a long sob. She wept for a few minutes, then she blew her nose and stepped deeper into the room, away from the window. Virginia listened. A faint whirr—the sound of a telephone crank. Now the woman was speaking again but her voice was too muffled for Virginia to hear the words.

Virginia stumbled back from the window and lurched forward almost blindly, barely breathing, as if someone had hit her. The shadows in the yard swirled around her. She reached out and touched the stone wall.

Clarke had been right! Giraud *was* Bayard. He had orders from Schaeffer—the same man Clarke had mentioned, the one Roger knew as an unscrupulous gallery owner in Paris. He must have sold Giraud the Corot landscape that hung in his office. And Giraud had power over Mrs. Ottlinger's husband, whoever, wherever he was.

A vague idea flickered in her mind but it faded in a flash of pain; Virginia clutched at her chest. Her heart was still fluttering. She told herself to be calm, thinking bitterly of Giraud: how easily he'd drawn her in, cajoled her with his dark, soft eyes, his demand for competence. How simple it must have been; playing on her sympathy for Anna, her need to prove that she and Bobbie were right, her desire to show that she was sane and strong and, above all, able. The memory of their conversation in the tea shop sickened her. It had all been lies. He'd only wanted to find out how much she knew, how much she'd told the police. But who was Anna? Who was Marie? Had they all been collaborators, pretending to be Belgian patriots? Or had Anna and Marie been duped as well; hadn't they realized that Giraud's real loyalty lay with the Germans?

She had no time, though. Clarke had to be told before he saw Giraud, before their meeting. She pushed herself into a loping run toward the High Street. Several passersby paused and stared, but she paid no attention. Her cape billowed out behind her, and she clutched her handbag to her side. She felt awkward and stiff; her breathing was ragged, but she kept at it. Don't think of anything but Clarke, she told herself, Clarke and Giraud. And Bayard. The names became a litany, a rhythm by which to pace herself, and finally she arrived at Hogarth House. She fell against the door, gasping for breath.

Leonard heard her and threw open the door.

"Where have you been? You've only an hour before Kerensky's speech. I'm supposed to introduce him."

She waved him aside and stepped to the telephone. The operator rang Scotland Yard and she waited, unable to stop panting. Clarke, she heard, was not available. "Then put me through to Commissioner Allington."

Allington's voice boomed over the line. "I'm very busy, Mrs. Woolf—"

"I have an urgent message for Mr. Clarke."

"I haven't seen him."

"You must warn him."

"About what?"

"Tell him—tell him," she thought quickly—"Tell him he was right about Giraud."

"Explain that please."

"Oh, bloody hell. Tell him I'll meet him at the Litchfield Arms at eight-thirty. Before he sees Giraud. That's important, *before* he sees him."

"What's this all about?" demanded Leonard as she rang off.

"I'll tell you on the way into town," she said, brushing past him and going upstairs to change.

On the train he listened, stunned, as Virginia recited all that she and Clarke had learned in the last few days.

"You mean Giraud's a double agent?" Leonard asked.

"MI5 has suspected Cranford all along. Now it seems that Giraud is the German agent they've identified as Bayard." She paused. "What's the term? 'Double agent'?"

He nodded, thinking.

Her expression changed. Inadvertently, Leonard had presented a possibility she hadn't considered, had held out one last glimmer of hope.

"Double agent," she repeated aloud. "Which means Giraud might only be pretending to be a collaborator—to trap the others, by forcing Mrs. Ottlinger to give information about the group as a whole."

Leonard's eyes were sad. "Please. You must leave this to the Yard."

"I can't believe I'd be so gullible, so damn simpleminded," she murmured. "But I have to warn Clarke, even if Giraud's on our side. There's no way of telling."

Suddenly she realized that Leonard was torn between ordering her not to go and offering to come with her.

"Don't worry," she said. "You have to introduce Kerensky. It's important, and this is something *I've* got to do. Inspector Clarke won't take any risks. Besides, I'm just giving him the book that Anna used for her code." She patted her handbag. "It's imperative. We can't even be certain for whom she was working, or to whom she was sending her messages. I'm just going to meet him, no more."

He nodded unhappily at her logic. She had prodded him

into thinking about his introduction of Kerensky, which he'd reworked all afternoon, and his nervousness returned. "But be careful, my dear," he said, looking at her directly.

"Of course. I'll probably be back before Kerensky's finished."

Recently organized by Leonard and several political allies, the 1917 Club was quartered in a dilapidated building on Gerrard Street. While Virginia rather liked the idea of a gathering place for friends, she distrusted the tendency of any organization to mire itself in propaganda and self importance. But Leonard took it very seriously, and tonight, for her own reasons, she was just as glad.

As she followed him up the stairs, festive voices echoed down from above, and when they entered the floor-through meeting room, Virginia saw Roger. He was waving at her and hurried down the aisle, gesturing her aside from the group beginning to gather around Leonard.

"What do you know about Clive buying paintings?" he asked straight out.

"So he's finally managed it," she said with a shrug.

"He's just spent the past twenty minutes bragging about a trip to Paris. 'A grand order for oils,' is how he puts it."

"What's the difficulty?"

"Because he's being so damned secretive. He wouldn't tell me for whom he was buying, or even which galleries he's dealing with. I don't like it."

She looked at him and wondered if he wasn't simply being jealous, though she had to admit that wasn't his style. She noticed Maynard staring at them from across the room.

"What's Maynard's feeling about this?" she asked.

"He knows nothing about it. Said it definitely has no connection with his buys for the government, none whatsoever."

A loud clamor of applause burst out behind them, and

they turned. A crowd was surging into the room. In its midst was Alexander Kerensky, his heavy face splotched with red as if he'd just made his escape from the Bolsheviks on a sleigh.

Leonard escorted the Russian to the speaker's table where he called the meeting to order.

"Shall we find seats?" asked Roger.

"I'm leaving early," she said and only shook her head when he asked why. They took seats on the aisle in the last row. "I think we'd better find out what nonsense Clive's up to," he repeated.

She stared straight ahead as if she hadn't heard him. She was lost in her thoughts of Giraud and she paid little attention to Leonard's introduction, much less to Kerensky's thundering remarks. When he shouted, "I have witnessed the death of democracy!" she rose quickly and hurried outside as the audience exploded in applause.

The air was heavy with fog. After a few grim blocks she crossed the expanse of Shaftesbury Avenue and passed through a group of soldiers. She kept her eyes down, ignoring the Tommies' remarks, and turned into the narrow streets beyond the broad avenue.

Figures lurked in the shadowy doorways, peering at her with glazed eyes. She increased her pace. In the second block, someone stumbled out in front of her, forcing her to stop.

"Looking for something?" beckoned the drunk. She drew back. "'Ere now, don't be in such a hurry. Me and Willie likes the ladies."

"Leave her be, Jimmy, or I'll thump you," came a loud female voice from behind her. Virginia turned to find a woman as tall as herself but heavier, with flaming red hair.

Instinctively, Virginia shrank back from the prostitute.

The woman laughed. "Don't take on, dearie, I won't hurt you." She guided Virginia past the man who now eyed her angrily. "And that rotter there, he won't give you no more trouble neither."

"Thank you very much," said Virginia primly. Then, annoyed by her reaction, she added, "I'm just going to the hotel up the street. This is very kind of you."

"The Litchfield Arms?" The woman fell into step beside her. "Blimey, what a crowd round there tonight. Never seen so much comin' and goin'. Filled with traps, it is."

"Traps?"

"Coppers. They're piping all of us. Nearly got meself arrested. The bloke wasn't in uniform, looked like a proper gentleman, he did. Big and tall, with a fancy mustache. Thank the lord, he was too bloody busy to pinch me. Told me to clear out."

At the corner the woman stopped. "I'd better not show my face down there. You be all right now, will ya dearie?"

Virginia nodded, peering up the darkened street.

"Across from the pub, it is. You be careful, and tell your gentleman friend to walk you home." The woman laughed again, then crossed the blacked-out intersection to join a group of Tommies lingering on the opposite corner.

Virginia hurried down the pavement, looking back once over her shoulder. She thought she heard footsteps behind her but she couldn't be sure; her ears still rang with the sneering laughter of the drunk. Now she could see the entrance of the hotel. The alleyway was this side of it and she said to herself, Oh God, let him be there. She stopped abruptly. She had heard the sound of voices. Oh, no, she thought, Clarke has already gone to meet him! She stood and listened. It seemed to be two men but she couldn't make out what they were saying. Suddenly there was silence.

She took a few steps forward, straining to hear. From the dark recess, still nothing. Then a crash.

A dustbin overturning, she reassured herself, though at once she heard footfalls, the sound of someone running back into the darkness.

The alleyway was narrow, the cobblestones wet and slippery. The bricks of the adjacent building were slimy with rainwater oozing from the crevices. She made her way slowly, reaching out to keep her balance. There were no more footfalls now, only the sound of her own labored breathing. She glanced over her shoulder and saw the dim light of the street and, at the mouth of the alley, a pedestrian passing.

Suddenly her foot struck something and she cried out in pain and fright. It *was* a dustbin. She reached out to stop its clatter.

Again there was silence.

"Clarke?" she called out tentatively. "Giraud?" Her mouth was dry, and again she rasped out their names. Off to her right, against the wall, it was all darkness but she thought she saw something. She forced herself to move closer. As her eyes acclimated she could just make out the baggy tweeds, the tan mac.

"Inspector Clarke? Is that you?"

There was no reply. She went closer. It was Clarke, all right, sitting with his back against the wall, his head slumped on his chest, a rain hat sitting low across his face.

"Inspector Clarke?" she repeated. With a trembling hand she reached down and touched his shoulder.

The touch was enough. The body slid sideways against the wall. Clarke's head lolled back as if he were looking up to greet her.

She froze in horror, staring dumbly at the long slash across his throat; the skin was parted evenly, almost surgically, the cut surging with blood.

She stumbled and lurched backwards against the opposite wall screaming. Waves of nausea overwhelmed her. She was spinning downward, sucked into a deep tunnel, the tunnel of her nightmares: the slimy walls closing in on her, trapping her in a vault, and once more a grotesque face before her: the man who'd throttled her in Josephs' flat; then Clarke with his gaping wound, and finally the deformed man from her childhood, more animal than human, whose pockmarked face leered at her with the grin of death.

She broke into a run, stumbling, sobbing. But the horrifying face was still in front of her. Now it was a harpy clothed in black, a looming figure clawing at her, trying to embrace her with great curled talons that tore at her flesh. Sharp shrieks echoed in her ears. Then another face, blurry, out of focus, rose before her: Giraud. She reached out. There was nothing, only silence and consuming blackness as she fell to the cobblestones unconscious.

27

The alleyway was bathed in the eerie white-green light of police torches. Two bobbies out of the reinforcements summoned from the Soho precinct held back the crowd which had poured out of the pub across the way, and a half dozen feet into the passageway itself another policeman was leaning over Virginia, trying to revive her. Further down, two men in civilian clothes as well as three in uniform waited while Commissioner Allington inspected the body.

Allington dropped the blanket back over Clarke's face. "One cut straight across and upward," he said. "From the Adam's apple to the ear. A clean cut, probably from behind." He spoke as if he were describing a vase on a table, pausing only when one of the younger men stumbled away to retch against the side of the building.

"Sorry, sir," apologized the precinct captain. "It's his first."

"Which of you discovered the body?" Allington asked, ignoring him.

An older officer stepped forward. "I did, sir. Sergeant James, Soho."

Allington copied the name into his notebook. "What time?"

"Came by about eight-thirty, sir, on my regular route. Takes me just under an hour to make my circuit. I was coming back down Dean Street here. There was a little dust-up outside the pub and—"

"Get on with it," growled Allington.

"I heard the lady's screams. I ran in and found her fainted dead away. Then him." He gestured without looking at the body. "That's when I blew my whistle and—"

"Whistle," repeated Allington, by way of cutting him off. "We'll have to wait for her to come round before we set he time more exactly. Detective Williams," he commanded, turning to one of the men in plainclothes, "get up to the hotel and see if Clarke stopped in there. Ask the clerk and anyone else you can find. Don't tell them who he is, just describe him. Find out if anyone knew what he was doing here."

He waited until the man had trotted away before turning to two plainclothesmen who had arrived after the others. "Yes, we've already identified him," he said. "He's one of us, so I want a damned good job done—every speck of ground covered, and I mean carefully. Don't let anyone touch the body until the medicos get here."

"Sir?" It was the older bobby who'd discovered the body.

"Keep it short, Sergeant," ordered Allington.

"Yes, sir. I just wanted to add that I heard someone running down the alley here. After the lady's screams, I mean."

"After the screams, you're certain?"

The bobby shrugged. "Can't say definitely. That was my impression. Down there." He pointed into the dark recess.

"You didn't go after him?"

"I was worried about the lady. I thought she might be hurt, sir."

"What's at the other end?"

Another policeman stepped forward. "Runs back seventy feet or so. To Wardour Street, with a fence at the end."

Without comment, Allington turned, disappearing beyond the circles of light. A few minutes later he returned. "Could someone have gotten over that fence?"

"I'm not sure. I'll check with a torch."

Allington turned to the bobby beside Virginia. "She conscious yet?"

"Just a tick ago, sir."

Walking back to her, he took one of the plainclothesmen with him. "It's a tricky situation," he said. "Clarke was MI5. I want you to make the usual telephone calls, but in this order: The Coroner and Warrants Office first, then Sir Basil Thomson and *then* Kell. Do you understand, Kell last? I want it made clear to both Thomson and Kell that Branch has already organized the investigation."

Virginia had heard the deep voice above her and now her eyes fluttered open. There was an ache at the back of her throat. She tried to struggle upward.

"Easy, Mrs. Woolf," said the Commissioner, resting his large hand on her shoulder. "You've had a nasty shock."

"What happened?" she asked in a frightened whisper.

"We'll talk about it when you're ready. First take some brandy."

Virginia choked down a few sips. The back of her head ached. She reached up and felt a lump. She tried to remember: she'd been falling, she'd reached out. Yes, she'd seen Giraud. Or had she? The harpy tearing at her flesh, the leering man. . . . Then it came back to her. Clarke, she'd found Inspector Clarke! She looked sideways, to her right. Less than ten feet away lay the covered figure. The image of the wound burned in her mind. "Oh, no," she sobbed. "Giraud?" she choked out, looking at the Commissioner wildly. "Did you see Giraud?"

Allington knelt down beside her. "What did you say? 'Giraud'?"

"Mr. Clarke was to meet him here, I told you. Giraud was

expecting me. I asked you to warn Clarke. He must have tried to arrest Giraud and—'' her voice broke into convulsive sobs. ''Why didn't you?'' she wailed, looking up into Allington's face.

''Here, here, Mrs. Woolf. Be calm. If Clarke had told me what he was up to, I might have been able to.''

Virginia took gulps of air. Allington's face was fading in and out of focus. She tried to concentrate, to speak slowly: ''Giraud uses the name Bayard. What Clarke suspected, what he was trying—'' The shadows began to spread again, and instead of the policeman, what she saw was only Giraud's face with its cheek-length scar. Then it faded into a blur and she closed her eyes. She heard a voice. She remembered there had been two men talking in the alley. One was insistent, just as this one was. She forced her eyes open. It was the Commissioner again. She shook her head. ''I'm sorry. I'm feeling—''

A voice called out from the darkness. ''Commissioner!''

''Excuse me,'' he said to her, standing. Virginia watched him, his broad figure receding, silhouetted against the carbide lamps of the police. Two men in white coats were coming down the alley with a litter.

It was like looking down the wrong end of a telescope. She could see what they were doing but it all seemed unreal. They talked too calmly, too methodically, as if they were clerks in an office. No one seemed to care about Giraud. Why weren't they sending anyone after him? Why was Allington just standing there, staring into his damned handkerchief, whispering to his subordinates?

She forced herself up, then stumbled forward, swaying slightly from side to side. ''Commissioner,'' she called. ''He's probably already at Cranford's. Giraud, I mean. Why aren't you—'' She reached out to steady herself. One of the bobbies took her arm.

''Look at this, Mrs. Woolf.'' Allington held out his handkerchief. There was a glint of metal. At first she couldn't make it out but Allington held it closer: a pocket knife, horn-handled with a long silver blade. She peered at it more closely; yes, Sam Josephs had sat at his desk the morning she'd first met him, opening and closing the very knife, using it to pare his nails. Without thinking she reached out to run her finger along the edge of the blade. Allington pulled it away.

"Evidence, Mrs. Woolf. There's no blood, I grant you, but it was probably wiped clean."

"Evidence? It's Josephs'. He kept it in his office."

For a moment Allington seemed surprised. Then a look of smug satisfaction accompanied his clipped, "Quite so. In his office. Indeed, Josephs was seen with Clarke in the lobby. The clerk claims they left together."

She forced herself to concentrate. Her reasoning was as blurred as the alley around her. "He's lying. Josephs is missing. Not even Bobbie knows where. He couldn't have known." She shook her head, trying to think clearly. Bobbie had said that Sam was trying to reach her. Had she told him? But even if she had, it didn't mean he was a murderer. Allington was turning everything the wrong way round.

"We know Josephs was here. I can only assume you told Miss Waters about your meeting."

"Yes, but—"

"Obviously she informed Josephs." He paused. "Josephs was in Paris over the weekend, that we know for sure. Whether or not he's working with Giraud remains to be seen." He wrapped the knife with his handkerchief. "But this, Mrs. Woolf, is certainly the weapon that killed Clarke."

"It can't be! Why would Josephs? For what reason? He's a good friend of Bobbie's. I've met him, we would have known."

"Met him. . . . would have known," he mused. "Perhaps, you would have known." He gave her a kindly look and stepped aside for the stretcher bearers.

A door had opened on memories she'd chosen to ignore.

Giraud *had* known about Anna's last message, he'd known about her use of the Joyce text but he'd only told her about the Michelet code. Josephs, too, when he'd burst into the Café Royal. He'd demanded the Joyce novel, as well. He'd known it was important.

Oh God, she muttered to herself. Now she remembered. She'd been bringing Joyce's *Portrait of the Artist* to Clarke. She wheeled away from Allington and ran to the opposite wall where she bent down and began feeling along the ground. Nothing. She pushed past the two bobbies and kicked along the cobblestones, working her way back into the alley. Suddenly Allington grasped her arm.

"You're disturbing the evidence!"

"It's my bag!" she cried. "It's gone. I had the book Anna used to code her last message." She stared up into the policeman's puzzled face. "Don't you see? Giraud must have stolen it. He's using it to send details of the offensive." She broke away, starting to run back up the alley. "It's Cranford. He's gone to Cranford, I'm telling you. And he has to be stopped!"

She didn't get very far. One of the bobbies restraining the crowd at the mouth of the alley turned, blocking her way, and in a moment Allington had pinned her against his chest.

"Cranford!" she screamed at him. "Don't you understand? Giraud and Cranford! Arrest them!"

"Quiet!" he ordered, turning her around to face him. "You must calm down. I know this is dreadful, but you're hysterical. It won't help, I promise you."

"Hysterical? Clarke's been killed and you stand there, you fool, and you think I'm mad!" Her voice was growing high and shrill.

Suddenly the Commissioner swung an open palm across her cheek. The blow wasn't heavy, just sharp enough to subdue her.

"Sorry," he said, his face rueful. "Now, I'll have one of my men drive you home."

❊ 28 ❊

At 7:30 the next morning there was a knock at the Woolfs' front door. Expecting another policeman, Nellie was startled by the young woman who pushed her way in demanding to see Virginia. Leonard came hurrying into the foyer to see what the commotion was about.

"But I need to talk to her. The police were at my flat with a warrant for Sam's arrest." Bobbie stopped, seeing Allington appear in the sitting room doorway.

"What's happened?" she asked, looking at Leonard. "Tell me! What's the matter?"

The Commissioner beckoned her into the sitting room. Keynes was on the sofa. Another man whom she'd never seen before stood before the fireplace, a black bag at his feet. Leonard quickly introduced Dr. Wright.

"Is Virginia ill?" she demanded in alarm.

"Mrs. Woolf's had a severe shock, Miss Waters. I've had to sedate her," Wright said.

"I warned you, Miss Waters," Leonard glared at her. "But, oh no, you wouldn't believe it, and now we're not sure she'll—"

"Please, tell me what's going on!" Bobbie looked from one man to the other.

"What's going on? Just this. Inspector Clarke was killed last night," Allington said. "Outside the Litchfield Arms. His throat slashed. A brutal killing, do you understand?"

"What?" gasped Bobbie. "And Virginia?"

"Virginia found him," interjected Leonard. "After going there to warn Clarke about Giraud."

"Warn him?"

Leonard turned away, tears in his eyes.

"Warn him about what? What about Giraud?" she persisted.

"Really, Miss Waters!" put in Keynes. "Mr. Woolf's had a terrible night."

She turned to him. "What are *you* doing here?"

Allington gave Keynes no time to reply. "My men tell me you refused to cooperate this morning," he said. "I still think you know where Josephs is and I need an answer."

"He has nothing to do with Clarke's murder."

"Nothing. . . . I doubt that. He was seen leaving the hotel with Inspector Clarke. A knife was found in the near alleyway. The knife has been identified as his. Even Mrs. Woolf recognized it."

"You mean the one from his desk? The pocket knife?"

To Allington's nod, she threw her hands up in the air.

"Ridiculous! Sam never takes it out of the office. He uses it to open his mail. Besides, it's a pocket knife. It isn't big enough to be a weapon."

"Don't be so sure. Mrs. Woolf says she told you of her meeting with Henri Giraud. Correct?"

She nodded. "She didn't say anything about Clarke, though."

"Didn't say anything about Clarke, but you saw fit to tell Mr. Josephs?"

Bobbie's mouth tightened. Unable to contradict him, she shifted her gaze.

"I know there's an explanation," she muttered. "But Giraud, where's he?"

"We don't know if he ever came to the hotel." Allington turned to Leonard. "That's another thing I'd like to confirm with your wife."

"I'm afraid it must wait," Dr. Wright said. "I want to see how she is after the sedative wears off."

Upstairs in her bed Virginia was drifting in and out of the drug-induced sleep. She felt as if she were wrapped in gauze, lost in a heavy, clinging mist. Her body ached. Flashes of light whirled behind her eyes and when she closed them the blackness came again. But so did the terrible faces. Once more she was stumbling, falling, moaning, and suddenly the claws of the grotesque harpy reached out to tear great hunks of flesh from her face; she could hear screams. Her hands were covered with blood. At last, she saw the end of the tunnel and a light. Dawn, an opening in the darkness and standing there, was it possible? Yes! She ran faster, she had to reach him. She called out his name, "Henri, Henri!" He smiled, rubbing the scar on the side of his face, then turned and hurried away from her. "Please," she sobbed, stumbling against the stone walls that pressed in on her. Only he could save her, but he'd deserted her. Now the harpy was again tearing at her shoulders. Then it was Sir Henry Cranford looming over her. And behind him his chauffeur, leering.

"No, no, no," she cried.

They heard her screams below. Leonard bolted for the stairs, Bobbie following. Virginia lay in bed, twisting her head from side to side, her eyes squeezed shut, tears running down her face. Keynes and the doctor came to the doorway; Leonard was standing transfixed. Bobbie pushed past him to the bedside and took Virginia by the shoulders, shaking her.

Wright came forward and tried to pull Bobbie away but Virginia reached up and clasped her arms around her friend's neck.

"Nessa? Oh, thank God, Nessa, you've come!" she cried.

Shrugging Wright away, Bobbie embraced her as if she were comforting a child. "It's me, Virginia. It's Bobbie. You're safe now."

Virginia's eyes fluttered open. Dazed, she stared up into Bobbie's face. Then she sobbed again as she pulled her close. "Oh, Bobbie, I'm so glad you're here. It was so awful. The face and the blood and—"

"I know. Shh, shh—"

Wright had turned from his open bag on the dressing table. Virginia saw him first. *"No!"* she shrieked, pointing a trembling finger at the syringe he was filling. "Damn you, I've told you, *no!* It makes me worse. I don't want it!"

"Nonsense," said Wright in his calm, authoritative tone. "Veronal helps you sleep, it doesn't cause your headaches. Give me your arm," he said advancing toward her.

"No! It's poison!"

"Virginia, please," urged Leonard. "You were hysterical, hearing voices, calling out for—"

"No!"

"Virginia, sh-h," Bobbie murmured. "It's all right. You were having a nightmare. It's perfectly natural after last night."

"That's right. And I . . . I . . . don't think," Virginia stammered, "the dreams, I can't go through it again." She looked back and forth between Bobbie and Wright.

The doctor said, "We want those dreams to go away now, don't we? Certainly we don't want to have another episode."

"Stop treating her like a child," Bobbie said. "Listen to me—" she turned back to Virginia "—anyone would have terrible dreams after what you saw. You're not going mad. Believe me, you're not!" She wheeled and struck Wright's hand. The syringe went flying. It hit the wall, the clear liquid running down the wallpaper in a glistening stain.

Wright's face became rigid and he looked to Leonard for assistance. It was Keynes, however, who intervened.

"Enough, Miss Waters. I suggest you leave. I can ask Commissioner Allington to remove you."

"Allington?" Virginia said. "Where?"

"Downstairs," said Leonard. "Dr. Wright asked him to wait below. I'll let him know you're awake." He left the room and they heard him calling down from the top of the stairs. When there was no response, he returned, shaking his head. "I suppose he's had to leave."

"He wanted to know if you saw Giraud last night," said Maynard. "I'd like to know, too."

Maynard's pompous tone sent new color into Virginia's cheeks and she pitched herself out of bed. "I don't have to tell you a bloody thing," she said. "Just who do you think you are, standing there gawking at me. And ordering Bobbie about!"

"Now, 'Ginia. Maynard's an old friend," Leonard objected.

"Certainly, and he's concerned about *his* friend, Sir Henry." Keynes lowered his eyes. "Sir Henry's been complaining about 'the mad Mrs. Woolf,' right? And, of course, you can't believe that the dear man's a traitor!"

Keynes stared at the floor, saying nothing. Bobbie watched him, Leonard and Wright too, a nervous smile playing at the corners of her mouth.

"I've had enough of all of you," Virginia shouted. "Get out of here. All of you. *Now!*"

Wright glanced at Leonard. "For God's sake, Woolf, do something!"

"'Ginia, please, there's no cause for this," Leonard said. "Leave it to Allington. You've done your part, you know that. Let Dr. Wright—"

"I don't want sleep. I want you men out of here!"

None of them moved. She saw them standing, unyielding, before her. Like so many bars, she thought, the bars of a cage. Suddenly her head cleared. No more, she told herself. This was a chance to prise open the locked room.

"Out!" she shouted again. "If you aren't out in three seconds it's all over. I've told you before, Leonard. I won't have it. All of you, get out of here, or I'm leaving, Leonard. For good!"

Leonard was trembling from head to foot, his face ashen with rage and humiliation. Before he could speak Keynes took him by the arm to lead him to the door. "There's no point in trying to talk to her," he said.

"Perceptive of you, Pozzo!" she yelled after them. She turned to Wright. "I'd follow his advice if I were you, Doctor. If you come near me, I'll charge you with assault."

Wright stalked angrily from the room. Bobbie closed the door after him. "Brava!" she said, clapping her hands. "That was wonderful!"

Virginia gave a mock bow. "Oh!" she exclaimed, straightening up. "My head really does hurt."

"Of course it does," Bobbie replied. "After what you've been through." She went to the wardrobe, pulled out a blue-green striped dress and tossed it across the bed. "But you don't have time to worry about it. We have a train to catch."

"A train?"

"I promised Sam. Now hurry up. I'll explain later."

Virginia dressed as fast as she could, feeling self-conscious as she slipped out of her nightgown and pulled on a petticoat and her dress. Then, as she twisted her hair into its bun, she paused a moment to look over at the table by the bed. Something was different. Then she realized what it was—she'd left her diary there last night.

"What's the matter?" asked Bobbie.

"My diary's gone."

"Are you sure?"

"Of course I'm sure. And, oh God!" She paused, remembering. "I didn't tell you. Last night, the book was taken, the

Joyce text. And Anna's message, too. It was in my handbag." Her eyes filled with tears. "But now my diary. I didn't want to take it into town with me. I left it here, I know I did." She rushed downstairs, Bobbie following.

"Please, Virginia, we've got to go. You can find it later."

"But that's the only copy of Anna's message," she said as she burst into the sitting room.

Leonard was on the sofa, his face cupped in both hands. He looked up at her sadly, defeated.

She spotted the diary immediately. It lay on the floor near his feet. She scooped it up. "Just taking what's mine." Her voice was edged with fury.

⇥ 29 ⇤

Giraud followed them. He had been watching Hogarth House from across the road, and now he kept far enough behind not to be spotted by the Yard man who was tailing the women as well. Bobbie, he saw, was aware of the detective, and at the Kings Cross Station she left Virginia in the ticket queue to lead the Yard man through the crowds and out the side entrance. Five minutes later, Giraud saw her push her way back to Virginia's side and the two sprinted down the platform, leaping into a compartment only seconds before the train steamed out of the station.

Giraud kept himself hidden behind the news kiosk. The detective ran past as the train pulled out. Obviously frustrated, he went to the call boxes at the far side of the waiting room to report his broken surveillance.

While the Yard man placed his call, Giraud sauntered to the ticket counter. A pound note soon refreshed the clerk's memory. The tall, thin woman in the long cape had bought two return tickets to Thetford.

"Who is she anyway?" the clerk said. "You're the second bloke who's asked." He gestured toward the call boxes.

"You mean the man in the tan mac?"

"No, the other one."

Giraud saw a man in a second call box, dressed in chauffeur's livery. Tucked under one arm was a visored cap and a flat leather envelope case.

Giraud slipped back into the crowd. The Yard man put up the telephone and left the station; a few minutes later the uniformed man hung up too, but strolled across the waiting room toward the kiosk.

Giraud bought a tabloid and as the chauffeur passed, he peered over the top of the paper to look at him. Now he was sure: the fleshy flattened nose and the heavy, square head were unmistakable. It was the man who'd followed Virginia to Marcus's, who'd threatened the bookseller: Cranford's chauffeur.

The chauffeur went into the men's lavatories. Giraud followed. The man was standing at the urinals at the rear of the long room and the Belgian went to the washbasins, watching his prey in the mirror. He was now wearing his visored chauffeur's cap, the leather folder still clamped tightly under his right arm.

Now Giraud moved quickly. When the chauffeur turned, he was staring into the barrel of Giraud's gun.

"What the bloody hell?"

"Shut up!" Giraud gestured toward the rearmost stall. The chauffeur moved slowly, sidling toward it. When he broke to his right, Giraud was ready. He whipped the butt of the gun into his midsection. The man grunted and doubled over, dropping the leather case and stumbling backwards into the stall. Giraud hit him with a fist to the throat. The chauffeur slumped down onto the seat of the toilet.

Giraud leaned over him. "Why were you following Mrs. Woolf?"

"I don't have to tell you—"

Giraud drove his forearm across his neck, using his body weight to increase the force. The man tried to move sideways.

Giraud pressed harder until the man's breath came in sharp, stifled gulps; his eyes began to bulge, glazing over as he writhed beneath Giraud's grip.

"Wha'?" he croaked.

Giraud shoved him now, and there was an ugly smack as the man's head slammed against the tile wall. "You heard me."

To no avail. The man struggled upwards, still trying to break free. Giraud pushed him back against the wall and wrapped his fingers around his neck.

"Stop," the chauffeur choked out. "I'm . . . I'm . . . Sir Henry Cranford's chauffeur," he managed to wheeze.

"But that's not all, is it?" Giraud menaced.

A look close to defeat crossed the man's face. His body began to tremble. "I do what I'm told."

"To follow Mrs. Woolf?"

"He said keep an eye on her. Crazy lady, he told me. Then I'm supposed to make a delivery."

"What's the delivery?"

"How should I know?"

"Where?" He squeezed harder. "Where were you going?"

"Gordon Square. Forty-six," he panted.

"Why there? Who?"

Giraud's face paled when the man choked out his reply. It startled him. He knew immediately what he had to do.

The chauffeur saw something in Giraud's piercing eyes. He looked up at him pleadingly. "That's all the guv told me. Honest, mate. Said it had to be taken today."

Giraud took tighter hold of the man's throat.

"Fool," he said, leaning close to the chauffeur's face.

"No!"

Giraud glanced over his shoulder at the empty room and now pressed both thumbs deep into the man's throat. His heavy face turned pink, then a violent red. He struggled, writing. There was a dull pop. Giraud still didn't release his grip, not until the body had jerked beneath him, spittle oozing from the corners of the chauffeur's mouth.

Finally he stepped back, letting go. The body slumped to one side; in one gradual movement it slipped down the side of the stall, the dead man's face coming to rest against the porcelain rim of the bowl.

Giraud emptied the chauffeur's pockets, then gave the body one last appraisal. Satisfied that it would be hours before the police identified the man, he turned and strolled back out into the train station, the leather case under his arm.

✤ 30 ✤

Northeast of London, the train to Thetford passes through the rolling downs and quaint market villages of the fen country but neither Bobbie nor Virginia was interested in the scenery.

Bobbie admitted she'd told Sam about the meeting with Giraud.

"But why? I told you in confidence," Virginia protested, lapsing into silence as she stared out the window. It was so unfair. To have had her reassurances, then to learn that Bobbie had turned around and told her lover. It was so typical. Most women's allegiances remained with men. No matter that the police suspected Josephs as much as Giraud, Bobbie still had faith in him. She herself was torn apart, even devastated by the mounting evidence against Giraud, but Bobbie was unwilling to believe the worst about Sam.

"He went to Thetford yesterday," Bobbie was saying. "I promised we'd come up when he phoned me in the afternoon. *In the afternoon.* That's when he said he had news about Giraud to turn over to MI$_5$."

Virginia slumped in her seat. She could still feel the effects of Wright's dose of Veronal and her own terrifying nightmares. Yet even more fatiguing was her sense of disappointment, not just with Giraud, but with Bobbie. Here were the two people who'd rescued her from the isolation of the last two years and now both seemed to be deserting her. Bobbie had no appreciation of how overwhelmed she was by the revelations about Giraud; all she seemed to care about was Sam's triumph. They would have their news scoop, just the two of them, and she herself had been stupid not to realize this. A scoop. No more, no less, she thought bitterly.

"I will sit like a cat in the sun, watching impassively," she murmured half aloud. She liked the phrase. Soon she was making up others; this is my true self, she thought, beneath my public masks. I want the hot, consuming quality of words, the melting of sentence into sentence. . . .

Vaguely, she heard Bobbie. She turned back from the window, her eyes glazed.

"Does your head still hurt?" Bobbie repeated.

Virginia gave her a faraway look. "The globe hangs heavy in the depth of the mind," she said. "Its radiance burns through, signaling the wanderer on her lonely journey. That is the flame in the flower, the moment of confirmation."

Confused, Bobbie looked down before meeting her gaze. "I'm sorry. I know you're upset but when you talk like this, I . . . I don't know what to make of it."

Virginia knew she'd built a wall between them, frightening the young woman by letting her thoughts bubble forth uncensored, but she couldn't help herself.

"I'm building phrases to capture the moment," she said. "That's my attempt to understand. I need reality to grasp, to fix in my mind. You see, I can tell our tale in astonishing detail, but what lies beneath it? How do I describe our rages and our passions?"

Bobbie shook her head in bewilderment but seized on Virginia's last phrase as something she could at least decipher. "Then you must realize how much I love Sam. It would have meant losing him if I hadn't told him about Giraud." She paused. "Besides, if he did go to the hotel last night, it was probably to protect you. He didn't know Clarke would be there, remember that."

"A lover is always a hero, isn't he?"

"That's not fair. Both of us were worried, Virginia. You took Giraud at his word and let yourself be seduced. Somebody had to look after you."

"Oh, dear," sighed Virginia. "The harshness, the twang, twang, twang of your unrelenting words." For a moment she looked at the passing trees and fields, then turned back. "I'd been thinking myself so unconfined, free and ready to enter the world. Suddenly, I'm weak, addled and insignificant."

"I certainly don't think that, and I don't mean to be so critical. I'm sorry about Giraud, really I am, but he may be the link to the other collaborators."

"There may be another explanation, however," said Virginia, getting a grip on herself. "We know Sam was there, the clerk told Allington. Yet for reasons unknown, your Sam didn't rescue me." She looked at Bobbie grimly. There was a long pause until she burst out laughing.

"Look at me. I'm defending Giraud by attacking your Sam. It's primitive, the protective instinct of women. I saw it in you and I abhorred it—the thread between us torn by your loyalty to Sam. Now I'm tearing at the same thread, forgetting what you did for me this morning. All because I want to believe in Giraud, to think that what I did for him was important."

"It may well *be* important. Only in ways you and I don't yet understand. That's why I insisted you come with me."

"Yes. And it was well worth it. If only for the look on Dr. Wright's face when you smashed the syringe—" Virginia laughed, pleased they were making their way back to firm ground. Whatever the outcome, the two of them might still be allies . . . against the world . . . the masculine world, she reminded herself, thinking of the way Wright and Leonard and Maynard had themselves banded together.

"Your husband and Mr. Keynes were certainly upset too," said Bobbie, reading her thoughts. "But I'd still like to know why Keynes turned up. Why is he so damned concerned?"

"His reputation," said Virginia. "It's not going to sit awfully well if his mentor turns out to be a traitor, especially when he's been buying paintings for him. Oh, and now Clive's been boasting about a buying trip to Paris too."

Bobbie had no chance to reply as the train was now pulling into Thetford's depot. Following the directions of the old stationmaster, they climbed the hill and turned into a narrow lane just past the village church.

Once the home of Josephs' mother, Number Four Jersey Walk was a small thatched cottage. The curtains were drawn and the patch of border garden looked long abandoned. Yet the door opened at once to Bobbie's knock.

Josephs was still unshaven and there was a fuzziness to his expression, as if he'd been napping.

"Thank God, you're all right," said Bobbie, burying her face in his chest. He held her and stroked her hair, meanwhile looking at Virginia.

"Why wouldn't I be?" he said with a smile. "Especially now that you're here." He gestured to the small kitchen off the living room. "Not much in the pantry but I could fix tea if—" He stopped. Virginia and Bobbie were both staring at him.

"What's the matter?" he asked.

"The police are looking for you," said Virginia.

"Oh, that," he said, waving his hand. "Clarke told me he was putting an end to it. MI5 has taken over—" He stopped, sensing there was more.

"You really don't know, do you?" exclaimed Bobbie.

"What? What is it?"

"Clarke was murdered," said Virginia.

He sat down heavily. "My God! When?" He rubbed his brow, squeezing his eyes shut for a moment.

"Last night, in the alleyway near the Litchfield Arms."

He buried his face in his hands, mumbling, "And he was worried about *me.*"

"So you did see him?" asked Bobbie. She sat down beside him. "That's why Allington thinks you had something to do with it. He had a Yard man tailing me but I lost him at the station."

"It certainly changes things, doesn't it?" He paused. "How did Allington know I was there?"

"The hotel clerk," said Virginia.

"That's what I get for trying to buy him off."

"It's worse," said Bobbie. "They found your knife in the alleyway."

"But I haven't been back to the office for days. Anyone could have marched in and taken it."

"Bobbie says you didn't know Clarke would be there," said Virginia. "You went to the hotel only because she told you I was meeting Giraud?"

He nodded. "Clarke stopped me in the lobby and took me outside. He didn't want us seen together."

"Which was when?" asked Virginia.

"About eight-fifteen. When was he killed?"

"I found him ten, fifteen minutes later. I have no idea how long it was before the police came. I fainted." She lowered her eyes, as if ashamed of the weakness. Then she looked up with a penetrating stare. "Bobbie says you thought it was dangerous for me to meet Giraud alone. Why?"

He shrugged. "In the first place, I'm a newspaperman. I know when I'm onto a story. But Clarke asked me to hold off for a day or so and I agreed. He was as worried about my safety as he was about yours."

Virginia was still incredulous. "He was afraid of Giraud?"

"Yes. We both knew he could be dangerous. That's why I didn't want the two of you mucking about in this. From the beginning."

"And if we hadn't, how far would you have gotten?" Bobbie asked. "You didn't think it was anything until Mrs. Woolf came round, and as far as I'm concerned, it's as much my story as it is yours."

"But *I* went to Paris, *I* was chased all over London, *I* managed to get a hold of the woman's suitcase—"

"What difference does it make *whose* bloody story!" Virginia cried. "I want to know what you learned about Giraud in Paris." She was tight with anger.

Sam crossed the room to pour himself a drink from a bottle of whiskey in the corner cabinet. "Either of you like one?" he said, lowering his voice.

"Sam!" shouted Bobbie, "answer her."

He tossed back the drink. "I congratulate the two of you. What do you call it? Women's intuition? You saw that the suicide story didn't hold together. Me, I suspected the Yard closed the case too quickly. I wondered about their reluctance to investigate. Bobbie had a hunch I was up to something— she knows me too well." He gave her a grim smile.

"Go on. When Marie Ickx was killed, you suspected a connection to Michaux?"

"Ah, Bobbie, my love. . ." He paused, looking down at the glass in his hand. "Yes. You see, I knew Marie. Met her last summer at the Center. I thought I'd do a story on refugees. I saw Marie off and on. After we became friends, I realized that waitressing wasn't all she did. I guessed it had something to do with the Belgian government. Last month, in fact, she seemed upset. She hinted she'd discovered something about some of the refugees here in London but wouldn't tell me exactly what. My guess is she discovered that Anna Michaux and others were working for the Germans."

"Impossible," said Virginia. "Anna and Marie were working together. They were his agents, if Giraud was telling the truth."

"He wasn't," said Josephs. "That's the problem. Anna was collecting information here in London and he was passing it to the Germans. Marie was loyal all right, but Anna and Giraud had switched sides."

"But the Germans killed Giraud's wife and son."

"That's what he told you. You know it for a fact?"

Virginia had to admit it made sense. She'd wondered why there were two different books for the codes. Giraud had readily told her about the Michelet but not about the Joyce. He'd known about it—the note he'd left at Marcus's made that clear. Yet Marcus, one of Giraud's Belgian agents, hadn't thought it important when she'd first shown him the Joyce book. So Anna and Giraud must have created another code for their messages to the Germans—based on "mistranslations" from Michelet keyed to Joyce's novel. Yes, that was it, she thought grimly: double codes—*double agents.* It was simple. And Marie must have realized it, too, once she'd seen the list of translations in Anna's room. Which was why she'd left so quickly without waiting for Anna's return; Cranford's housekeeper had told them how upset Anna had been that night. Marie must have taken the pages of "mistranslations" and hidden them in her copy of Michelet, and just as obviously it was why Marcus had given the book to her and not to Giraud.

Excited, Virginia repeated her reasoning aloud. "Giraud asked me to bring the Joyce last night," she continued. "When I fainted my bag was stolen." She lowered her eyes, her lips quivering. "I suppose Giraud took it because he needed the book to code further details of the tank attack. Which means," she added almost with a sob, thinking of Clarke, "that it must have been he."

"So the Germans must now know the tank attack was set for Flanders," said Bobbie matter of factly.

"That was the message," Virginia said, forcing herself to speak calmly. " 'Meeting Sunday, Tank Attack Tuesday Flanders, Details Follow.' Here. I'll show you."

She flipped through the diary, looking for the right page.

"Oh, no!" She ran the tips of her fingers down the book's inner binding. "They're gone. Someone's cut them out! All the pages about Anna. Not just where I decoded the message. Even the pages where I wrote about Anna's suicide note." She looked at Bobbie. "It must have been Leonard. He probably did it while I was drugged. Wright must have told him to destroy the pages so I'd stop thinking about Anna."

"What about Keynes, though? He was there. Or it could have been Clive at Garsington." She paused. "Couldn't it have happened Sunday? You know how Bell's been trying to find out what we're doing."

"I don't think so. I wrote in my diary yesterday. I'd have noticed it. It has to be Leonard. Remember? He had the diary in the sitting room, on the floor by his feet."

"That's not really important now," interrupted Josephs. "What matters is Giraud. He may already be on his way to Paris."

"The Schaeffer Gallery?" Virginia asked.

"How do you know that name?"

"Why?"

"Just tell me," he insisted.

"Roger Fry mentioned it in Le Havre, all right? He thought that a painting in Giraud's office came from there." She frowned. "And yesterday I overheard Giraud threatening Mrs. Ottlinger. He said something to the effect that Schaeffer wasn't happy with her. Something about her husband, too."

"Well, that confirms what I discovered in Paris," said Josephs. "Giraud has often been seen at Schaeffer's."

Virginia felt her pulse pounding, like waves on the shore,

crashing in and then receding, churning up the bits and fragments of the past two weeks. She was exhausted by Josephs's ready explanations. Something glinted in her mind but it was barely glimpsed, as if in the froth of a wave. Over and over again, she tried to focus on it.

From outside she heard a low rumble, the sound of a motor, and closer now, the engine cut and dying. Then the slam of the car door as footsteps sounded on the cobblestones in front of the cottage.

"What the hell?" exclaimed Josephs, moving to the window where he saw two policemen coming up the path. "Christ! I thought you lost them."

"I did," Bobbie said, taking a look. "Their car says Norwich constabulary. They're from here."

"Police!" a voice called out as Sam was already at the door, opening it wide enough to verify their badges.

"What's this all about?" he said in a calm voice.

The policemen exchanged glances. "You *are* Sam Josephs?" the taller one said.

Sam nodded.

Again it was the taller one who spoke. "Come with us then, please."

Sam reached for his coat, turning to Bobbie and Virginia. "Go back to London. But watch for Giraud. Don't worry about me, I'll ring up Kell at MI₅. This'll all be set straight in half a tick."

"I wouldn't be so sure of that, sir," said the bobby. "It was MI₅ that ordered you brought in."

⇥ 31 ⇤

On the return to London, Virginia sat dejected in the corner of the train compartment. Neither of them spoke. All along she'd counted on the Belgian, imagining him as the embodiment of all she cared about—all the personal values the war had so terribly tarnished, and no small part of her faith had been rooted in his request for help. But he'd manipulated her. He'd played on her inherent dislike of Cranford, choreographed her deepest bias against the munitions maker.

Still, perhaps she hadn't been totally wrong, she told herself, now remembering what had been nagging at her while she listened to Josephs: The Schaeffer Gallery! Clive's secrecy, all his talk about a buying trip to Paris. Cranford must have easily enlisted Clive. The damned fool, he had been so eager to worm his way into the industrialist's good graces. She stopped herself. He could be in danger, too. She had to find him. He probably hadn't a clue as to what he'd gotten himself involved in.

When they arrived at Kings Cross Station and Bobbie asked if she would come with her to see Allington, Virginia shook her head. "I'm going to have a chat with Clive."

"Hardly see the point of that," Bobbie said with an impatient shrug, hailing a cab. "But suit yourself. Scotland Yard," she commanded the driver. "As fast as you can."

"They did *what?*" Allington leapt from his chair.

"The Norwich police arrested Sam in Thetford," she repeated. "It's all a terrible mistake. He admits seeing Clarke in the alley, but Clarke was alive when he left."

"Clarke in the alley," repeated Allington. "Hold on. Let's take this a step at a time. When did they arrest him?"

She gave him a puzzled glance. "Kell didn't tell you?"

"Kell?" he said, stiffening in his chair.

"The bobbies said MI₅ ordered it."

"Damn Kell!" he exploded. "Josephs belongs to us. We hold the warrant."

"That doesn't matter. Sam has information from his trip to Paris about Giraud and the Schaeffer Gallery. Will you listen or do I go to Kell myself?"

He apologized, giving her an avuncular smile, and listened as she repeated Josephs's account of Giraud's visits to the gallery.

"You mean Clarke also knew that Giraud is actually Bayard?" he asked when she was finished.

"Sam thinks Clarke had more information, even who the collaborators are. That's why Giraud killed him. Giraud must have seen Sam with Clarke in the alley and realized Sam had discovered his true identity." She paused, adding, "God knows how Giraud got hold of the knife." Her voice turned insistent again. "So you see, you must let Sam go and—"

"Let Sam go—well, that may be sticky," he said. "I'll need to verify all this. Meanwhile there's Bayard." He cocked his head to one side and looked at her questioningly. "I hope Mrs. Woolf hasn't taken it into her head to try to find him herself?"

"Oh, no! She realizes how dangerous it's become. Though she's quite upset he duped her."

"Duped her, yes. But both of you had your ideas about all this. Weren't about to give them up on the word of a middle-aged Yard Commissioner, were you?" He gave her a warm smile, then became serious. "I'll want to speak to her. She's at home?"

"She went to her sister's in Gordon Square. I don't know what she was on about." She stopped, annoyed at herself for criticizing Virginia. "She's all right," she reassured him. "I'm sure she'll cooperate."

He picked up the telephone, put through the call and boomed, "Kell? Allington here. What's all this about Josephs' arrest?"

His eyes narrowed as he listened. "I don't care if you did have a tip. By rights Josephs comes to us. It's a Branch investigation, especially as you dropped Clarke in my lap in the first place!" He paused, listening. "That's ridiculous. You can't hold us responsible. I didn't even know about the meeting."

He darted a look at Bobbie, then stared down at the papers on his desk. "When are you bringing him into town?" he asked. Kell's reply brought an angry flush to his cheeks.

"Dammit," he shouted. "I intend to be there. Whatever he knows belongs to us too—" Allington stopped abruptly. As Kell went on his face slowly stiffened.

"What is it?" Bobbie asked when he hung up.

"Sir Henry Cranford's chauffeur has been murdered. Strangled, at King's Cross Station. They've just identified him."

"Giraud?" she asked.

"That's Kell's hunch, yes."

32

"Can't you do something about Julian and Quentin?" complained Maynard as Vanessa's two sons raced around the tea table. Both were naked, having just had their baths. Vanessa reached out and caught them around their waists. She tousled their hair. "Boys! You're disturbing Pozzo."

Quentin, the younger of the two, stuck his tongue out at Maynard, then at his mother.

"He's a silly old blimp," grumbled Julian, racing his brother upstairs.

"As I was saying, you're welcome to use the flat," said Maynard. "Especially as Clive will be away in Paris, too." He paused. "Has he told you his secret?"

Vanessa shrugged. "I've given up paying much attention to his intrigues. Besides, I'm much more worried about Virginia. Leonard rang to see if she'd turned up here. He's even talking about sending her back to the nursing home."

"That won't be necessary," said Virginia from the doorway. She'd let herself in with her own key and hearing her name, had listened from the landing.

"Oh, Goat!" cried Nessa, trying to embrace her. "I've been so worried."

Virginia pulled away. "Pozzo's had a great deal to tell you?" she said coldly.

"Sit down, Virginia. Have some tea," he said.

Virginia shot him a hostile look, then turned to Vanessa: "Where's Clive?"

"He went round to the Omega. But you should ring Leonard—"

"I don't have time." She turned to go, pausing at the head of the stairs. "I've got to see Clive at once. Before he gets into real trouble."

The Omega Workshops, founded by Roger Fry four years before, were halfway up Fitzroy Square, at number 33. In the middle of the main room stood a row of tables laden with bolts of silk-screened cloth, baskets, and hand-painted crockery. Along the white walls hung paintings by Vanessa Bell, Duncan Grant and Fry himself, all in what Roger called their Post-Impressionist style.

Roger and Clive were bent over some papers at a rear table; both looked up as Virginia came in.

"Clive! I want to talk to you!"

"Well, you'll have to queue for it," he replied. "Roger's giving me a lecture."

"It's not funny," said Roger. "As usual he won't listen to reason." He waved the sheets of paper at her.

"I take it you've come from Gordon Square," said Clive. "Has there been a delivery for me?"

"How should I know?" Virginia snapped. "Roger, what's that?"

"The painting orders Clive's supposed to bring to Paris. I'm trying to convince him how stupid this is. No reputable person would go near Schaeffer."

"The Schaeffer Gallery!" she exclaimed, certain now that Clive was involved with Cranford. "That's what I was afraid of. You mustn't, Clive!"

"Why are you so concerned?" he huffed. "Don't tell me you're coming all over patriotic, too? There's absolutely nothing wrong with the Schaeffer Gallery."

"Tell him," Roger urged her. "Everyone in the art world knows that Schaeffer's collection includes paintings seized by the Germans in occupied countries. Look here, these provenances are patently false—" he pointed to the page where numbers and titles of paintings were listed—"I don't know who's drawn up this order, but it reeks to high heaven. I wouldn't go near it and neither would any knowledgeable buyer."

"Roger, you've *never* been one to take risks," said Clive. "What neither of you understands is I'm talking art, not politics. If the Germans are selling their collections, why shouldn't we take advantage of it?"

Virginia was no longer listening. What at first glance seemed to be innocent order numbers now leapt from the page at her. With as much certainty as she'd ever felt in her whole life, she knew exactly what they were. Set off in three columns, *just as Anna's and Marie's codes had been, sets of three numbers,* it was the enemy's code. This was how they'd been sending information to the Germans. And now Cranford had Clive carrying the details of the tank attack in Flanders to the so-called Schaeffer Gallery in Paris.

Her hands trembled, and even as she felt a glow of triumph, she was overcome with sadness too. The sign in the waves—the vision she'd long been seeking and yet the discovery appalled her. Her brother-in-law, one of her oldest friends, had inveigled himself into it too. First Giraud, then Clive—both somehow working for Cranford. A lump rose in her throat. Perhaps, though, Clive was an unwitting fool who'd wheedled his way in.

She stared at Clive who was still defending himself. "There's no reason why I can't find a Dürer woodcut for myself—"

"Dürer!" she exploded. "Look at this." She pointed to the first order number. "This has nothing to do with paintings. It's a code, damn you. It refers to a book—page, line, and word numbers. All of these do." Her voice rose. "You've got to tell me—who's sending you? It's Cranford, isn't it? Did you convince him you'd work for him, no questions asked? Is that how you managed it?"

Clive only laughed. "Leave it to you, Goat. This one tops them all. It really, really does."

"Dammit, Clive. Listen!"

He stared at her mutely, looking like an angry turtle withdrawing into its shell. "Tell me," she said. "It *was* Sir Henry, wasn't it? You saw his chauffeur take his own case, then you used that to blackmail him. Tell me. I'm only trying to save your bloody hide."

She stopped. Clive was staring past her toward the front door and she whirled.

"Giraud!" she exclaimed.

He was still wearing the disguise of a refugee but carried a flat leather folder under one arm. His other hand remained in his coat pocket. His dark eyes drilled through her. She felt pinned like a moth, watching now as a slow smile crossed his face. He was sneering at her, mocking her vulnerability. She forgot her fear. Her hatred for him thickened inside her.

"Murderer! Traitor!" she burst out uncontrollably.

Then she fell silent. In one sweeping motion Giraud had brought his arm up from his side, his hand holding a gun. He walked slowly toward her. She stared, hypnotized, into the small black eye of its barrel.

⋙ 33 ⋘

Bobbie had rushed from her office to Hogarth House in response to Leonard's frantic phone call. He'd cried, broken down weeping after announcing the kidnapping, and now Bobbie found herself equally distraught as he recounted what had taken place.

"Giraud dragged her out of the Workshop at gunpoint. Roger and Clive couldn't stop him. He threatened to shoot—" he gulped hard, unable to finish.

"What's the Yard doing?"

"Special Branch is out looking for her. Allington thinks Giraud will use her as a hostage."

"My God!" said Bobbie, fighting to control her panic. "I should have realized he'd be that desperate. But Virginia insisted she had to go see Clive."

"I know. Roger told me. But now Clive's gone too. No one knows where. He didn't even wait for the police. Just went running off, swearing about some papers Giraud took from him."

"Papers?"

"Something about painting orders, I don't know. Do you expect me to *care?*"

Bobbie turned away, only half hearing him. The police,

she realized, had spared him the news that they suspected Giraud had murdered Cranford's chauffeur.

"All we can do is wait," she said. "If he needs her to get out of the country, he won't hurt her."

"You may be right. But, oh God, I wish I hadn't listened to her when she insisted she had to see this through. She actually had me convinced that she had to help the police . . . ."

"All those 'ifs' don't help much. Besides, you couldn't have stopped her."

She sat down in the armchair in front of the fire. Leonard was hunched on the sofa, his hands hanging helplessly between his knees. After a moment he looked over at her.

"That chair, Miss Waters, it's—"

"I'm sorry, what?"

"That's where Virginia sits to write in her diary. Sometimes I'd watch her . . . the firelight across her face, her beautiful secret smile when she'd written something that pleased her. She'd lean back and burst out in that special laugh. You know, more a hoot than a laugh."

His eyes filled with tears. "I'm afraid I complained. She'd interrupt my reading, or insist on telling me a bit of gossip. I thought it trivial, a waste of time." He slammed his fist on his thigh. "Damn! Damn!"

"Don't blame yourself. None of us knew where it would lead."

He looked up at her with brimming eyes. "But you have no idea what it's been like for Virginia and me these past two years."

"Virginia told me about Wright's regimen. I saw how much she despises him. That was certainly one reason she went on with this: to prove herself. That's why she was eager to help Giraud. She believed him because he didn't treat her like an invalid."

"But dammit, she *is* an invalid." He caught himself and softened his voice. "I've spent the last twenty-four months watching her suffer. I've had to calm her when she's heard birds speaking Greek or imagined her mother standing by her bed. I've seen her writhing from the pain in her head, the voices echoing in her ears."

Bobbie started to interrupt, but he waved his hand to keep her quiet. "You may think me an ogre—locking her up, the doctor, the Veronal, sending her friends away. But all that was necessary. She's tried to kill herself. Did you know that? And more than once. So when she fastened on the woman's suicide, I *had* to be worried. I should have been *more* worried when she started going on about spies and codes and murder. It's too much for her. We don't know what sets off those hopeless moods. I thought the sight of Clarke's body had sent her over the edge again."

"Anyone would have been terrified," Bobbie said. "And today she was fine. Worried, yes, but no headaches, no tears."

"But there's no telling how dangerous Giraud is. Virginia's worst nightmares are of physical assault. Beneath the skin of civilization she imagines cruelty and evil and violence. She has no defenses. The only cure I've devised is careful control of her sleep and diet. She can't do anything strenuous, anything that overexcites her." He sighed, casting his eyes around the comfortable room. "She'd almost recovered. She was working on her novel a few hours every day. She was even able to see people once in a while. This could destroy everything."

"She's not as fragile as you think. Look what she's been through the past two weeks. If anything, she's stronger for having tested herself."

"Yes, in certain ways she's resilient," he said. "I sometimes forget that. I've been so busy taking care of her, I've ignored what attracted me to her in the first place. Her courage, her spirit. . . ."

The ringing of the telephone shattered his reverie. He ran into the foyer, Bobbie close behind him.

His face turned ashen as he listened. "I won't do a damn thing unless I know she's safe," he shouted. There was a pause. Bobbie could see his relief as Virginia must have come on the line. "Yes, yes, my dear. I understand. You're sure you're all right?"

There was silence again. "Yes, Virginia," he said finally. He lowered his voice. "Please be careful, darling. I . . . you know I love you." There was another pause. "I warn you, Giraud, you harm her, I'll—" He stopped, listening. "But what if I can't reach them all?" He listened again briefly, then hung up.

"She claims she's fine," he said, turning to Bobbie. "Giraud's given us two hours to gather Clive and Maynard and get them to Cranford's house." He waved off Bobbie's quizzical look. "He says he has something to tell us. He won't do it any other way. For Virginia's safety. . . ." He shook his head. "Oh, God!" he burst out. "I'm so worried about her!"

"She'll be all right." Bobbie tentatively reached out to touch his arm. He seemed to flinch, and she withdrew her hand. She bit her lip and lowered her head.

Noticing the sorrow and guilt in her face, he clasped her hand between his. "I'm sorry. You shouldn't blame yourself either." He sighed and turned back to the telephone. "But I'd better get on with this." He clicked the phone for the operator, saying nothing further until he had gotten the connection.

❧ 34 ❧

The reading lamps cast pools of light in Sir Henry Cranford's study. Cranford, roused from bed, wore a maroon silk dressing gown. He looked at Clive and Maynard, then back to Leonard and Bobbie. The ticking of the clock on the chimney piece echoed in the silence.

Soon the clock struck midnight, its leaden chimes cutting the tension-filled air. They waited. After another moment they turned as one, all five of them, hearing footsteps in the anteroom.

"It's Virginia," cried Leonard.

And there she was.

The room broke into noisy confusion as they rushed toward her, surrounding her with questions.

"I'm fine, really I am," she said, striding through their midst and with an oddly flamboyant gesture, tossing her cape across the back of a chair.

Leonard and Bobbie glanced in surprise at each other, then hurried after her. She turned and embraced each of them. Beneath her calm expression was a glow of excitement.

"What in hell is going on?" Cranford burst out. "Where's that bloody Belgian? He rousts us out of bed, threatens us with your life—"

"Absolutely," Maynard joined in. "Virginia, let's have an explanation. This is no tea party, you know."

"Unless it's one of Goat's pranks," said Clive. "And I for one, Virginia, am going home now that you're safe."

He was half-standing when the voice boomed at him. "Stay where you are, Mr. Bell." It was Giraud. Still unshaven and wearing his tattered clothes, the Belgian blocked the doorway. Clive shrank back into his chair as the others raised cries of alarm and protest.

All but Virginia. She watched calmly as Giraud crossed the room and came to her side. "Quiet!" he commanded the others. Then, in a lower voice: "Sit down. All of you." He gestured to the chairs in front of Cranford's desk. Then he took Virginia's arm. "You stay here with me."

"Get your hands off her!" said Leonard, starting forward. Giraud stopped him: "I wouldn't if I were you, Mr. Woolf."

Leonard stopped, his face flushing bright red, then retreated to the chair next to Bobbie's. She took his hand to comfort him.

"Look here, Giraud!" exploded Cranford. Then reversing himself and adopting a reasonable tone, he said, "Just tell me what you want. I'll arrange it. Money . . . safe passage . . . whatever."

Giraud waved him quiet. He was staring over Cranford's head at the rear doorway, a faint smile crossing his lips. The others, following his gaze, turned in their chairs.

Lord Ladbrooke entered.

Virginia gave Giraud a sidelong glance as Cranford rose from his chair in alarm. "Oh, Christ, Alex, this is no place for you!" he cried. "This madman's holding Mrs. Woolf hostage. Us, too, and now you—"

"But you didn't tell me to bring him," Leonard interrupted, giving Giraud a puzzled look. Giraud paid no attention. Leonard stared at Virginia who showed no reaction either as Bobbie looked accusingly at Maynard and Clive.

Maynard shook his head, but Clive looked down, his cheeks flushing.

Ladbrooke crossed the room and faced Virginia. "I was worried about you. When I heard what had happened, I had to come immediately."

"Yes," she said. "And I appreciate your concern. But as I've told everyone, I'm quite all right." Her face betrayed no emotion.

Ladbrooke turned to Giraud. "As for you, now that I'm here, perhaps we can negotiate. I'm perfectly willing to use my connections to guarantee Mrs. Woolf's safety."

"All in good time, all in good time," said Giraud. He glanced at Virginia as if this were her cue.

"Yes, Lord Ladbrooke, as long as you've been summoned—" she stared pointedly at Clive who squirmed and ducked his head—"I'm sure you'll want to hear what really happened to Anna and Marie. It's a complicated tale."

"If you've gotten to the bottom of it, yes, by all means." Without taking his eyes off her, he sat down.

Maynard looked with amazement at Ladbrooke's calm expression, then whispered to Cranford, who shook his head in bewilderment. Clive nervously jiggled his knee. Bobbie furrowed her brow, staring up at Virginia, while Leonard wrung his hands as if to control their trembling.

Lord Ladbrooke folded his arms across his chest and leaned back in his chair. "I suppose Giraud—sorry, it's Bayard, isn't it? I suppose you have a great deal to tell us. Since the two Belgian women worked for you."

"What are you talking about?" said Cranford. "Anna worked for me."

"Of course, she did," said Virginia, giving him a slight smile. "For good reason, too, it seems. But," she paused like an actress scrutinizing her audience, "we'll get to that in a moment." She turned to Ladbrooke. "You see, sir, it's really *my* story to tell. Not Giraud's."

"Then by all means, go on, my dear," he said obligingly. Cranford sputtered his objection again, but Ladbrooke shushed him. "Henry, really! Let Mrs. Woolf speak."

Virginia leaned back against the desk, bracing herself. Her cheeks were pink, her eyes flashing.

"My husband, my *dear, dear* friends," she said with a sarcastic edge. "This all began with a few simple questions about the suicide of Sir Henry's governess."

"What the devil?" Cranford interrupted again. "Are you still nattering on about that?"

"Yes, I'm still going on about that. Leonard, you were afraid it was simply my obsession with suicide that led me on. You managed to convince Maynard and Clive, even Roger and Vanessa, that I was on the verge of another breakdown. No, please—" she raised her hand to keep him quiet. "You even had me sedated while you ripped pages from my diary."

"I did not!" he protested.

"The diary entries about Anna Michaux weren't cut out while I was asleep? It had to be you."

"I didn't do it," he objected. "I admit I was reading them, but I was with Dr. Wright. I was worrying about you, then fending off Commissioner Allington. Remember? He wanted to question you."

She put her finger to her lips, thinking. She looked over at Bobbie, then as if deciding to let this drop, she shifted her gaze to Cranford. "You, Sir Henry. You were also opposed to further questions about Anna. A man in your position couldn't afford the publicity, you said. Miss Waters's interest in the case made you especially wary." She paused. "But that wasn't the real reason, was it? You wanted the case kept quiet. Not because of your reputation but because you realized Anna's death wasn't a suicide. It was murder."

"That's ridiculous," said Cranford.

"That's what you all said. Even Scotland Yard. It was so

easy for everyone to dismiss the notion. And do you know why?" She glared at her husband. "Leonard?"

He shook his head, staring down at the floor.

"You allowed it," she said. "You let everyone know about my breakdown, my own attempts at suicide. It never occurred to you that several people were taking an active interest in my questions about Anna. You thought they were simply worried about Virginia's latest problem." Her eyes flashed. "Weren't you just, Maynard—old Pozzo, the Woolfs' dearest friend?"

"Virginia! I was!"

"And I too," insisted Clive as if to head her off.

"Always so convenient, isn't it?" she said. "Virginia imagines she's being followed, she's convinced a woman's been murdered. Well," she drawled out her words, "don't mind her, old boy, she's bonkers. Just calm her down and lead her off to the nursing home. The crazy lady of Bloomsbury, eminently certifiable."

Maynard stood up. "For God's sake, Leonard, stop her." Leonard ignored him. He was staring at Virginia as if he'd recognized an old friend whose name escaped him. "Be quiet, Pozzo," he growled.

"Thank you, Leonard." Virginia strolled behind them to the small table where Cranford displayed the photograph of Anna Michaux with his two daughters. She brought the photograph to the front of the room and placed it on the desk directly opposite Sir Henry.

" 'Poor Anna,' you said, Sir Henry. She'd been so depressed and you hadn't been able to help her. I'm sorry, but I didn't believe you. Call it my novelist's instincts, my feminine intuition. You were too ingratiating. You were trying too hard. Your grief was too obvious."

"Your instincts be damned. My sorrow was real. We were all very, very upset. Why do you think my family's away in the north? They're trying to recover from this terrible tragedy." His eyes were wide and slightly moist. "Anna *did* drown herself, and I *do* blame myself for not helping her."

Virginia gazed at him, startled by his outburst. Then she pointed to the inscription at the bottom of the photograph. "Then how do you explain the suicide note?" she asked with renewed conviction. "Once you'd shown me Anna's handwriting here," she tapped the photograph—"I knew she hadn't written the suicide note."

"But the Yard explained that," objected Cranford. "Allington had a specialist in. Said it was the difference between writing and printing, something like that, but it was still the same hand. . . ." His voice trailed off in thought. "But anyway," he continued, "the Yard reopened the investigation. I certainly didn't stand in their way."

"You could hardly object, not with Lord Ladbrooke insisting." She cast a slight smile in Ladbrooke's direction and he gave her a modest nod. "And there was no question of suicide in the case of Marie Ickx. Commissioner Allington might have liked his 'Belgian Butcher theory,' but poor Inspector Clarke, of MI₅, by the way—" she waited until a few murmurs of surprise had subsided—"yes, Mr. Clarke had different ideas, especially after he'd seen the lists of numbers hidden by Marie Ickx."

She gestured toward Giraud. "Once Bobbie and I realized that Marie and Anna had been sending coded messages, Giraud had to admit the truth: Anna and Marie were both working for him, trying to find out who was sending military secrets to the Germans. That's why Anna took the job with you, Sir Henry. There was reason to believe you were collaborating with the enemy."

"Outrageous!" Cranford shouted. He jumped from his chair and turned to Leonard. "We've all heard your wife's mentally unbalanced, Woolf. But I'll have her up on charges if you don't stop her."

Leonard folded his arms across his chest and slowly shook

his head. "Actually, it seems quite plausible, Sir Henry. Why would she say it if she weren't sure?" He looked back at Virginia.

She said nothing, but they exchanged the bare flicker of a domestic glance in which she expressed her gratitude. Then Virginia clasped her hands together and touched them to her chin as she scrutinized Cranford once more. She seemed genuinely confused by the man's outbursts, but continued nonetheless, her words building slowly.

"You see," she explained, "Giraud had managed to convince the people at the Schaeffer Gallery in Paris that he was their trusted agent, the man called Bayard who was being tailed by MI₅ as a German courier. Still, the Schaeffer agents were always careful to keep the names of their London counterparts a secret."

"So that's why Sam was sure you were a German agent?" interrupted Bobbie, sitting up in her chair and addressing Giraud. "He had the right information but the wrong way around."

Giraud gave her a nod, but before he could say anything, Clive burst out: "Schaeffer Gallery! Collaborators!" He buried his face in his hands, muttering, "Oh, my God."

"That's right, Clive. That's what Roger and I were trying to tell you," said Virginia, picking up the thread of her story. "And that's why Giraud staged my kidnapping."

"Staged?" said Leonard and Bobbie in unison.

Lord Ladbrooke cut them off. "You mean you were never in danger?"

"Lord knows, I was scared—the gun, being slammed into a taxi and all. But Giraud took me to the Litchfield Arms, and we worked out the real story. You see, Sir Henry, Giraud thought he had more evidence against you. Evidence he'd taken from your chauffeur—"

"But my chauffeur was killed—you madman, you were the one!"

Above the cries of outrage, Giraud said: "It was necessary. All of you, quiet. Just listen."

"I know. It shocked me, too," said Virginia. "But let me finish. Your chauffeur, Sir Henry, was making a delivery. He was carrying something. Giraud didn't understand why until—" she held up three sheets of paper she'd retrieved from her bag—"he took these from you, Clive, back at the Omega."

"The painting orders!" Clive exclaimed. His face drained of color.

"Quite. The ones you were to present as a purchase order at the Schaeffer Gallery. But we didn't know its precise meaning until Giraud showed me what the chauffeur was carrying." She looked at Cranford.

"I didn't—" he objected.

"I know," she said, cutting him off and reaching into her bag again. This time she brought out a book which she thrust in front of them. It was blue, its title, *Art,* spelled out in white letters across the cover.

"That's my book!" exclaimed Clive in bewilderment.

"Confusing, isn't it? Because you didn't give it to Sir Henry. You gave it—" she paused and turned dramatically— "to this gentleman here. To Lord Ladbrooke!"

Ladbrooke met her gaze while calmly flicking an imaginary piece of lint from his trouser knee. "When Sir Henry's chauffeur came round to my house yesterday with some papers to be signed," he said, "I simply asked him to drop the book at Gordon Square. It was convenient. That's all. What are you muddling up now?" He looked at Virginia with pity and forbearance.

The casual reply stunned her for a moment. "You know what I'm getting at," she said.

She'd been controlled and methodical. But now she felt her face grow hot. "You stupid, stupid man. You thought you were so clever, forcing Sir Henry's chauffeur and his governess to work for you. To spy on him!"

"Ladbrooke?" exclaimed Bobbie, shrinking back against Leonard who was wide-eyed in shock. Clive and Maynard sputtered, staring at Ladbrooke. Cranford, meanwhile, had leapt from his chair, shaking his head.

"You can't be serious," he shouted. "This is too ridiculous. First me. Then Alex. . . ." He looked from his mentor to Virginia and then back again. Ladbrooke remained silent, unperturbed. Cranford turned on Giraud: "You! You're behind all of this. You're lying to protect yourself. I . . . I'll," he stammered.

"You'll sit down!" Giraud gave him a frozen stare. "Hear Mrs. Woolf out."

"Right, Henry," said Ladbrooke. "Do calm yourself." He seemed oblivious to the storm swirling around him.

"I know it's true," Virginia went on, aware that everyone was watching her as she held Ladbrooke's gaze. "I deciphered your message. You didn't change the basic method. You made up your so-called painting order, lists of numbers in three columns. I recognized it immediately, but anyone else would believe that Clive was simply taking a list of orders and provenances to Paris. How innocent it would seem. Only Clive was also supposed to bring his own book to the Schaeffer Gallery—" she looked at Clive who nodded—"and the agents there would put two and two together. *Voilà!*" She snapped her fingers. "The Germans have the details of the tank offensive. It's all here in code, these numbers keyed to Clive's book."

"Oh, Christ! You . . . you're right, Virginia." Clive turned on Ladbrooke. "You bastard, you had me carrying military secrets—"

"More than that, Clive," said Virginia. "The message in the painting lists also ordered your death. Look." She handed him the three sheets on which she'd written the decoded letters next to the numbers. Clive read through it and blanched. Virginia went on. "Ladbrooke also ordered the death of Bayard," she gestured at Giraud, "since Ladbrooke

· 252 ·

had discovered he was a double agent, really loyal to Belgium. So, Sir Henry, shocking though it may be, there's no doubt. The proof is there." She pointed to the pages in Clive's lap. Clive nodded, too frightened to speak.

A swell of confused shouts washed over them as they all watched Lord Ladbrooke rise slowly from his chair.

"Quiet!" he ordered, his voice cutting through the noise. He turned to face Virginia, a look of amused congratulation in his eyes. He spoke almost casually. "Well, Mrs. Woolf. *I* never thought you were mad . . . and in fact I'm the one person who never doubted you."

"How true," said Virginia, honing the edge of his irony. "And ever so eager to help when you heard I questioned the suicide, going so far, even, as to take my side against the Yard. But, of course, now we all know why, don't we?" She paused, her eyes narrowing. "You were afraid. You had to know how much Bobbie and I had uncovered. You had us followed, you had us threatened. And when people got in your way—like Clarke, like Anna and Marie—"

"Clarke and Marie, yes, I had them removed," he interrupted. "As for Anna, I still don't know what happened to her. Just as you suspected, she did work for me. Well, perhaps it really was suicide." He thought for a moment, then gave a slight shrug. "No matter. That's not important to the plans. Final success is what counts. And I mean to ensure that tonight."

His tone had changed, as if force of will had obliterated any hint of hesitation. Everyone heard it, the coldness of his voice, the menace of his words.

Clive and Maynard glanced at each other. Cranford gripped the arms of his chair, his knuckles white. As if by instinct, Virginia drew back toward Giraud, who steadied her by putting his hands on her shoulders. Bobbie sat rigidly, her breath coming in short, fast gulps as Leonard hugged his arms to his sides.

Ladbrooke ignored them all and turned to Giraud. "As soon as Bell told me you'd taken the painting orders, I knew whose side you were on. I also knew that it was only a matter of time before *you,* Mrs. Woolf, decoded them and exposed me." He paused and bared his teeth in a smile. "So did you really think I'd come here unprepared? Hardly."

He gestured around the room. "Of course, it will appear a terrible tragedy, all of you destroyed by another Irish bombing. But then the Yard knows the Sinn Fein are ruthless. Remember the bombing at Swan and Edgar's last week? And the Irish have threatened you before, haven't they, Henry?"

Cranford blanched. "You can't be serious, Alex!"

"My God, you *are* vile," said Virginia, shuddering at the memory of the cavernous pit she'd had to step round in front of the department store.

Ladbrooke ignored her. "My men are setting the fuses now."

"You won't get away with this," shouted Cranford. His eyes betrayed his desperation. He looked to Giraud as if the Belgian might save them.

Giraud showed no sign of fear, but gave a slight nod to Virginia. As if she were rousing herself, she stood straighter and looked over at Bobbie and Leonard who were still cowering together. "Look here, Ladbrooke," she said, trying to sound brave. "At least tell us *why* you're doing this."

He seemed eager to explain. With a sneer at Cranford, he said, "None of this would have happened if Sir Henry had done what I suggested." He turned to the munitions maker. "Didn't I warn you Mrs. Woolf would cause trouble? I advised you against talking to her. To avoid publicity, I said. But you talked to her anyway."

"Then you *are* involved in this, Cranford?" Maynard cried.

"I'm not. Alex said I couldn't afford a scandal. . . ." Cranford's body was quaking as if gripped by a terrible palsy.

"Oh, but you were very cooperative," said Ladbrooke. "Just as you were, Keynes. All of you were willing to discuss the latest decisions taken in your meetings. And what you wouldn't tell me, Henry, your chauffeur and Anna found out. Remember how eager you were when I suggested you hire them? When I said that you needed a full staff of servants?" He laughed, shaking his head as if at the stupidity of mankind. "Then, too, I arranged your art purchases through Keynes, set up contracts in Sweden for your postwar expansion on the Continent. Didn't I just, and you never objected, did you?"

He turned toward Clive, who flinched. "And you, Bell, you were just as eager. Practically begging me to send you to Paris. And when you saw Sir Henry's chauffeur give me his valise, you didn't go to the police now, did you?" Bell flushed a deep red and bent his head in remorse. "Oh, no," said Ladbrooke, "you sounded me out. A touch of blackmail, one might say, and I was only too happy to oblige with a buying trip to Paris, as you'll recall."

Clive sat with his head still bowed. Virginia felt sorry for him, and for Maynard, too. All her anger was directed now at Ladbrooke; the snideness of his tone, the small, predatory pleasures he was taking, it was disgusting, as yet the fullest measure of what the man was capable of.

"But why?" she cried. "Why are you helping the Germans?"

"It's not that simple," he said in a tutorial voice. "What I'm doing is necessary for progress. For survival."

"A German victory?"

He shook his head. "Hardly. What I've done is bring together eminent men of every nation, businessmen, economists and financiers committed heart and soul to a new order —an order superseding all national affiliations. Our objective is to ensure a prosperous and efficient postwar society, nothing more, nothing less."

"Economists like Maynard, I suppose," said Virginia.

"Yes, Mrs. Woolf, men like Keynes and Sir Henry. They've been working for the same thing, although doubtless they would have objected to my methods if they'd known."

"For this you betray your friends? Your country? Murder innocents? Why?"

Quietly, almost modestly, he said, "I am saving England. The war must continue for another year, until our group consolidates its power." He paused, giving her a grim smile. "A British victory now and we'd all be stopped. That's why there cannot be a successful Allied offensive. The terms of peace must protect financial interests on both sides. A German defeat now would destroy Europe's economic future—reparations, subsidies, partisan forgiveness of national debts. Disastrous. You agree, don't you, Keynes?"

The economist refused to meet his eyes.

"He doesn't care to admit it, Mrs. Woolf, but he's been saying the very thing. I assure you, my ideas are simply the logical extension of his own."

"Bloody rubbish," Keynes burst out. "That's not what I meant at all."

"And Henry, you too agreed in principle," said Ladbrooke, ignoring Keynes. "Of course, a little profit here, another contract there, all helped convince you."

"And the ends justify your means?" Virginia suddenly started to laugh. "Don't any of you recognize this? It's Nietzsche's worn-out melody played on an out-of-tune piano." She glanced round the room at their frightened faces.

Ladbrooke folded his arms across his chest. "Very good, Mrs. Woolf. I agree that Christian morality is fit only for shopkeepers—"

"And Englishmen, and women, and cows, too, as I remember the passage. A charming sentiment. I for one will gladly stay on the side of the cows, even the shopkeepers." Her voice lost its flippancy. "That's been my point from the beginning. Ladbrooke manipulated all of you because you're

· 256 ·

interested in power. You want to dominate and control, whether it be women or men, servants or countries." She gave Maynard a pitying look, then turned to Leonard, "Now do you see why I call it betrayal? Because of your own needs you've all helped him. And you, Sir Henry, you tried to cover up your governess' murder—"

"But I told you, I didn't know. I thought it was suicide. Alex told me it just wouldn't look proper, one's servant killing herself."

For a moment, Virginia seemed stymied. "You really didn't know, did you?"

He shook his head.

She wheeled around and glowered at Ladbrooke. Giraud stepped within inches of her but said nothing.

"You've said quite enough, Mrs. Woolf," Ladbrooke glared back at her.

"What's the matter?" she shouted. "Don't you like the truth? You're a monster!" She caught her breath, knowing she had to go on.

Ladbrooke's normally pale face had flushed to a deep red and he seemed ready to strike her.

"You see?" she said. "I hold a mirror up to you and you cringe at the sight."

She stopped, thinking she heard footsteps outside. She'd had to stall for time, and it had worked. But who would ever have believed the arrogance of this man? She'd guessed that Clive would tell Ladbrooke that Giraud had not only kidnapped her but taken the painting orders. And once she'd deciphered Ladbrooke's message, she and Giraud had planned this gathering, making sure as well that at the right moment Kell would hear Ladbrooke's confession.

And Kell must be at the door now, she thought, falling limply against Giraud as if she'd finally taken her last hurdle in a steeplechase, looking straight ahead, without paying any mind to the crowd. The man they'd expected had arrived. She stared at the door, waiting. By now he'd surely heard enough. She sighed in relief as the door opened.

Standing in the doorway was not the head of MI₅ but Nigel Allington.

Where was Kell? Stunned, she turned to Giraud who, with more calm than she could muster, put his arm around her shoulders. Vaguely she heard Leonard cry, "Thank God, Commissioner! This maniac was about to blow us up."

Virginia stiffened as Ladbrooke walked toward the door. "Hello, Nigel," she heard him say.

Suddenly she saw it all. And although she sensed what would happen, her feet wouldn't move, she had no voice.

Giraud had seen it, too. He grasped her shoulder roughly and spun her around, pulling her against his chest.

✦ 35 ✦

A roar filled the room.

Bobbie screamed. Leonard grabbed her hand. Maynard ducked to the floor as Cranford sprang from his chair, Clive dodging behind him.

A second shot followed the first. Bobbie screamed again. Giraud had sheltered Virginia against him and she felt the roughness of his jacket, then the pounding of his heart. She was dazed but her mind was racing.

Releasing her, Giraud went to Ladbrooke.

The aristocrat was clutching his chest and had lurched against a table, falling to the carpet. Virginia watched as he tried to get to his knees, but, with a moan, he now collapsed. Motionless, he lay face down on the floor.

Giraud crouched down, examining him. "He's dead," he announced to the room.

Allington held his gun limply at his side. "Well, the bloody fool left me no choice." As Giraud stood up, Allington leveled the gun once more. "All right, Bayard, you're coming with me. You're under arrest. The rest of you," he said to the others without taking his eyes from Giraud, "wait here for my men. We'll need to question you."

"Where's Kell?" demanded Virginia, rushing forward, oblivious to Ladbrooke's body. "You came here alone?"

"Please, Mrs. Woolf, step aside," said Allington.

She stood her ground. "Don't move!" she said to Giraud over her shoulder, then called out to the others: "Did any of you tell Allington about this meeting?" There were murmurs among them, but they all shook their heads. Giraud muttered in French under his breath, but she didn't quite hear it.

"So *Ladbrooke* must have told you," she turned to Allington. "That's why he was so calm when you came in, Commissioner. He had nothing to fear from you. And he was about to say so." Her words rattled against each other, as she said breathlessly, "And that's why you shot him. To shut him up. Before he gave you away." She paused, staring at him. "And you . . . *you* were at the hotel the night Clarke was killed, weren't you? I remember now. A prostitute told me a Yard man threatened to arrest her." Catching her breath, she realized something else and exclaimed, "And I'm the one who stupidly told you about the meeting when I gave you the message for Clarke."

"But this afternoon he denied knowing about it," interrupted Bobbie excitedly. "You made a point of it with Kell on the phone, Commissioner."

"From the beginning," Virginia stumbled on the heels of Bobbie's words, *"you* tried to close the investigation, Commissioner, I know you did. You probably ordered Anna's cremation, too." Her voice rose in excitement. "Don't you all see? He's one of them. Clarke must have suspected it. That's why MI$_5$ assigned him to Special Branch."

Allington grabbed Virginia by the wrists. "That's enough!" he shouted.

Giraud tried to push him aside but Allington was too fast. Yet as he pulled Virginia away she broke his grip. Suddenly she clutched her chest and fell to the floor, moaning.

"My God!" Bobbie screamed. Leonard rushed to Virginia, pushing Allington away as he knelt down beside her. "Look what you've done," he shouted.

Virginia was writhing on the floor. "Fear no more the heat of the sun," she ranted, her voice rising. "Fear no more. The code, the code's the key." Her eyes were closed now, her head rolling from side to side: "Falling down, down into the flame, the flame in the flower, the flame in the flower." Her eyes fluttered open. She stared up at Leonard as if she didn't recognize him.

"Virginia!" he cried. "Can you hear me?" He was smoothing her brow.

She moaned again. "Anna, Anna. He burned you, burned you in the flame of the flower."

As if unaware of what was happening, Giraud watched Allington. The Commissioner was staring down at Virginia's twitching figure. "This proves it, Woolf," he announced officiously. "You'll have to have her certified. I told you she was mad. And now this. 'Fear no more,'" he repeated with a scornful shake of his head.

Virginia began to babble in Greek. Bobbie knelt beside her, too, and tried to hold her flailing hands.

"For God's sake," Leonard shouted up at Allington. "Do something. Ring Dr. Wright, Maurice Wright in Harley Street."

"No, no, there isn't time," said Allington. "Put her in my car. I can take her to hospital."

He turned toward the door, then stopped.

There stood Sir Vernon Kell with two of his men from MI$_5$.

Allington backed slowly away as Kell motioned one of his men to attend to Ladbrooke's body.

"Right, Vernon," said Allington, recovering his poise. "If you'll see to that, I'll take care of Mrs. Woolf. She's had a fit. Poor woman . . . found all this too bloodcurdling!"

"Bloodcurdling! Indeed!" Virginia struggled up from

the floor. Ignoring Leonard's attempt to hold her back, she came forward to stand beside Giraud. "We expected you a little earlier, Sir Vernon. Hence my feigned 'mad woman of Bloomsbury'!"

Her face was flushed now as she turned to Allington: "And you've just made a dreadful mistake, Commissioner. You think I found it too 'bloodcurdling.' 'Bloodcurdling' is it? That's far too melodramatic for a Yard man. In fact, it isn't *your* word at all. It's *mine.* I wrote it in my diary. About Anna's death. So you must have cut the pages from my diary, you must have studied them carefully." She paused. "I'm sorry, Leonard. Of course, it wasn't you. It was *you.*" She turned back to Allington. "And with your weird habit of repeating what people say, you remembered, didn't you?"

"What?" interrupted Bobbie, the reporter once more.

" 'Bloodcurdling.' That's the word I used in my diary. I said *The Mail* ran the story of Anna's suicide because they had nothing else more bloodcurdling—"

"Nigel! Of course!" Cranford fell heavily into the armchair. "That's why you wanted Anna's case closed. I thought you were just being helpful. Didn't want to put me and my family through it. So that's why you and Alex kept telling me not to talk about the suicide. And Mrs. Woolf was right. You had to shoot Alex before he could give you away."

With evident relief Clive and Maynard returned to their chairs, their eyes darting between Cranford and Allington. Kell stood off to one side, smoothing his mustache and watching Allington as Bobbie and Leonard reached Virginia's side. The three of them stared at Allington, awaiting his reaction.

Giraud, however, wasn't looking at the Yard man. Instead, he fixed Virginia with a stare, as if she were the only other person in the room. "You were always right about Anna's suicide," he said. "Allington and Ladbrooke realized she knew too much."

Virginia nodded, but a puzzled look crossed her face. Just then, however, she was diverted by Allington's heavy breathing. His face had folded in on itself. His mouth worked frantically without uttering a word. For a moment he seemed paralyzed. Then he bolted, crashing past Bobbie and Leonard to the French doors behind Cranford's desk.

One of Kell's men had drawn his gun but Kell pushed him aside, watching Allington disappear into the darkness of the terrace.

Everyone ran toward the open doors, shouting. Leonard turned back. Seeing Kell still rooted in his spot, he called out, "Good God, man, he's getting away!" The others turned too, begging Kell to do something.

"My men are out there. They'll bring him in," Kell reassured them above their clamor.

Then a shot rang out, stunning them into silence. They heard the sound of running feet echoing on the terrace, followed by shouts. Kell pushed through, ordering them back as he hurried by. But Bobbie scrambled after him. Virginia started forward, too, only to be restrained by Leonard.

As the sounds of the scuffle subsided, Bobbie quickly reappeared.

"Mr. Josephs!" Virginia exclaimed.

And indeed, with an arm around Bobbie's shoulders, there stood the rumpled Irishman.

"What happened out there?" Giraud demanded of him.

"Chap's gone and shot himself."

"But you?" Virginia asked. "What were you doing on the terrace?"

"Waiting with Kell's people," Sam replied. "He's been holding me for my own 'protection.' When you and Giraud cooked up this meeting," he gave her a slight smile, then turned to Bobbie, "he kindly let me come along. Told him I'd like to be in on *your* story, dear."

Virginia stared at him, ignoring Bobbie. The full impact

of the evening was just hitting her. The violence, the horror of it all. "But Allington?" she burst out. "He's dead?"

Josephs nodded. "For a Yard man, Mrs. Woolf, it was really the only honorable thing to do."

❈ 36 ❈

Leonard and Virginia were driven back to Hogarth House at dawn. They'd all been questioned individually in MI₅'s Whitehall offices, then sent home.

Leonard closed the front door and helped Virginia off with her cape. "Come. Sit with me," he said. "No. Here, beside me." He pointed to the sofa before she could take her usual chair.

She sat down, giving him a questioning look. He put his arm around her. The gesture was tentative, but she felt comforted by it and rested her head against his shoulder.

"I want you to know, I'm very proud. I mean—well, I didn't have a chance to tell you. Kell says you saved the Cambrai offensive. They brought it off this morning." He caressed her shoulder. "You must be exhausted."

As if by instinct she pulled away. He laughed, guiding her head back to his shoulder. "Don't worry. I'm not telling you to go to bed or that you need your rest. I'm not even ordering you a glass of milk. I've learned. If you hadn't ignored my instructions, Ladbrooke and Allington would still be plotting to betray the Allies. And God knows what might have happened to Clive and Maynard."

Tears brimmed in her eyes. It was the closest he'd come to an apology in all their years of marriage.

"Thank you," she whispered. "That matters a great deal." She sighed. A moment passed. "I don't know if I really care about the Cambrai tank offensive or this damn war. And I don't know if I'd ever want to go through something like this again. But I do care about us, about the way you see me. I don't want my health to be a screen, keeping you out or locking me away."

Leonard stroked her hair. "But let me worry sometimes?"

"Of course. You wouldn't be Leonard if you didn't."

They sat in silence for a few more minutes. Then Leonard roused himself. "I'm going up for a nap. Promise me one thing, though. Don't ever stage another fit. It was awful. You damn near gave me a heart attack."

She laughed. "At least it got everyone's attention."

Later, after a bath, she sat in the dining room drinking coffee and staring out the front window at the astonishingly bright sunshine. She already missed Bobbie. They'd been separated at MI₅ and hadn't had a chance to talk. As much as Leonard's words had warmed her and given her hope, she needed Bobbie and Giraud too. She was not a single self for whom there was one all-consuming love. No, she told herself, she had various selves; some had been called forth by Bobbie, others by Giraud. That was love, too, but she would probably never see them again. She felt dispirited and empty, and to console herself, she asked Lottie to bring her diary from her bag in the living room. The missing pages were another reminder of loss as well; she turned quickly to a fresh page. "*I was glad to come home,*" she wrote,

& feel my real life coming back again—I mean life here with L. Solitary is not quite the right word; one's personality seems to echo out across space, when he's not there to enclose all one's vibrations.

This is not very intelligibly written; but the feeling itself is a strange one—as if marriage were a completing of the instrument, & the sound of one alone penetrates as if it were a violin robbed of its orchestra or piano.

She closed her diary as Lottie brought in the morning post. On top of the usual circulars and printing orders, she saw a thin blue envelope. It was Elise Robert's reply to the letter she'd sent last week. She tore it open.

In a few brief sentences, Elise described, as Virginia had requested, the man who'd identified himself to her as Inspector Brown: he had large brown eyes, dark hair that needed cutting and—Virginia ran her fingers along her cheek—a scar on the side of his face. So it *had* been Giraud, she thought. But why had he been so anxious to recover Anna's copy of Michelet? Because it was their code book? Or because he knew Anna had also used the book as a basis for her messages to the Germans? And why had he hidden his identity from Elise?

But even more startling was Elise's final paragraph: Anna had definitely known that her mother and father were alive; Giraud knew it too. In fact, Elise said, as a last resort she'd written to Giraud last summer in Le Havre, asking him to help find them.

Virginia looked up from the letter with a frown. The pieces of the puzzle hadn't yet fallen into place. Why had Giraud continued to lie about Anna's parents? Then, too, there was Ladbrooke's comment last night; he'd denied knowing anything about Anna's death. Virginia was troubled by something she could not yet put her finger on. She concentrated: what was making her uneasy? Was it Giraud? What was it he had said last night? Suddenly she remembered. Giraud had made a point of saying that Ladbrooke and Allington realized Anna knew too much.

The ringing of the doorbell broke into her confused

thoughts. She stood up as Lottie led Bobbie into the dining room. The American was grinning, although the blue shadows under her eyes betrayed her lack of sleep.

"The pussycat's swallowed a canary?" teased Virginia.

Bobbie spread out the newspaper she was carrying, the morning edition of *The Daily Mail.* Emblazoned in huge type was the banner headline: *Boche Collaborators Foiled by Scotland Yard.* Above the two-column story was the byline: *B. A. Waters.*

"B. A.?" asked Virginia.

"Not to give my sex away."

Virginia laughed scornfully, but as Bobbie refused to see the irony, she relented: "But why *The Mail?*"

"Sam arranged it as my reward. He admits he should have been more candid with you. He didn't realize what a good investigator you'd be." Bobbie smiled to herself. "He can't say it himself, Virginia, but he's really sorry." She shrugged happily. "And when Draper axed me this morning, Sam offered me a position at *The Mail.* I may even get sent to the Front."

So it had all worked out for her, Virginia thought. She had her story and Sam Josephs, too. No fears, no doubts, nothing clouded the young American's triumph.

"Let's see the story," said Virginia. Bowing her head to hide her awkwardness, she pulled the newspaper closer and began to read:

Wednesday, 21 November, London—Lord Alex Ladbrooke (58), a peer of the realm widely respected for his government service, was killed today while resisting arrest just after midnight in a townhouse in Belgravia. After months of investigation by MI5 and Special Branch, Ladbrooke had been identified as a German agent. During the struggle that ensued, Deputy Commissioner Nigel Allington of Scotland Yard was killed in action.

"Townhouse in Belgravia?" repeated Virginia. "Allington killed 'in action'?"

"Kell insisted. The story had to be cleared with Whitehall."

Virginia turned back to reading. The ensuing paragraphs described the intricacies of Ladbrooke's selling military information to the enemy:

> ... information to which he had access by virtue of his political and financial affiliations. Through his association with the Schaeffer Gallery in Paris, a known center of German intelligence agents, Lord Ladbrooke attempted to establish a network of collaborators in Britain while amassing a personal fortune in foreign bank securities, business contracts and priceless paintings. According to Special Branch, his activities had long been under surveillance and information passed to the enemy had been carefully constructed both to mislead the Germans and to trap the conspirators.
>
> According to the same informed sources, Lord Ladbrooke had tried unsuccessfully to recruit agents among the most respected citizens of the realm. Failing that, he employed a number of known criminals whom the authorities have already apprehended.

" 'Known criminals'?"

"The clerk at the hotel. Others too, like Cranford's chauffeur and those two terrible hoodlums that attacked us in Sam's flat—supplied by Allington. He kept a rogues' gallery, from his days running Dartmoor."

Virginia shuddered at the memory of the fat man with his breath on her neck. "But what about the murders—Anna and Marie? And Clarke?" She roused herself. "They're not even mentioned."

"Kell again."

Virginia read the rest of the story, her mouth set grimly. Much of it was MI$_5$'s official statement that the enemy had received no vital information. The final paragraph was a tribute to Allington, praising the policeman for his ultimate sacrifice "on behalf of the realm."

"My God!" she exclaimed. "The traitor comes off a hero. And what about Cranford? Even if he was tricked by Ladbrooke, he was still involved." She stared at Bobbie, her eyes blazing. "How could you write this?"

"I had no choice. Otherwise Kell would have arranged for someone else to do the story."

"Maybe that would have been just as well."

"That's not fair, Virginia. . . ." Her voice quavered. "I wanted you to be pleased. This is an important story, you have to understand that."

"I can't pretend. It's all on their terms. Whitehall forced you to lie."

Bobbie began to weep. Virginia watched her for a moment, then softened her tone. "I care about you, I want you to succeed. But if being a reporter means telling lies, perhaps it's not worth it. You have to consider what it's likely to do to you. Men are trained to covet success and power. But we women have more of a choice. Let's protect our real loyalties. If that means having principles, so be it."

Bobbie took her time folding up the newspaper. She studied the page as if a reply was buried there. "That's all very well for you to say, Virginia. But you can't be a reporter and shut yourself away from the world."

"That's not what I want, either for you *or* for me. But don't let them bully you out of your own principles. It never works. Believe me." She stopped. There was no point in lecturing. Bobbie would learn it on her own.

Suddenly Lottie appeared at the door, slightly flustered, a visitor standing behind her. Without waiting to be announced the man entered, a handsomely tailored gentleman in a grey suit and so closely shaven the scar down his cheek stood out like a corded pink welt.

"Still sleuthing?" Giraud gave them both an uneasy smile. "I gather you kept Kell and his censors busy, Miss Waters."

"He told you?" she asked with a sidelong glance at Virginia. "The official version—" She gestured towards the paper on the table.

"Of course. The government can't have the public worrying about traitors in the upper class or at the Yard."

"But why omit Cranford's name?"

"Because Cranford agreed to supply the names and details, the contracts that Ladbrooke arranged for him."

"He'll simply go back to making barrels of money!" Virginia muttered. "No one will ever know the truth."

"The government needs him to manufacture guns."

"And journalists to manufacture lies." Once more Virginia glanced at Bobbie. The young woman refused to meet her eyes.

For a moment they were all silent. Uncomfortable with the tension in the room, Giraud looked back and forth between the two women. "I just came round to say goodbye," he said. "I didn't mean to intrude, but I wanted to thank you both. We'd never have suspected Ladbrooke if you hadn't realized those painting orders were a code keyed to Bell's book."

"I still find it hard to believe," Bobbie said. "Ladbrooke actually thought he'd take over the government."

Virginia shook her head in exasperation. "I've been trying to tell you. Ladbrooke was a fanatic but his ideas are only an exaggerated version of what one hears over dinner in Mayfair. The way Englishmen are traditionally educated, conspiracies are inevitable."

"But to think—"

"Inevitable. It's not conspiracies so much as the obsession with power and competition. The ethic which permits one to subvert the rules."

"Aren't you overstating it?" asked Giraud.

"No," she insisted. "It's why I've always distrusted politics. It's all based on ambition, domination. The seeds of it are in every man, everywhere—in England or Germany or America."

Her face was sad. Why couldn't she stop? she asked herself. The tide of loss and loneliness she'd felt this morning was carrying her to sea, far away from these people who'd become important to her. Each time they approached she sent them away with her bitterness.

Giraud turned and walked into the foyer.

"No, wait—" She got up from the table.

He was back in a minute. He held out a book to her. It was a copy of Joyce's *Portrait of the Artist as a Young Man*.

"Kell gave it to you?" she asked.

He shook his head. "No. I took it when I saw you'd fainted in the alley."

"So you *were* there. I didn't dream it." She sat back down, suddenly more tired than she'd realized.

He nodded, pushing the book toward her. "I've inscribed it."

She opened the flyleaf. Something flickered in the depths of her eyes but far back and dimly, as if it had been there for some while but was only now coming to the surface. She looked up, her face pinched.

"I'm sorry, Bobbie but I must speak to Henri alone."

❧ 37 ❧

As Virginia lit a cigarette her hand was trembling. She read Giraud's inscription aloud: " 'With gratitude for the work you've done for Belgium'." She stared at him, pained. " 'Work'?" she repeated. "You shouldn't have used that word."

"Perhaps I wanted you to know," he said.

"I wouldn't have, but for that one word. When Allington showed me Anna's suicide note, I realized Anna hadn't written it. The letters were too rounded, broad and thick. Like these. 'No mother, No father, No *work*'." She emphasized the last word. "And the 'w' and the 'k' had the same strange, curlicued tails. Just as you've written them here." She let her eyes fall to the inscription in front of her. "Why did you do it? It's senseless . . . unless . . ."

"Go on, say it. Unless I killed Anna. Yes, then. I killed her when I learned she'd become a double agent. I wrote the suicide note and pinned it to her dress."

Virginia's face was a ghostly white. She seemed to have stopped breathing.

Giraud leaned over the table towards her, pressing his knuckles against the surface. "Look at me. Yes! It was me. It was necessary."

"Why didn't you tell the police?"

"Kell knows. He also knows the reason. Why do you think no one was charged with Anna's murder?"

She was sobbing now. Giraud raised his voice to force her to listen.

"I made it look like a suicide so that there'd be no investigation. I wrote, 'No mother, No father, No work,' so the police wouldn't try to track down her parents. I even hoped they wouldn't realize she worked for Cranford, since we suspected he was involved. But most of all, I didn't want the collaborators to guess that I knew about Mrs. Ottlinger, only I didn't realize that Allington was one of them, covering up Anna's death for his own reasons."

Her head had come up. "Mrs. Ottlinger!" she exclaimed through her tears. She stopped, remembering. She'd nearly stumbled on it before. But now the two faces were fixed in her mind. "Mrs. Ottlinger was Anna's mother?" she said. "And that's how Anna was forced to work for Ladbrooke?"

He nodded. "The Germans arrested both parents when her father fired at troops crossing his farm. The mother was brought here through Ladbrooke's Relief Committee. They gave her a new name, set her up at the tea shop, all the while using the father as hostage. Then they went to work on Anna. Ladbrooke needed information beyond what Sir Henry was giving him. Anna had no choice. But neither did we."

"So you killed her!" she said in a rising wail. "Why didn't you protect her? Go to the Yard?"

"Listen to me!" he said. His eyes were black stones in his pale face. "What alternative was there? I couldn't trust Anna with my life." He touched the scar on the side of his face. "This was a part of it, too. When I fled Brussels a German cavalry officer tried to stop me: he used his bayonet. I killed him. There was no time to consider the morality of it. So yes, I learned to kill. And afterwards I learned not to think about it. I learned to endure loneliness, to live a life of disguises and masks. And to do what's necessary."

"Murder's never necessary—"

"In your world, perhaps. I had to protect our organization, however. She knew I'd infiltrated Schaeffer's group in Paris."

"And that's why you went to Elise Robert, posing as Inspector Brown?" She pointed to Elise's letter on the table. "I wrote her to ask for a description. It was you."

"I had to know if Anna had said anything to Elise, or sent anything which could give me away."

Virginia stood up, rigid with anger. "Don't give me bloody reasons! I won't sanction it. All these lies, all this violence. I hate it. It's the same whether it's you or Ladbrooke! You all say it so easily: 'It's necessary! That's the way it must be done!' Well, I'm sorry. No, I don't accept it."

Wearily, he rubbed his eyes. "Again, I don't have the luxury of your high-minded, philosophical position. You scold Miss Waters, you condemn me. But life's more complicated."

He took her by the shoulders. "Don't you see? I hate all of it, but for the time being we must live with it. Call it finite but inescapable. Hate it, but don't hide from the reality of it. When the war's over, we'll all have changed."

"That's what I'm so desperately afraid of," she said. She looked into his eyes and saw the sadness there. For all his rationalization, he still had to live with Anna's memory.

Suddenly he embraced her. "I'm afraid, too," he muttered. Then he kissed her, his mouth trembling over hers. She resisted. But his arms were warm and comforting, and she clasped her own arms around his neck and lifted her face to his. Her lips parted slightly. She felt his strength engulf her and she returned his kiss so hungrily as to surprise herself.

He stopped and pulled away. He took her hands from his neck and held them for a moment, looking down into her glittering eyes. "I must go. Someday I hope you'll understand. Perhaps when the war is over. . . ." He left the sentence unfinished.

"Perhaps. . . . But as you say, then we'll all be changed. There'll be all the memories, the ghosts—" She didn't trust her voice to go on. He nodded solemnly, then rushed from the room. Swaying slightly she reached out to the back of a chair to steady herself. When she heard the front door slam shut, she stared out the window, watching him. He gave a brief wave, then walked up the street, his head bowed. After a moment she went to her study and collapsed in her armchair.

He had asked her to understand. Now she thought she did—but in the red heat of emotion, not the cold light of truth. His intensity had conquered her. She hated the idea of Anna's murder but she couldn't hate him. Not when he grieved so, when he admitted he was afraid. But still he went on, she thought. Just as they all must—she and Leonard, Clive and Maynard and Nessa. And Bobbie, too. He had been right. She'd been too hard on all of them, though perhaps too, finally, everyone's necessity was no greater than her own.

So Giraud had taught her this much: she had to go on as well. The war might alter everyone's values but her personal fight had to be on her own terms. It was what she'd told Bobbie. She wouldn't wage it by adopting men's ways, not by repeating the worn-out conventions like a broken record. No, she thought, taking up her writing board and resting it across her lap. Only as an outsider, alone with her writing, could she remain as faithful to her vision as Giraud was to his.

She wiped away a tear, remembering the frightening things he'd said—he'd learned to kill, learned to accept loneliness. She shook her head to clear it. But so, too, had she learned something in the past fortnight. She could be pushed to the edge and still come back; she could endure pain and loneliness and fear and still survive. But her source of strength was here, in a room of her own.

Soon she was hard at work. By midafternoon, she'd created a new character for the novel she'd set aside two weeks ago. A young woman, she would call her "Mary"—a plain, substantial name. "Datchet" would be her family name. She said it aloud, pleased that it sounded blunt, like "dash it." It suited the character who would be cynical and brusque, a little like Bobbie, she thought, spirited and determined as well. She would be independent, have her own flat in London, and earn a living. Valuing integrity and personal freedom above all, Mary would have a unique talent for understanding the feelings of others. Yes, thought Virginia, it was a good balance for her other character, Katharine; the two women would be as opposite but as inextricably related as night and day.

The afternoon light was fading. As Virginia reached over to turn on the lamp beside her, the image of a magical moment, a globe of time, came to her: She would use it at the end of the book. Mary's room would be seen from the street below, a sanctuary but a beacon as well. She began to write, her pen racing across the page. She felt as if she'd finally glimpsed the elusive meaning of these last strange weeks:

From below the golden light of Mary's large steady lamp was an expression . . . of something impersonal and serene in the spirit of the woman within . . . it was a sign of triumph shining there for ever, not to be extinguished this side of the grave.

She paused. The phrase "this side of the grave" took her by surprise. Too morbid but still not inappropriate, and she dipped her pen into the inkwell to continue.

Suddenly the windows began to rattle and the house shuddered on its foundation. She could hear sounds of a heavy motor accompanied by excited shouts and the pealing of bells. She hurried to the already open front door.

From the stoop she saw her servants running down the street to join a crowd gathering on Richmond Green, where a massive brown and green armored vehicle was circling the grass. Soon it came to rest. Across its front was fastened a roll of what appeared to be wooden slats. At its top a long cannon protruded from a slowly rotating turret. Then the turret stopped. Its lid swung open and out popped a soldier like a jack-in-the-box. Visible only from the waist up, the man began to address the crowd with expansive gestures, using a loud-hailer.

Nellie and Lottie turned. Catching sight of Virginia on the front steps, they ran back to her.

"Sorry, mum," said Lottie. "I expect you're wanting tea."

"There's no hurry," Virginia said. "What's that chap going on about?"

"It's a tank, the Tommy says, with things on it to look like a hedge. He calls it a 'Tank Bank' on account of he's selling war bonds in honor of the attack at Cambrai."

How ironic, thought Virginia as she turned and went back inside, finding her diary on the dining room table. She went into the sitting room and stirred the fire, musing. All afternoon she'd lost herself in her writing. Now the war had virtually arrived at her doorstep. She sighed in despair and opened her diary. Tracing her finger along her lips, she remembered Giraud's kiss. Then she thought of the kiss she'd given Bobbie. A tremor went through her. Both moments were gone forever; still, each was a timeless illumination.

But she couldn't put her feelings into words, at least not yet. Instead she wrote:

The uproar & potency of Richmond . . . worshipping a Tank was like the hum of bees round some first blossom.

She looked up. Leonard was watching her from the doorway with a tentative smile on his face. She held up her hand.

There was something more, something she'd seen in his wary hesitation, and at the top of the page she added in parentheses:

(What word will express the stir of life still cased in a soft velvet sheath?)

Then, closing her diary and putting aside her pen, she turned to see what he might want.

Epilogue

In 1937, with war once again threatening Europe, Virginia Woolf wrote *Three Guineas,* her indictment of masculine aggression, German fascism and incipient totalitarianism at home. Four years later, in 1941, her body was found in the river Ouse behind Monk's House, her home in Sussex. To this day, her death is commonly believed to have been a suicide.